The
Hau
o
Tyle

B J MEARS

First published in Great Britain in 2012 by The Dream Loft
www.thedreamloft.co.uk

ISBN 13: 978-0-9574124-0-8
ISBN 10: 0957412401

For Henna, Talitha and Kayla.

Special thanks to Joy for your support and the blurb,
to my editor, Edward Field
and to all those who have helped along the way.

'Nothing in all the world can be hidden from God. Everything is clear and lies open before him, and to him we must explain the way we have lived.'

Hebrews 4:13 (New Century Version Bible)

'Courage is the first of human qualities because it is the quality which guarantees all others.'

Winston Churchill

The Bag

Tyler May stared at the bag. It looked just like hers, was identical in every way: blue canvas, black edging, black straps. Except that it was *not* her bag. She checked the name tag a third time, still not believing what she read.

She sounded the name aloud as though that might help it sink in.

"Lucy Denby."

Taking the wrong bag home from school was not the only strange thing to have happened that day. She'd had a notion ever since leaving the school gates that someone was watching her. It intensified as she walked home printing perfect, crisp shoe prints on the snowy path. It was Friday the twelfth of December and it had already grown dark when school had finished. Her walk home had felt creepy, but a man *had* followed her. She was sure of it. The small hairs on the back of her neck stood up at the recollection. The feeling was still with her, an intangible gremlin clinging. She searched from her bedroom window but could see no one on the lamp lit road outside her house.

Tyler checked her watch.

9:15p.m.

It would soon be bedtime, though she didn't feel like sleeping. She had a project to do this weekend but it was in her bag, along with her lists. The bag she no longer had…

She considered looking in the bag. She lifted the flap, peered at the toggled drawstring, but then gave up on the idea. It felt wrong. It wasn't her bag. It wasn't her stuff. It was Lucy Denby's. There was nothing else for it. She would have to forget about the homework until Monday when she could confess to her mistake and apologize for taking the wrong bag; apologize for not being able to do her work. But the problem was she had made *no* mistake. The more she went over it in her head, the more certain she became. She had taken the bag from her peg, the peg with *her* name on it. With *her* coat and scarf on it. If it wasn't her peg then why had she collected the right coat and scarf? She looked at the label on her coat.

Tyler May

Tyler picked up the book she was halfway through and tried to forget about the bag, her homework and the man. She planned to make a new list for Saturday in the morning. Today's list was gone, infuriatingly beyond reach.

*

A long, uneventful weekend followed; uneventful except for the feeling that never really left her. Tyler went about her business as normal, but whenever she was out she found herself looking over her shoulder, peering into shadows and doorways. She told herself she was being silly, but a little voice in her head disagreed. Once, she was in town and had started to cross the road to visit Smiths, but she turned back when she changed her mind. Apparently two other people also had the very same notion: to her left a tall man with a grey beard and thick glasses, to her right, further down the bustling street, a glamorous woman in a green fur-lined coat. Were they following her? She had to wonder.

Several times over the weekend Tyler sat in her room and gazed at the bag, strongly tempted to riffle through it. Still she resisted.

*

Monday arrived with a sense of relief for Tyler. At last she would be able to put things straight. She couldn't get to school fast enough. It had snowed again overnight and the deeper layer made the walk slow and hard. She arrived in her form classroom just in time to hear Miss Sedgewick begin the register, narrowly missing a telling off for lateness. It meant she had no chance to see Miss Sedgewick before class as she had hoped, so she sat at her desk, dumping the bag on the floor by her feet.

Names were called and each child answered, barring Jimmy Lawrence, who was still off sick, and Nora Jacobson who was also absent (nothing new there). The name that woke Tyler from her worrying about the bag and the homework was 'Lucy Denby'.

"Lucy Denby?" Miss Sedgewick called a second time.

Tyler looked around the class, found an empty desk where Lucy usually sat.

Beneath a bristling brow, Miss Sedgewick's keen eyes flicked over the room. She marked the register and continued to call names.

This posed a new problem for Tyler. How was she to return the bag to Lucy and get her own bag back when Lucy was absent? She couldn't believe things were actually getting worse, but little did Tyler May know that this was only the start of her troubles.

"Don't worry," Miss Sedgewick told her when she finally had a chance to explain without the whole class listening in. "I'm sure Lucy will be back tomorrow and you can swap your bags back and then do the homework."

"Okay. Thanks, Miss Sedgewick."

She checked Lucy's peg anyway, just to be sure that her bag was not there, but the peg was empty.

The little voice in her head was talking again, bothering her.

'Don't you think that's odd?' it was saying. 'Lucy is not in school. Why is Lucy not in school? And why do you have her bag? Did Lucy swap bags on purpose? Lucy Denby… Lucy Denby… Lucy Denby…'

Lucy was one of those girls who seemed to have too much confidence for her own good. She was brash and sly. She was always getting in trouble at school for breaking the dress code, wearing makeup or the wrong shoes or the wrong colour tights. What had Melissa called her? A *goth*? Tyler had seen Lucy out of school looking like a vampire: black clothes, big boots and black lipstick, snake earrings and a thick silver chain about her neck.

Tyler didn't like her much.

Knowing that her teacher knew about the issue put Tyler's mind at rest over the project work, but her thoughts were never far from the strange accumulation of events and feelings of late.

"What's eating you?" Melissa asked at break time.

"Oh, nothing," fibbed Tyler. "Do you know what's wrong with Lucy Denby?"

"Yeah. She's an arrogant, stuck-up, spoilt, blood-sucking bitch from Hell."

"I mean, do you know why she's not in school?"

"No, but she's bunked off before. So there might not be anything actually wrong with her. Despite the fact that she shouldn't be bunking off, I mean. Why the sudden concern?"

"Oh, no reason."

"You going Dance Club tonight?" asked Melissa.

"I guess."

Tyler checked today's list.

Go to school
See Miss Sedgewick about project and bag
Get bag back
Check Friday's list
Buy new pencil case
Gymnastics
Dance Club
Complete project

She ticked off the first two items and breathed a deep sigh of frustration as she contemplated the next two with rising anxiety. *OCD* she reminded herself. She wasn't officially diagnosed, but Miss Sedgewick had said she definitely had Obsessive Compulsive Disorder to some degree. Tyler knew she was not like others. Others didn't feel the need to make lists all the time and, if they did, they certainly would not get upset about not being able to tick something off.

When the school bell rang later that day Tyler waited until everyone had gone before making a brisk search of the classroom. She hoped she might find her bag in a cupboard or a corner somewhere, but no such luck. She checked the pegs outside her form room again and also the pegs along the rest of the corridor. Nothing. Every peg was empty except hers, which held her coat and scarf and Lucy's bag. So begrudgingly she took her things and the bag. She was at the school entrance when she had a thought. It was that little voice again.

The desk was empty. Lucy was not at her desk today. The desk... Check the desk!

Tyler double-backed into the corridor and made her way to her classroom. She made sure no one was around before lifting the lid of Lucy's desk. Books, a few pens and pencils, a transparent shatterproof ruler. Nothing of any help. In frustration she sorted through the books, no longer knowing why she was still there. Most of them she recognised as the same text books she had in her desk and in her bag. Only one was unfamiliar. She lifted it out, letting the others fall back into the desk. It was a small dark red book with an old leathery cover. At first she thought the gold-lettered title read 'Ghost Hunting', but when she read it again she saw that in fact it said 'Ghost *Haunting*'.

Ghost Haunting… What's that?

She flinched when a noise from the corridor startled her. Someone was coming. Quickly she pocketed the book and let the desk lid gently down. She froze, waiting. The footsteps passed the classroom door and she caught a glimpse of the school caretaker through the door's fire-glass window. The footsteps died away. She sighed with relief and left the school building as swiftly as she could.

Outside the day had darkened and the school car park was empty. She realised she must have been lingering longer than she'd thought as everyone had gone already. She looked down the street in the direction of her house and saw two school kids walking home, but they were miles away and everything else was still and quiet. It gave her the creeps to feel this alone so she squeezed swiftly through the tall gates intending to catch up with some of the others. Snow was an icy slush under her feet. She walked fast, doing her best not to slip, but that feeling once more made her check over her shoulder. A movement sharpened her focus and jarred her heart.

Someone was there, following her from the shadows of the school wall.

Tyler quickened her pace, slipping, almost crashing, into the pavement. The man seemed familiar somehow, yet she could see no features from this distance of thirty metres or so. Tyler checked ahead to see the last of the kids disappear around a corner. She shivered. The man was making her nervous. She hated that, begrudged it. She stopped and turned, meaning to tell him go away and leave her alone or she would call the police, but he was gone. This freaked her out even more. If the man was innocently walking the street, why would he suddenly conceal himself?

Tyler checked the road. Nothing coming. She left the curb and ran along a tyre track where cars had worn the compacted ice away. Her grip was better here. Athletic and fit with long legs, she was the county gymnastics champion and people told her she looked like her heroine, the gold medal winning Sanya Richards-Ross.

Tyler put her strengths to good use now as her heart pounded with fear. When she thought she must have put some distance between herself and the man, she turned, jogging backwards on the road so she could see if he was anywhere behind her, but the road there was empty. She turned back and ran into him with a thump. Grey beard, thick glasses, tall.

She flailed and fought, smelled stale tobacco smoke.

He grasped at her but she was strong and determined. Breaking loose, she swung the bag at him and something hard within the bag met his head. He cried out and staggered. Tyler bolted across the road. It wasn't the way home but she didn't care. She just wanted to get away. She slipped and slid her way up another road seeing with dismay that here it was even darker with fewer streetlights, but she had known instinctively it would be easier to hide in the dark.

He was coming still, slipping just as she had done and nursing his head, cursing. She was slowly getting away from him, but to her horror she saw that others had joined him. She wasn't sure how many.

The road climbed and Tyler had a sense of *déjà vu* as though this was some kind of recurring nightmare; a slippery uphill road and a frantic need to escape. She found a narrow tread mark on the road and hammered her legs as fast as she could. She didn't know this part of town well. It quickly became very unfamiliar. One left turn soon brought her to a junction. She went right. Tyler unzipped her coat. She was sweating. Up ahead she saw a bus stop with a single figure waiting and she couldn't believe her luck when a bus turned into the road. She found a new turn of speed. The bus passed her, slowed and the figure stepped on. Tyler reached the sliding doors as they were closing, but the driver noticed her and let her on. She sat panting for several minutes not bothering to count the number of stops the bus made. Diesel fumes were nauseating. The other passenger, a strawberry blond woman clutching a briefcase, eyed her suspiciously.

Tyler's head reeled. Why were they after her? She became nervous of the woman and left the bus at the next stop.

Now she didn't turn, didn't slow for anything. Head down, she pushed herself until she could run no more. She searched about desperately for somewhere to hide, conscious that even now they could be following somehow.

The houses around the school were gone, along with the thin scattering of shops she frequented on her walk home. She was surrounded by large grey buildings hunkering like monsters in the gloom, concrete and brick, dark glass and grubby boards: an industrial zone. It wasn't a friendly place and few of the lights were on, but she didn't care. Anywhere was good if it hid her from the men. She found an old warehouse with broken windows and ran down its side where a doorway was boarded up with flimsy wood. She prized the sheet of ply back and slipped easily through.

Once inside she dug out her mobile phone and called 112. Unnerved she hung up before anyone answered. She stood still and listened. Silence. She pocketed her mobile. She had lost him. She was sure of it.

Before her a dusty old desk was strewn with cobweb-laced office equipment. She tried the lamp but the bulb had blown long ago. Sweeping the top clear with one arm, she upended Lucy's bag. Books scattered. She saw the tell-tale shape of a torch in the gloom and grabbed it, switched it on. A feeble yellow beam showed her the spilled contents more clearly: a pencil case, a black A5 spiral bound notebook. Light glinted from something shiny, a metallic surface. Tyler shoved books out of the way and snatched the metal object to hold it up in the torchlight. It was a chunky, silver medallion on a chain, but strange, different from anything she'd ever seen before. And heavy. There were odd markings on one side and, turning it, she saw what looked like a large jewel in the centre of the other side.

A wrenching sound from the doorway startled her. Flicking off the torch, she threw the jewelled medallion around her neck, tucked it inside her shirt and swept the rest of the things back into the bag. Throwing the bag over her shoulder she ran deeper into the dark warehouse. She flew up steel checker-plate stairs as more noises came from the blocked-up doorway. They had found her. She cursed under breath. She must have left a very obvious trail of prints in the unblemished snow leading to the entrance.

That was dumb.

The stairs opened out on level two: a grimy landing, shadowed corridors and dim doorways. Somewhere below she heard male voices, at least two of them. In fear for her life, she darted up a second flight of stairs and down a corridor full of doorways. Gloom, dust and cobwebs. An unloved place. The end of the corridor. Tyler tested doors and fled through the first one that gave. Behind her, metallic footsteps echoed. An empty room. Through another door into a smaller room with a pile of broken chairs. Mouldering carpet. Grubby shattered windows fighting moonlight. She reached a dead end, cornered.

She turned as they entered the room. Three men in suits and long dark coats stood considering her.

"Where is it?" demanded the tall bearded man with glasses. "Give it to me." He dabbed at a small wound on his temple with a white handkerchief.

"Where is what? Give you what? Why are you chasing me?"

They each took a step closer. Tyler backed away towards the broken windows.

"You know what we have come for. Give it to us," demanded the shortest of the men.

"I don't know what you're talking about," said Tyler. "Who are you? What do you want?"

The three watched her for a moment as though curious to see what she might do.

"I phoned the police already. They'll be here any minute. You'd best get out of here."

"Give me the bag," said the tall one, showing no sign of leaving.

Tyler was not stupid. She knew the jewel about her neck must be important in some way and that they would probably kill her once they had it. She did not intend to let that happen. With all her might she hurled the bag at them and made for the windows. The men scrambled for the bag and began searching it, throwing books aside.

Tyler climbed nimbly up onto the windowsill and toed her way through an empty pane to balance precariously on the slippery ledge outside.

"It's not here, Mr Bagshot," she heard someone inside the room shout.

"STOP HER! SHE'S GETTING AWAY!"

Men lunged at her through broken panes. The shorter man cut his arm and recoiled hissing.

Outside, Tyler inched her way along the ledge. Further on the outside wall she could see a fire escape ladder just out of reach. There were several window panes still intact giving her cover for now but she wondered how many seconds would pass before the men smashed those with the abandoned chairs.

"Grab her!" commanded the tall man. "Don't let her fall. We need her alive. We need to know how much she knows."

Closer she edged, teetering to the very end of the icy ledge to lean out hoping to reach the fire escape, but it was too far to stretch and, while she was wondering what to try next, she slipped and lost balance. She made a grab for the ledge as she fell but only grazed the tips of her fingers on brick.

Tyler knew she was going to die. It would all be over very soon. Free falling, she hurtled towards the unforgiving, cold ground.

That's it. I'm dead.

The Device

As Tyler fell, she felt a pulse from the thing about her neck. It radiated from the silvered jewel like a shiver of electricity. She slowed, watched the concrete yard approach her face. When she came to a stop she was still some five centimetres from the ground, screaming. She hovered there briefly, inexplicably, before descending the remaining short distance to gently land, very much alive but in a state of shock. Above her they watched, cursing.

"She has the device," the tall man named Bagshot screamed. "After her!"

Tyler did not wait. She had a head start and she planned on making the most of it. Whilst they descended floors within the warehouse, she fled. She found an alley a short way down the road and guessed it might lead her in the right direction. She wanted to get off the roads, away from the main routes. The alley narrowed before joining a claustrophobic footpath; six foot brick walls either side, a no-cycling sign on a bent pole. She jogged down the track, seeing no one behind. Breathless and shaking, she allowed herself to slow. Melissa's house should be this way, she hoped. It would still be a bit of a hike, but she would find it one way or another. Then she could get off the streets properly, hide away and begin to work out what exactly was happening to her.

Her phone rang. A tinny mechanical rendition of Beyonce's *Run The World (Girls).* She killed it without looking to see who was calling. She already knew it was her mother, wondering where she was.

Twenty minutes later she was round the back of Melissa's house, throwing tiny gravel pieces up at her bedroom window, hoping to catch her friend's attention and avoid her parents'. She was relieved when Melissa's curly blond hair and friendly, if a little podgy, face appeared at the glass. Melissa opened the window and squinted disbelievingly down at Tyler.

"Is that you, Tyler? What *have* you done to your hair?"

Tyler drew a finger to her lips signalling to keep it quiet. She knew she must look a state.

"Can I come up?"

Melissa nodded and disappeared.

A few moments later she was at the back door, nervous energy making her eyes sparkle.

"What's wrong? I was just getting ready for Dance Club."

"Are your mum and dad in?" Tyler asked.

"Yes, watching the news. We finished tea about ten minutes ago."

"Good. Can I come in? I need some help. Can we go to your room?"

"Sure, come on."

Tyler wiped snow from her shoes on the mat and went in. They crept upstairs to Melissa's room. Melissa closed the door and they sat cross-legged on a shaggy white rug.

"What about Dance Club? We'll need to leave soon if we're going to make it."

"Forget Dance Club. Something is going on. It's to do with Lucy Denby. I've been followed for days and just now I was chased and I nearly died. I *should* have died. I don't know why I didn't die. Except…"

"What? You're not making sense. What's it got to do with Lucy and who's chasing you?"

"A man called Bagshot and his men…" Tyler went on to explain what had happened. She trusted Melissa, who was undoubtedly her best friend. She was at the point in her story where she was about to climb out onto the window ledge when she felt that old anxiety building up again. She began drawing quick, deep breaths and soon she was close to hyperventilating.

"Say… uh, uh, uh… Say it'll be alright… uh, uh, uh. Say it for me… uh, uh, uh…" Tyler managed to say whilst clutching at her throat.

"What?" asked Melissa becoming concerned. She edged tentatively towards the door.

Tyler shook her head to let Melissa know she didn't want her to fetch her parents.

"Say… uh, uh, uh… Say it'll be alright… uh, uh, uh… I know it's weird, but… uh, uh, uh, I just need to hear the words… uh, uh, uh…"

"Ok, calm down now. It will be alright. It *will* be alright. Do you need a paper bag or something?"

Tyler shook her head. The panic attack was already subsiding. Her breathing slowed.

"It *will* be alright," said Melissa with conviction. "You know that don't you?"

Tyler nodded again, her breathing almost back to normal.

"Sorry about that. I know I'm odd, but for some reason, that always works."

"Did you have a panic attack in the warehouse when you were being chased?"

"No. It only seems to happen when I start to think about things too much."

"What do you do if you're having a panic attack and there's no one around to say the words?"

"I don't know. It hasn't happened yet." Tyler continued with her story.

"You're joking…" said Melissa when Tyler had concluded and drawn out the silver object from her shirt. She took it from around her neck so they could examine it more easily. Now that she could study it in proper light, Tyler could see the intricate designs incised around one side. At the top was a skull and then working round a central switch in a clockwise direction it was followed by a staring eye, a heart, something that looked like a stylized pair of wings, an eye facing anticlockwise, a tree, a tower with battlements, a spiral, an eye facing clockwise and a symbol that could only be interpreted as a flame or fire.

"That's odd," said Melissa.

"And there's this…" Tyler turned it over to show her the jewel.

"Wow… Do you think that's a diamond?"

Tyler studied the gem. It was like dark, smoky glass, a crystal cut with multiple faces about its edge and a large flat surface at the front.

"It's the wrong colour for diamond. I think it's magic," she said. "It's a magical device. How else could I float?"

"I agree," said Melissa. "It's the only explanation… Unless you hit your head and imagined it all, or something. Did you? Hit your head, I mean?"

"No!" Tyler objected. "It happened like I said. I think this thing stopped me from hitting the ground. I think it saved me." She put the chain back around her neck and tucked the device away in her shirt. She suddenly felt very possessive about it. She didn't want anyone to see it.

"What are you going to do?" asked Melissa.

"I don't know. I can't go home. They know where I live. They've been following me for days. Ever since I got Lucy's bag. Do you think she swapped bags on purpose? Do you think they were following her and she knew it? Maybe she needed to get rid of it, or hide it… I don't know."

"And she swapped bags with you? That makes sense because, after all, you *are* best friends…" Melissa's sarcasm was obvious.

Tyler sniggered.

"I don't know… Who *would* she choose to give it to if she needed to lose it somewhere? Maybe she didn't have time to think about it. Maybe it was in her bag and suddenly she knew she was going to get caught with it. Maybe she needed to stop Bagshot and the others from getting it. I think they're bad men."

"Wait a minute. Your bags are both the same type. She couldn't just swap with anybody or it would have been too obvious. It wouldn't have worked."

"Of course," agreed Tyler. "What was I thinking? This whole thing has got me pretty freaked."

"Don't worry. We'll figure it out. First thing is I need to tell Mum and Dad. They'll know what to do." Melissa jumped up.

"Wait! No." Tyler didn't really know why, but she wanted this kept secret, wanted to keep it all quiet, at least until she'd worked out what was happening. "Don't tell them yet. Go and tell them I'm here and that we can't go to Dance Club. Make up a reason. I need some time to think and I've nowhere safe to go. I need your help."

Melissa returned a minute later.

"I told them I hurt my knee at school today and I want to rest it. They know you're here. Why don't you sleep over? We can ask my mum and dad and then phone yours. I've got spare stuff if you need anything and there's a new toothbrush in the bathroom closet you can have."

"Great idea. Thanks. I don't know what I'd do without you."

"What are friends for?" Melissa shrugged and left to talk to her parents again.

Tyler took a long, deep breath before drawing out the device again to gaze into its dark glass. She wasn't sure, but for a moment it seemed the smoke within the crystal was moving faintly. She turned it over to the side with the symbols and looked closely at the switch at its centre. Cautiously she tried the switch. It moved easily with a soft click. It was similar to one she'd seen on an electric guitar in the school music room. The one on the guitar was used to select one guitar pickup or the other, but this switch went ten different ways. Each selection made the switch point to one of the ten symbols. As she watched, the place where the chain connected shifted of its own accord with a soft clicking until the selected symbol was at the top of the device. She became nervous and quickly set it back where it had been, pointing to the skull icon. If it really had saved her from death, perhaps she'd better leave it in that position. The device rotated again until the skull was back at the top. She heard the voice in her head as though someone else was thinking aloud.

Of course! The skull is the symbol for death…

So logically, did that mean the device saved the wearer from whatever was selected? If so, some of the symbols did not really make sense. She had a thought and flicked the switch to a different symbol again, this time the spiral. The device rotated as before, stopping when the spiral was at the top by the chain. She turned it over and put her eye to the dark glass. She was amazed to see within the crystal a swirling pool of mist. This time she was in no doubt. There was movement within the glass, but what the mist *was* exactly, she could not say. She looked at the edge of the device where the front and back surface met like the edge of a coin, and she could see miniscule gaps in the metal telling her it was made of at least three individual sections of silver, a facetted front section with the crystal, a similar back section bearing the symbols, and a very narrow central ring which joined the front and back together.

Melissa returned, interrupting her examination. Tyler tucked the device away quickly.

"It's all sorted. My mum called your mum. Your mum was about to phone the police 'cause you weren't home from school. You better give her a call before too long. She's going off her face. But it's official. We're having a sleepover."

"Great, thanks. At least that's bought us some time to think."

"Maybe you should disappear for a few days. I mean, if bad people are trying to get you. It's either that or go to the police and tell them everything."

Tyler considered this.

"I don't want to go to the police. Those men could be the police for all I know... They looked kind of official. They had these long coats like you see in the films. Like the secret police or something.

"This is big. It's important, but I don't know who to trust. I'm not taking it to anyone until I've figured that out. Anyway, what do you mean, *disappear*?"

"Well, I don't mean really disappear. I mean I can help you vanish for a while. People will think you've run away from home or something, but really you'll just be hiding out somewhere."

"What about Mum and Dad?"

"We can let them know you're alright somehow... Send them messages or something."

Tyler nodded.

"I like it. I don't think I should go home right now anyway. And I certainly can't go to school. They're watching the school. That's how they found me in the first place. I'll stay here tonight though."

"Yes. Then tomorrow you can leave for school with me, but double back once my mum and dad have left for work. I'll give you a spare key. You can let yourself back in and hang out here. After that, we might need to find somewhere else for you to hide."

"Perfect! I don't know what I'd do without you. I really mean it!"

Tyler phoned her mum and let her know she was okay and that she planned to go straight to school the next morning with Melissa. She began working out a plan of action for the next day whilst Melissa found her some food from the fridge as she'd missed her evening meal. By the time she crawled into her makeshift bed on Melissa's bedroom floor she had made a list and was feeling a little less on edge. All the same, she could not sleep. They talked long after Melissa's mum had told them to go to sleep, just like any other sleepover. When Tyler thought her friend had fallen asleep, she took out the device and looked into the glass.

It was dark and she could see nothing within the jewel so, turning it, she flicked the switch back to the spiral symbol and then checked the glass. She let out a small gasp. Through the dark eye piece she could see the ubiquitous fog once more and now the image was lighter than the bedroom so that the glass appeared to glow. But that was not what made her gasp. There, standing alone with haze shifting all about, was a small figure; a boy. He looked quite odd, dressed in old ragged clothes. Tyler thought he was like someone from the war times. There was something else strange about the boy. He was not solid. Rather, he was translucent. Tyler could see fog moving on the other side of him. She could see right through him. The boy looked sad and was carrying a violin, but was not playing it. She noticed a yellow star stitched roughly to the front of his shirt. As she stared, he turned his head slowly and with haunting eyes looked right at her. Tyler gasped.

"You okay?" Melissa asked, startling Tyler. She turned over and tucked the device into her borrowed nightshirt.

"Fine. Just can't sleep."

"It'll be okay, you know. We'll work things out."

"Of course we will. Sorry if I woke you."

The Book

Tyler awoke feeling exhausted after a long, almost sleepless night. Mornings worked quickly in the Watts' household. Before she knew it, Melissa was heading out for school and Tyler tagged along feeling dishevelled and not ready for the day. Five minutes down the road she waved Melissa goodbye thanking her for all her help and turned back.

'If there are no cars on the drive, it means Mum and Dad have both gone to work,' Melissa had told her earlier. Now Tyler stood peering through a gap in a bedraggled hedge, watching Mr Watts pull away in a blue Ford hatchback. When he and the car were out of sight, she crept round the back and let herself back into the house with the spare key she'd been loaned. She jogged up the stairs and sat on Melissa's bed cradling the device. It was as she'd left it, with the switch pointing to the spiral. She looked into the crystal lens. The boy was still there as if waiting, looking for her, only this time he was playing a mournful tune on his fiddle. She heard the long notes clearly, a high, sweeping, sad melody. When she took her eye away from the lens she could no longer hear the music.

"Boy, can you hear me?" she asked.

The boy stopped playing and watched her for a moment.

"Can you hear me?"

The ghostly figure nodded and a chill ran the length of Tyler's spine.

"Who are you? Can you talk to me?" she asked.

The boy shook his head slowly and then repositioned his violin to resume his tune.

Wondering what each of the different symbols meant, Tyler flicked the switch onto each one in turn, every time flipping the device to peer into the lens. Some of the positions made the crystal go dark, almost black, some were more interesting. She stopped when she viewed the lens with the switch pointing to the tower symbol.

"Wow," she heard herself say aloud.

There in the swirling mist was a dark scene. Bone-like, blackened trees clawed inwards to the centre where an ancient looking tower rose upon a ragged hill. The tower itself had a portcullis and several narrow windows but something odd was happening. Ominous birds circled the gothic tower and she noticed the tower itself was being built. Nobody was there actually *doing* the building, but it was being built just the same. Block by block the tower was ever so slowly raising. Behind the tower a full moon shone like a huge silver penny hanging in a moody dark sky.

"What an odd thing you are," she said to the device while feeling she might be losing her mind. She placed the device on the bed and took out her list from a pocket.

Leave for school
Go back to Melissa's (don't forget the key)
Disguise yourself as a boy
Go home and collect everything you need
Leave a note for Mum and Dad
Find somewhere safe to hide out
Find out who Bagshot is
Figure out what the device is for
Figure out what the hell is going on
FIND LUCY DENBY

It was one of the more interesting lists she had made so far.

Tyler found a red baseball cap in Melissa's wardrobe. It was deep enough on top to take all her hair once she'd pinned it up in a bun. She went for blue colours other than that. A pair of jeans, a light blue sweater and an old quilted coat Melissa didn't wear anymore. Now she looked pretty boyish in the bedroom mirror. She still had full lips, fuller than most boys she decided, but then she knew she could suck them in a little if she thought she was being watched. The cherry on the cake was a Liverpool FC scarf she borrowed from Melissa's brother's room, which was particularly useful as she was able to wrap it several times round, hiding her neck and lower face. Now she was quite sure her own mother would not recognise her and this was just as well, she thought, because she might well bump into her quite soon.

She was fetching her house key from her coat pocket when her hand found the small dark red book. She pulled it out and read the gold title on the front; *Ghost Haunting by Zebedee Lieberman*. She noticed a faint additional line below the title which read *With closing comments by Orealia Stephensen*. She'd forgotten all about the book she'd shoved into her pocket in the classroom. Why did Lucy possess a book called *Ghost Haunting*? She checked the back cover of the book for some explanation but it was empty, so she opened the book and read down the contents page, wondering if the book was a story book or something else.

<u>Contents</u>

She flipped straight to the chapter entitled *A Definition of Ghost Haunting* and read the first paragraph.

Ghost Haunting: the utilization by force, enticement or coercion of spirits (living or dead), ghosts, geists or any other such spiritual entities for the purposes of controlled supernatural empowerment in the physical realm. Ghost haunting often involves the trapping of ghosts inside an object or container of some sort,

spirit device or ghost machine (see 'A Brief History of Ghost Haunting', 'Objects of Power').

Tyler glanced quickly through the book from start to finish. This chapter was the shortest in the book except for the chapter entitled *The Dangers of Ghost Haunting.* Here the pages had clearly been torn out and an odd page, which didn't match the rest, had been crudely taped in place. The added page was written in an elegant freehand script. It said simply, *The Dangers of Ghost Haunting. Ghost haunting is extremely hazardous. In no circumstances should anyone attempt to do it, ever.*

Tyler swallowed hard. The connection was obvious. The thing now hanging about her neck was a device that used the power of trapped ghosts. Ghosts trapped within the device. She'd even seen one of them. It was a ghost machine.

She slipped the book into the inside pocket of the blue coat she now wore and headed out of the house. She had things to do. Too many things. The book would have to wait until later when she knew she had somewhere safe to stay for the night.

Outside the rear of Melissa's house all was still. It was easy to leave unobserved. She locked the back door behind her and followed the path to the gate which edged a quiet back road. Tyler pulled the scarf high over her chin and walked boldly to her house, slowing only when her home came into view to be sure that no one was watching for her. Out front, on the opposite side of the road, a black van was parked. She imagined the interior packed with spy equipment and headed round the back. She noted the family car was not on the driveway, though this only told her that her father was at work. Her mother might still be home.

The back garden was at the end of a long, thin, ramshackle road that also serviced five other houses, so if someone did see her going down it, they could still not be sure which house she was visiting. The garden gate was tall; six feet high like the fence, but she'd done this before and found it easy to find a hold and hoist herself up enough to reach the bolt on the inside. The gate swung open and Tyler peered up the garden towards the back of the house. She did not wish to encounter her mum; too many questions. It looked empty. The kitchen was dark and still beyond the windows. Tyler made a dash for the back door, rapped on it twice and ducked beneath the window where a dwarf conifer tree in a planter hid her. No response. No one was in. She unlocked the door and went in.

It was comforting to be back home. It felt like an age since she'd left for school the day before. All the same, she knew she could not risk staying long. She went to the fridge and drank some orange juice from a carton. She found notepaper and quickly scrawled a note to her parents.

Hi Mum and Dad,
Something has come up and I need
to disappear for a few days. I don't
have time to explain now. Please
don't worry and DON'T call the police!
I'm fine and I'll be in touch very soon.
Love you.
Tyler.

Then she made a beeline for her bedroom, took a rucksack and filled it with clothes. She smashed her china piggy bank (one she'd had since turning five) and stuffed cash into her jeans pockets. She packed her mobile phone charger and fetched a sleeping bag and a camping roll.

Tyler left the same way she had come, leaving the note in the centre of the kitchen table. She figured she had maybe a couple of hours before Mum returned and all hell broke loose.

Tyler checked the list and ticked off the first few items before considering at the next one.

Find somewhere safe to hide out…

…preferably somewhere she could make comfortable enough. That was going to be tricky. In the meantime, she needed somewhere to think and, in any case, she'd left some of her things behind, so for now she headed back to Melissa's.

The Notebook

Tyler woke up with a jolt. She had not meant to fall asleep but fatigue had overcome her. She wiped cold sweat from her forehead and looked about wondering if she was safe. Melissa's bedroom was comfortingly silent. She relaxed, letting her head fall back onto the pillow. She took out the ghost machine and held it up to her eye. It was still set on the tower but now the darkly brooding image was different. The tower was slowly crumbling. Block by block it was shrinking as though someone was demolishing it. Perplexed, Tyler set the switch to the skull symbol. She felt safer with it in this position.

She checked her watch.

2:10p.m.

How had that happened? She must have collapsed on Melissa's bed meaning just to rest for a few minutes. She estimated she had less than an hour and a half to get ready and get out of the house. Not long after that, it would be growing dark anyway and she didn't want to be on the streets when that happened. She packed her things and checked her image in the mirror. With a rucksack on her back, the bed roll, the baseball cap and the scarf she looked like a boy going on a trip. Her face was grubby and the little of her hair that was visible was now dishevelled. She looked nothing like the girl who was followed by Bagshot and his men. She left Melissa's once more and headed out not really knowing where she was going to hide.

She had not gone far when she had a thought. There had been many rooms in the abandoned warehouse where she had hidden. The men were not likely to go back there looking for her as they had seen her run away from the place. It would have to do for now. She changed direction, hoping she could find the warehouse before darkness fell. Her phone beeped twice. The text was from Melissa.

U might want 2 turn ur phone off. They can trace mobiles from the signal ;) X

Tyler swore and held down the *on* button until the phone went blank. Her mum was sure to freak when she tried her mobile and found it was off, but that was just too bad.

Tyler retraced her steps as best she could. She became lost for a while but then recognised the no cycling sign on the bent pole. She had found the alley close to the warehouse and from there it was easy to track her way back to her hiding place.

The area was still quiet even at this time of day. A few cars came and went as she staked it out. Several workers walked past her and she did her best to look like she was waiting for a lift, striving to not look as afraid as she felt. Her fears began at being caught out of school and ended with being captured by Bagshot and his men. Of course there were probably many bad things that could happen to her in between, but she tried not to think about them.

Tyler waited until the road was quiet and then, when she could see no one moving and no cars coming or going, she walked quickly to the side of the road by the warehouse, careful not to approach it from the front. She wanted to find a back way in; a way that would be safer for her and less watched. So with this in mind she skirted the next building seeking a way through. She found just such a route three buildings along where a wide driveway led up a slight incline to a small car park on the side of a cinder block building. The car park was edged with a chain-link fence, so it was easy for her to see through to the back of the warehouse where she wished to be.

She checked about for movement. A solitary red car sat in the car park. Steam issued from a grill up on the building's wall. Someone was in there but there were few windows on this side. She figured she stood a good chance of not being noticed as long as no one came out, so she dashed up the incline and hugged the wall. Now the chain-link fence was all that stood between her and the warehouse. It was mostly in good condition but she noticed a few links broken at the edge where it met the building and it was bent out of shape at the bottom as though a dog or someone had tried to get through. This suited her fine. The corner was not overlooked.

Tyler checked round the building for CCTV cameras but found none. She made her way along the wall, ducking beneath windows, until reaching the fence. She prized it up and crawled under. The chain-link snagged on her borrowed coat and the baggage she was carrying made it impossible to pass beneath. She backed up and slipped off the coat, the rucksack, almost her whole disguise. Sweating with the fear of being discovered, she shoved everything through and ducked under the fence again. This time she made it through quite easily. A moment later she was running for the warehouse, arms laden with gear.

She didn't wish to hang about now, searching for a better way in. Instead she went straight to the door she'd used the first time and squeezed through, again pushing all her things in ahead of her.

Once inside she was more at ease. She stood for a long time wondering if she had been seen, waiting for footsteps which never came. She was alone. She was safe, for now.

She took out the ghost machine and switched it to the tower symbol. The little dark tower was rising again. She didn't know why but that felt good. She wanted the tower to be finished, to be built right to the top. She switched back to the skull.

She was itching to read the book and to experiment more with the device but these things would have to wait. First she needed to find a room she could use, get a bed made, make the place safe. Then she could relax a bit and learn what she could from the red book.

She was searching through the warehou
grew longer when she stumbled upon the ro
had been cornered by Bagshot and his me

was still there, its contents scattered. She went to the window and peered out at the ground three floors below. It was a long way down and it was clearly a fall that nobody could ever survive. She had *not* imagined it. Not any of it. But she *had* survived and that meant the ghost machine was real. It really worked. She wondered what else it could do.

Lucy's text books were the same as her own school books. Tyler touched nothing just in case the men did come back sometime as she meant to leave no clues to her presence there, although she examined all to be sure she had missed nothing that might tell her something. She stopped when she found a black spiral bound notebook. It was small enough to fit into a large coat pocket. She wondered if Lucy had written anything in it. Suddenly she felt it was too important to leave. She grabbed it and opened it at the beginning. She was stunned to find a pencil sketch of the device.

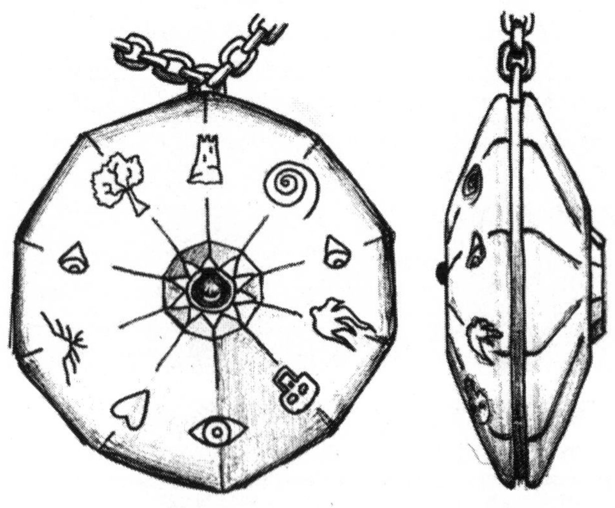

There followed pages and pages of notes and names, other strange diagrams and sketches of people, amongst them a tall man with a beard and thick glasses. There was no name on the drawn figure but she was sure it was supposed to be Bagshot. It surely could not be anyone else. Lucy was quite an artist. More reading for later…

Tyler found another metal staircase and climbed to the top level. This floor seemed to have hardly been used. It was cleaner. Most of the rough blue carpet tiles were still in place and it felt safer. She thought if someone came into the building after her, this would be the best place for her to hide. It would take longer for them to find her and she would probably get more of a warning that they were on their way up. She decided she would set up an early warning system to raise the alarm should they come in while she was asleep. As a last resort she could find a window, make sure the device was set to the skull, jump and hope she didn't go *splat*.

The rooms offered little choice in the end. She found one not much bigger than a store cupboard but it had no window at all. The room next-door had more space and windows but two of them had been smashed and a cold wind whistled through. These were the best and cleanest rooms on offer and in the end she decided to make use of both of them. She needed light to read, which she had in the form of Lucy's torch and a spare she'd packed, but that meant after dark anyone outside the warehouse would see the light through the window and know someone was there. Also, the small room was warmer because there were no broken windows, so she settled on that room for sleeping and reading. The rest of the time she could use the bigger room, block up the broken windows with something, eat there, move around and keep an eye on the road below.

By the time darkness had fallen, she was ready. She had her makeshift bed made in the claustrophobic room and, using an old screwdriver she'd found, she'd taken a bolt from a door on the floor below and fixed it to the inside of the storeroom door so she could lock herself in whenever she wished to.

Now for the early warning system.

She switched on Lucy's torch and crept her way around the grim warehouse by its feeble beam. The place wasn't completely empty. Here and there were abandoned desks, some with stuff still in the drawers. She found two old filing cabinets and a chunky old computer that clearly hadn't worked for years. She searched for wire; a thin wire, if possible. At length she unplugged the computer's power cable and stabbed it open with the old screwdriver. It took some effort but, little by little, she drew out the thinner wires from inside until she had three lengths, each about two metres. Tying these end to end she made one long wire. This she fixed across the stairs, knotting one end around the side at the bottom of the tread and letting the other end of the wire fall from the other side. Now all she had to do was tie some metal objects to the trailing end and if someone came up the stairs in the dark they would be sure to catch the trip wire and make a din. Or so she hoped.

Finally, she took out her list and read it by torchlight. She smiled to herself as she ticked off another item. Now it was just a list of several mysteries she had to solve. She intended to attempt this from the safety of her new room.

Tyler bolted the door and made herself comfortable in her sleeping bag. The old building was terribly cold so she kept a coat on as well. She took the ghost machine and peered into the glass. It hadn't changed, just a dark crystal with a faint misty haze. She flicked the switch to the tower. The *Tower of Doom*, she thought. It was something she'd seen in a film one time. The creepy tower was now very slowly, almost imperceptibly, building. That felt better than when it was falling down. She set the switch back to the skull and tucked it away in her shirt. She dug out the red book from the bag beside her and began reading the foreword.

Have you ever wondered if ghosts really exist, or if there are any facts behind popular myths and legends? Are fairies real? Did trolls once walk the earth? Did Aladdin truly have a genie in a magic lamp?

What would you say if I told you it was all true; that every strange tale, every ghost story you ever heard was true in some way and had its origin in fact?

The chapter went on with many more rambling questions which all seemed to be suggesting there was a good reason for every strange thing that had ever been reported or written. Yet there were few real statements or answers to the questions, just many suggestions. Tyler quickly became frustrated with this chapter and so, having the gist (that all these things were because of ghosts in one way or another), she moved on to the next chapter, skipping the definition.

This chapter was entitled *A Brief History of Ghost Haunting* and was broken down into subheadings and peppered with black and white images, each one in a different style and illustrating a different story. The first heading was *Objects of Power.* This had smaller subheadings, so Tyler scanned through those quickly, turning page after page, wanting to get a general feel for what was in the book and not really wishing to plough through a load of boring history. The headings were *The Rings of Power*, *The Holy Grail*, *The Spear of Destiny*, *Swords of Power*, *Magic Wands & Staffs*, *Magic Cauldrons*, and *Brian's Boat & the Eight Mystical Objects*. There came another heading: *Common Fairytales*. Beneath that were several headings spanning a dozen or so pages including *Pinocchio & Other Possessed Toys*, *Aladdin & the Genie of the Lamp*, *The Gingerbread Man*, *Talking Animals*, *Jack & the Beanstalk*, *Rumpelstiltzkin*, *The Nutcracker*, *The Magic Carpet*, *The Frog Prince*, *The Golden Goose*, and *The Musicians of Bremen*.

The book went on under another subheading of *Myths and Legends*. Here the stories were about *Celtic Talking Heads*, *Amulets & Talismans*, *The Egyptians Explained*, *Norse Gods*, *Saxon Fairies & Other Evil Spirits*, *Black Shuck & Other Demon Dogs*, *Monsters & Ghouls*, and finally, *The Classical Mythologies*. This last heading contained a vast number of pages and Tyler got the impression that the author had rather given up on subheadings and just spewed out story after story onto the page.

From what she could gather from this quick skipping through of the pages, it seemed that each of these stories, myths or legends, was being explained in a new light. The writer, Zebedee Lieberman, was explaining how all these legends had come about because of ghosts in one form or another. Sometimes the ghosts were ghosts; sometimes the ghosts were pretending to be something else. Sometimes Zebedee Lieberman did not seem entirely sure *what* the ghosts really were. It was an interesting concept, Tyler considered; one she had not heard of before.

She closed the book, tucked it back into the bag and then took out Lucy's black notebook and turned to the excellent illustration of the ghost machine.

The following page was interesting. It had a list of the symbols, both a sketch of the actual symbol and a name next to each one, in Lucy's spidery handwriting. Tyler studied the notes.

Skull ~ DEATH

Eye (front) ~ SECOND SIGHT
FORTUNE TELLING ?

Heart ?

Wings ~ FLIGHT ?

Eye (Left) ~ HISTORY ?

Tree ~ KNOWLEDGE ?

Tower ?

Spiral ~ GHOSTS !

Eye (Right) ??

Fire ~ HAVEN'T A CLUE

It seemed to her that Lucy had been trying to guess what each of the symbols was for.

Tyler scanned the rest of the pages, looking for helpful clues to what was going on. She found the sketch of Bagshot again and wrote his name beneath the sketch in pencil. She noticed Lucy had written a date in the top right corner of the page.

9th December.

Lucy had drawn this just three days before swapping bags with Tyler.

Tyler found a page with some notes about something called the NVF. Like the list near the front, it seemed to be guesswork about what the NVF actually was. Lucy seemed uncertain, but among the garbled notes, Tyler saw something that set her hairs on end. Just after Lucy had written with a blue pen in a careful, neat hand, *something not right – NVF not what it appears*, she had scrawled quickly in pencil, *Steal the device! Dangerous!*

Ghosts

Tyler turned the page. There were no more references to the ghost machine. She saw that Lucy had begun to fill the notebook with information and notes on this and that, but nothing was very clear. There were odd diagrams of things that Tyler thought might be similar devices or magical charms, strange symbols, but the notes were never very specific. It was as though Lucy had not wanted to write too much down in case someone found the notebook; as if she had taken notes on something but also tried to keep secrets.

Tyler shrugged, shut the notebook and slid it into her bag, next to the red book. She devoured an apple and a packet of salt and vinegar crisps.

She took out the ghost machine and checked the *Tower of Doom* again. It was building nicely. That made her smile, though she didn't know why. Frustrated that she had nobody to ask about the device, she thought again about the ghost boy she'd seen in the lens and wondered if he could help.

Wind whistled through the windows of the room next door and moaned against the side of the building. The storeroom was an all-encompassing concrete coffin. Tyler shivered even though she was warmly wrapped in her many layers.

Nervously she set the switch to the spirit symbol and looked into the lens for several minutes. Within the device, mist continued to drift slowly, but the boy ghost had gone. She shook the thing as though that might rouse someone.

"Come on," she muttered, viewing the glass once more. "Speak to me!"

A small shape appeared some way off in the miasma. It grew slowly until it became a grey figure. As it neared she could tell it was a boy and, for a moment, she thought it was the same boy she'd seen before, but it wasn't. This boy was dressed differently and was a few years older. He wore a cloth cap and dark grey, knee length shorts, a tattered, grubby, off-white shirt and over that, a torn black waistcoat. She couldn't see his feet, though she imagined he was barefoot. He looked Victorian, like someone Charles Dickens might have written about, and was also translucent. The boy's face was smudged with grime and soot, as though he'd just climbed down a chimney. He was searching around for something and soon moved out of Tyler's view, leaving the glass completely.

"Don't go!" she said, pressing her eye to the glass, though all the time presuming he couldn't hear her. After all, why *should* he be able to hear her?

"Come back. Pleeease!" Tyler begged.

Then, just when she was convinced he was gone for good and the whole idea was utterly useless, he reappeared and looked directly at her. Tyler instinctively backed away, taking her eye from the glass. She'd wanted to talk to someone, but now that someone was actually there, she baulked at the idea. What if the boy was nasty, an evil spirit? Lieberman had suggested more than once in the book that ghosts might well be evil spirits just pretending to be ghosts. He'd even said that some evil spirits might well be ghosts pretending to be evil spirits. But all that didn't really help Tyler very much.

Tentatively she looked into the lens once more.

"Lucy?" said the Victorian ghost boy. "That you, Lucy Loo?"

Tyler blinked several times, but resisted the urge to pull away. She could hear him. He was speaking to her!

"No," she mumbled. Afraid he might vanish, she said, "I mean, I'm not Lucy. Lucy is a friend of mine… Well, not really a friend…"

"What ya' want? Who are ya'?" The boy screwed up his brow and craned his neck to peer intently at Tyler. His hair was dark, short and wavy, with tighter curls about his ears. His face, when he was not screwing it up, was bold and handsome beneath the smudges of dirt. He spoke with a strong London accent.

"I… I want help. Can you help me?" Tyler asked.

"That depends, don't it. Who are ya'?"

"My name is Tyler May. I have this thing. This silver thing. And you are in it."

"Oh yeah, the 'device'… Lucy told me about that. She alright? I only saw her once before she vanished. Seemed a bit upset about some-fing…"

"I don't know where she is or if she's okay. What did she say to you?"

"Not much really. She seemed like a nice gal though."

"She mentioned the device?" Tyler prompted.

"Oh yeah, she told me all about it. She were trying to work out what it were for… Were goin' on an' on about all these little pictures. I didn't really know what she were talkin' about."

"I see." Tyler was disappointed. "I think it's some kind of ghost trap. You are a ghost? Aren't you?"

"…Last time I looked. We're all ghosts in'ere, ain't we."

"How many of you are there?"

"What? Ghosts? Thousands."

"No. I mean in there. How many are trapped in there with you?"

"Oh, I don't rightly know. Hard to tell really. We're not strictly trapped though. Oh no. We're kind of… tied to it. It's 'ard to explain. We can come and go, but there's this kind of a pull on us. Sometimes it's so hard, ya just can't fight it."

"I saw this boy. A quiet boy with a violin. He wouldn't speak to me. Is he alright?"

"Oh that's old Marcus. I calls 'im *the silent fiddler*. He's alright really, just a bit down. Don't take 'im personally though, will ya'. He don't talk to no one. They say he saw some 'orrible fings back in the war. Ain't said a word to no one since."

"That's sad."

"I shouldn't worry. 'E's dead."

"I suppose he is."

"I'm Albert, by the way. Albert Goodwin."

"I'm pleased to meet you, Albert."

"Likewise."

"Can I ask you. I mean, do you mind me asking – if you really are a ghost - then how did you die? Was it painful? Do you remember it happening?"

"Yeah, yeah, I remembers it like it were yesterday. Come to fink of it – I thought it was yesterday..." Albert scratched his head as though he'd managed to confuse himself. "I were cleanin' some toff's stack an' I got stuck, din' I. My ol' gaffer left me up there. Nuffin' 'e could do I suppose. The rest of me's still up there as far as I knows."

"You were cleaning some *toff's stack*?"

"You know. A chimney. A bleedin' tall one too, I tell ya'. And that's why I'm 'ere, I suppose."

"What do you mean? You became a ghost because you died up a chimney?"

"In a manner of speakin'. There's always a reason."

"A reason?"

"A reason why you become a ghost instead of going on to the other place. You know…"

"I don't think I do. Not really."

"There's always a reason why. It's some-fing to do with the way you been buried. Or rather, I should say, the way you ain't been buried. Get it?"

"So, what you're saying is that, if you don't have a proper funeral, you end up becoming a ghost?"

"Some-fing like that, yeah. You become a 'restless spirit' an' all that…"

"Will I see you again? I mean, if I go away now, but want to speak to you again… Will you be there?"

"Can't guarantee it. But I'll keep the mince pies open."

"Great. Thanks. I'll look for you tomorrow, then."

"You do that, Missy. Time don't mean much to the dead, though. Sorry about that. I won't really know when tomorrow is. But I'll be 'ere if I can be. Will that do ya'?"

"Thank you, Albert. Will you do something else for me?"

"Sure. If I can."

"I need to know more about the device – the one Lucy told you about. Can you see if anyone in there knows anything about it?"

"I'll see what I can do." Albert gave a cheeky wink.

"Thanks. Bye for now, then."

"Fare thee well, Tyler May." He waved his cloth cap and bowed low.

Tyler flicked the switch back to the skull. She was sorely tempted to try some of the other settings on the device, but the hand-written warning she'd found in the red book made her think twice. If she'd understood Zebedee Lieberman's definition correctly, ghost haunting had nothing to do with people being haunted by ghosts. In fact, it was completely the other way round. It was people haunting the ghosts, bothering them, pestering them. Making *them* do things they didn't want to. She didn't really like the sound of it but realised with horror that she'd already done it. She had talked with a ghost and had asked him to do something for her. She was already *ghost haunting*. This concerned her and she wished she could read the real chapter, *The Dangers of Ghost Haunting*, which was missing from Zebedee's book.

In any case she was beginning to work out how Lucy had come by the device and, in part, what it was for. Tyler took a last look at the day's list as the torchlight grew weaker. She was still some way from ticking off the last four things, but she had made a start and that would have to do for now.

Exhausted and anxious, she decided she should try to get some sleep. She wanted to call her mum and dad to let them know she was alright and tell them all about the ghost machine. She considered turning her mobile back on so she could text Melissa. In the end she did neither, deciding she would do both the next morning when she was away from her hideout. That way, if the calls were traced, she could still return to the warehouse and nobody would know where she was hiding.

She put the list away, set the alarm on her wristwatch, switched off the torch and tried to sleep. Tomorrow was going to be a busy day.

*

Something was beeping in her ear. Tyler woke and felt better although she had the feeling she probably needed to wash. She was grubby and realised she hadn't showered in days. She checked her watch and killed the alarm. Twenty minutes before she needed to be somewhere.

*

Melissa was walking to school, moving quickly because she was late. She was passing a phone box when an arm shot out and dragged her in. She screamed, but then saw who it was.

"Euuuw! You smell," she said with a grin.

"Pleased to see you, too," said Tyler. "Thanks for your help. I need to see you."

"After school? You can use the house by the way. Just check Mum and Dad are out of the way before you go in. Get a shower. Get cleaned up. Find something to eat. You still got the key?"

"Yes. Thanks. I will."

"You okay?"

"Fine. I need to fill you in. I found out quite a lot of stuff. I think Lucy's in big trouble."

"She's missing. It's official now. Posters are up all over town and the police were in school asking questions. No one has seen her for days. Apparently her parents are going to be on TV tonight making an appeal."

"Right."

"I'd best go. I'm late. I'll see you later. Oh, your mum's having a fit by the way…"

"Right. See you later then."

"Bye!" Melissa dashed away.

It wasn't long before Tyler came across a poster taped around a telegraph pole. It was a respectable picture of Lucy, just her shoulders and head, with tidy hair and a green jumper. Above it was printed in large black letters 'MISSING'. It didn't look like the 'Lucy' Tyler knew, but then she figured it was probably a picture her parents were proud of. They wouldn't want to use a photo of their daughter looking like a deranged vampire. Under the image of Lucy were the words 'Have you seen this girl? Please contact the police.' There followed a hotline phone number to call. Tyler was tempted to turn on her mobile and call the number. She hadn't seen Lucy but she did know a few things that might help. She thought better of it and pocketed the phone. She had a feeling that the authorities wanted this device and probably wanted to use it for something bad. After all, why had Lucy decided she should steal it? Why would Tyler go to the police when Bagshot looked like he was one of them?

*

Melissa's house was a luxurious respite from Tyler's grimy hideout. She stood in the shower for forty-five minutes, dried and dressed in clean clothes from Melissa's drawers. She checked to see what the *Tower of Doom* was doing. It was slowly dilapidating. Clearly she'd been hanging around for too long and the old tower had become... What? Bored?

Tyler checked the contents of her purse. She made a new list and binned the old one.

Buy torch batteries
Buy food
Buy a cheap mobile
Buy hair dye
Text Melissa
Text Mum
Dye hair
Break into Lucy's house
Fill in Melissa
Google Lucy Denby
Research the NVF
Find out who Bagshot is
Figure out what else the device does
Figure out what the hell is going on
Speak to Albert the ghost
FIND LUCY DENBY

She read and reread the list. It was beyond doubt the most outrageous list she'd ever written. Her watch told her it was nearly ten-thirty. She'd need to get a move on if she was going to get all that done.

An hour later she had all the shopping and she'd sent a text to Melissa with her new mobile to say she would see her later and with her old phone she'd sent a text to her mum saying she was okay and would come home soon. She turned her old mobile off again and returned to Melissa's place.

Tyler dyed her hair jet black. It was the furthest she could go from the streaky blond look she usually had. When it was done and she'd dried it, she stared at her reflection. Just changing her hair colour made her look very different, but it wasn't enough. She found a pair of scissors in a kitchen drawer and took a deep breath before hacking off the lower ten centimetres of hair so that it ended at her jaw line. It was rough looking, but better. She borrowed makeup from Melissa's top draw and soon she looked a few years older too. That was good. She was happy she didn't need to dress like a boy any more. In fact, she quite liked the new look.

She wondered if she should arm herself with something. She planned to break into someone's house and men were already after her. It seemed like a good precaution, so she made a cursory search of the house for something she could borrow. Ten minutes later she gave up. She didn't want a carving knife shoved down her jumper or a fire poker hanging from her belt. Instead she turned her attention, guiltily, to Mrs Watts' bedroom drawers with a vague notion she might find an old forgotten rape alarm or something similar.

She eventually recovered a lurid pink and black aerosol from the very back of the lowest drawer, a seventeen gram canister of Mace UV Defence Spray. She smiled to herself at the thought of giving old Bagshot a good dose of the stuff right in the eye.

Next she went into town because she remembered seeing Lucy and a few of her goth friends hanging around outside a pub. She wondered if she wasn't imagining everything and it occurred to her that Lucy might be found safe and well in one of her old haunts. Lucy was not at the pub. Several other hangouts came to mind, but these also turned up no clue to Lucy's whereabouts.

Tyler passed public toilets and, following a whim, went in to check the device. The place was empty so, after locking herself in a cubicle, she flicked the switch from the skull to the *Tower of Doom*. The tower was building, the sky behind it as stormy and brooding as ever. Good. She switched to the spirit symbol and peered into dark mist.

"Albert," Tyler whispered. "Are you there?"

She waited and then repeated the words.

A moment passed as mist stirred. Someone was coming. She could tell by the way it was swirling faster. Someone was disturbing the air, or whatever the stuff was. Suddenly a hard face pressed itself up against the glass and it was like looking through a wide-angle lens. Tyler let out a small, shrill sound and pulled away.

The ghost was a bristly old man in a tunic and chainmail. Even his head was covered in a mail coif. His face was lined with wrinkles, pockmarked and scarred and distorted in a malicious leer. When he'd backed away a little, she could see his tunic bore a coat of arms, two golden lions on a red shield.

"Bonjour, my lovely…" the ghost growled in a French accent. He bowed, mockingly, tilted his head and peered at Tyler as though he wasn't sure what he was looking at. "Who might you be then?"

Tyler didn't want to give her name.

"Is Albert there? I want to speak to Albert."

"And, who is this… Albert?" He pronounced it Al-bear, the French way, and he sounded like he planned to eat him. Or perhaps her. He rubbed grubby gauntlets together with delight.

"He's my friend. Is he there?"

"Ah, mais oui! I am your friend now! Entré, entré… Come in! And I will 'elp you with anything you want! Come in, come in…" The words were friendly enough but the way they were said made Tyler's skin crawl. Going in, or going anywhere near this creepy old man, was the last thing she wanted to do.

"So how did you die?"

"Ah! That is a good question. It is like this, you see… I was a knight; one of the knights who came over to England across the channel with William the Bastard. I fought in the battle of Hastings where I defeated many English warriors."

"You mean William the Conqueror. So you actually died in the battle of Hastings," Tyler concluded.

"But no! I survived the battle! It was in revenge that I was murdered a year later by some of the English *dogs* who endured our invasion…"

The outer door to the washroom squeaked open. Tyler froze, listening. Footsteps crossed the tiled floor. A shadow passed at the base of the cubicle door. Tyler turned the device and flicked the switch to the skull with a soft click. The footsteps halted. She had a bad feeling and tucked the device into her shirt. Carefully she put her hand on the edge of the door. It was badly fitted and, with a little applied pressure, a miniscule gap appeared between the door and the frame. She squinted out as best she could, caught a glimpse of a green, fur-lined coat, long black boots. She released pressure slowly. The green figure moved again and Tyler heard a tap running.

She'd had enough. The feeling was mounting and she feared things would only get worse. Tyler flushed the toilet and left the cubicle, head down and walking fast.

"You there!" a voice shouted after her. "Wait!"

Tyler bolted for the door and ran into the first shop she came to, not daring to look back. The chemists was big. It was her good fortune that it had two entrances. She lost herself amongst row upon row of medical supplies, hair driers, razorblades and deodorants. Having weaved her way around the store for a while, she used the other exit and dived into another shop.

The NVF

Lucy Denby's house was larger and smarter than Tyler's. It was daunting to think about going through with the crime she now contemplated, yet it seemed the right thing to do. She knocked on the front door, planning to ask 'Is Lucy home?' should anyone be in. Lucy's parents did not know Tyler but nobody answered the door anyway.

The bathroom window on the second storey was high, but the ladder had been easy to find in the unlocked garage round the back of the property. Tyler double checked the ghost machine to be sure it was set to the skull. She did not want to fall from this height without its protection. She was thin and agile enough to squeeze through the top window and then make her way, hands first, past the sink with its toothbrush clutter, to the floor.

Very nice.

Mr and Mrs Denby clearly had some money. A central, free-standing tub, glossy wood flooring, plush paintings on the walls and Victorian moulding. It looked even plusher than it did from the outside, and that was only the bathroom.

Tyler had the impression that Lucy was an only child. A quick search of the upstairs rooms confirmed this. Lucy's room was a confused mismatch of what her parents wanted her to be and what Lucy truly was. A white china lamp with a frilly, patterned shade graced the bedside. An elegant landscape painting on the largest wall dominated beautiful white painted furniture. In contrast, Lucy's character made itself apparent with a grim spewing of gothic posters, a life-size cardboard cut-out of Marilyn Manson and some equally morose posters of goth bands Tyler had never heard of. Her wardrobe was mostly black and a few items had been left draped over the foot of the grand, renaissance style bed. Under the frilly lamp lurked a shiny white skull incense burner, the last stick half burned. Yet none of these things held any interest for Tyler. She was after more books, more notes, more sketches. Anything that would help her on her quest to find Lucy. She had a thought and took out the ghost machine, setting it to the tower and, watching through the lens, moved about the room searching for any change in the tower's growth. Near the wardrobe the tower built slowly. No change. By the bed, the same, but when Tyler neared the bookshelf the tower began growing faster.

The bookshelf held several books of interest which Tyler took. Each one was about vampires or ghosts and the supernatural world. She repeated the action and the tower led her to the desk, again visibly speeding up construction when she pointed it in this direction, slowing down when she turned away. A search of Lucy's desk turned up little valuable information, except a big sheet of what looked like doodles and random scribbles. Tyler slipped this out from under everything else, folded it and put it with the books.

Next the device led her to some drawers, which she pawed through, clothes mostly. She found it, a cardboard file bearing the initials NVF. She was opening the file to take a quick look when a rattling sound alerted her. She left Lucy's room, following the noise. It was coming from the bathroom and she realised it was the ladder she could hear. Someone was climbing the ladder to the bathroom. Tyler dumped the pile of books on the landing and ran to the window. She unclasped the larger window beneath, threw it open and pushed at the ladder with all her might. The ladder fell away and, with it, the smart looking woman in a green fur-lined coat and black boots, belatedly trying to climb back down. Tyler did not wait to see the woman hit the ground.

She snatched up the pile she'd left and dashed downstairs knowing she'd not have long before the woman recovered from the short fall. She scrambled through the hallway searching for a front door key, found one hanging from a hook with several smaller keys, and was gone.

Back in Melissa's bedroom she opened the file marked *NVF* and flicked her way through it. Notes in Lucy's spidery handwriting crawled over pages. There were photographs of places, more sketches of people and a few seemingly random documents. One of these was an invoice with an official company logo at the top and, below, a printed list of items with dates and costs next to them in columns. The logo bore the initials NVF.

Underneath were the words *New Vision Frontiers*, in a small font. The image behind it all was a globe overlaid with a spiral. Beneath all this was a line which, Tyler thought, was meant to explain what the NVF did.

Specialists in New World Logistics & Technology

What the hell was that supposed to mean?

Tyler's hands shook with nervous energy. She put the file down on Melissa's bed and took out Lucy's notebook from her pocket, flipped through pages, stopped at the page where she'd seen the NVF mentioned the previous night. She found the place where Lucy had written with a blue pen in careful, neat hand writing, *something not right – NVF not what it appears* and, beneath, had then scrawled in pencil, *Steal the device! Dangerous!*

NVF not what it appears…

Was Lucy suggesting that the NVF did not really stand for New Vision Frontiers? That it was not a company who dealt with some kind of logistics and technology? Tyler folded the corner of the page so she could easily find it again. She turned back a few pages and found the sketch of Bagshot. Taking a pencil she wrote in small letters above the image *NVF*, followed by a question mark. She went through the notebook again, searching for other sketches and hoping to match them to the other two men she'd seen with Bagshot, but she couldn't be sure she recognised any.

Leaving the file aside she rifled through the other things she's taken from Lucy's room. She unfolded the paper from Lucy's desk and marvelled at the multitude of doodles and patterns. It was like a weird landscape made up of individual shapes and marks. Every now and then there was a note, a line of words or a recognizable image like an eye or a heart. Spiders and their webs were commonplace. Tyler found a dagger dripping blood and a creepy silhouetted figure. She also found a little sketch of a sleek woman with tall black boots. What really drew her eye to this image among the many was the coat that Lucy had coloured green. Was it the woman who had been following her, Tyler wondered? It seemed too big a coincidence not to be.

She turned to a clean page in Lucy's notebook and began adding her own notes.

Woman in black boots and green coat – NVF?

She took out the ghost machine and switched on the ghost viewer. Nothing. She called for Albert but, finding only mist, switched it back to the skull.

She knew Melissa's mum and dad would be returning from work before too long and didn't want to be discovered there, so Tyler went all through the house making sure she'd left no signs of her presence. She found the hair dye box in the bathroom and binned it, wiped up the few tell-tale drops of dye from the basin. She cleared a space under Melissa's bed and tucked her things away out of sight in the closet. When she heard someone at the back door she slipped under the bed and began reading more from Zebedee Lieberman's strange book.

She heard pots and pans downstairs, the fridge door, water running in the sink and guessed it was Mrs Watts.

The next chapter was titled *The Other: Fact or Fiction*? Unlike previous chapters it had no subheadings. The pages simply ran into each other in a sprawling mass of arguments about what ghosts, spirits, genies, demons - whatever you like to call them – actually were. At one point Zebedee stated they were most definitely the souls of the dead, an essence that lived on, one not reliant on a house to live in, such as a human being. In another place he argued they were demons or, at least, that they could become demons over a period of time, once they'd truly forgotten who they used to be in life, and subsequently taken on new characteristics. It all seemed pretty farfetched to Tyler, but she felt she needed to read it nonetheless.

A short way in, she came upon several pages of black and white illustrations. Most of them looked like etchings, quite old, and they each had images of the discussed entities. Indian demons leered with a concerning number of arms, English ghosts levitated, Egyptian figures with animal heads walked sideways and eastern genies spouted from various glimmering containers.

By the end of this long and rambling chapter, it was Tyler's opinion that Zebedee himself was quite unsure about the truth of the matter.

She heard the back door again and hoped it was Melissa. It was.

"Tyler?" whispered Melissa when she came into the bedroom and noticed her things disturbed. "You in here?"

"Under the bed," Tyler whispered back.

"Good. Stay there a minute. I'll fetch my tea. Make some excuse. Mum won't mind and Dad's not back yet. We can share it. You hungry?"

"Starving."

When they'd eaten, Tyler told Melissa all she had discovered and asked if they could use Melissa's computer to look a few things up.

"Are you crazy?" asked Melissa. "You broke into Lucy's house?"

"It seemed like a good idea at the time."

"This is nuts."

"Hey, it got us the file on the NVF, didn't it?"

"Okay, okay. Let's take a look on the web. See what else we can find."

They Googled the NVF and found the company had a website. The site, however, was vague about exactly what the NVF did. It mentioned research projects and funding, new technological advances, though it didn't go into what they were specifically, and there was a section on opportunities within the company. Tyler clicked on that link and was taken to a page where company jobs were advertised. The NVF was currently seeking a secretary and a new lab technician. They found a contact page with a map and an image of the NVF building; sleek glass, shimmering metal and concrete. The futuristic building looked like it could well be harbouring all manner of scientific experiments. By the door was a small metal box she recognised as a security keypad. Tyler was stunned to learn that the listed address they gave was in Watford, less than two miles from Melissa's house.

"We have to go there," stated Tyler. "Lucy could be in there. Bagshot has got her and he's taken her there. I bet you."

"Yeah? And how do you suggest we do that? We're just two fourteen year old girls. We can't get in there. Be serious. Plus we don't even know if Bagshot is really with the NVF. He might have Lucy, but he could easily have nothing to do with that place."

"What if I'm right?"

"Well…"

"I'm right. You know I am."

Melissa studied Tyler briefly.

"Alright. I'll help get you in, but then you're on your own. See what you can find out and stay out of trouble. This is nuts…"

"Let's Google Lucy Denby."

"What? Why? No wait!" Melissa tapped out a name into the Google search bar and hit return. A list of search results for *Bagshot* filled the screen.

"There…" Tyler pointed to the third one down.

"Leopold Bagshot-Mcguire, director of the NVF since August 2010…" Melissa read aloud.

"See?"

"Oh my gosh! You're right."

"Don't sound so surprised." Tyler jotted down the full name beneath the sketch of Bagshot in Lucy's notebook. She tapped away on the keyboard of Melissa's computer. Lucy's Facebook page popped up and they skipped through an album of photos of Lucy and goth friends.

"Weirdos," sung Melissa, rolling her eyes.

Tyler nodded. "She has some pretty freaky friends." She scrolled through a whole bunch of profiles, each listed as *friends of Lucy Denby.* She stopped and stared at the screen, open mouthed. One of the profile pictures was not a photo, but a cartoon of a witch dressed head to foot in green and riding a broomstick. The name was also not a real name but an obvious pseudonym, *The Green Goddess.* Tyler wrote in the notebook again.

"What are you doing?" Melissa asked.

"I think I've seen this woman. The woman at Lucy's house. The woman in green. It's just a hunch, but…"

Tyler followed a message thread on the screen; conversation about what a real witch was and whether the wiccan religion was a modern perversion of the true practice or something else.

"She's a witch. The Green Goddess is a witch."

"Looks that way," Melissa agreed. "What exactly *has* Lucy got into?"

"In the last twenty four hours I've talked with two ghosts, broken into a house, skipped school, run away from home and become a thief… Who am I to judge?"

"Good point."

They read more about Lucy on her Facebook page, learned she was in several dodgy-looking clubs and that she had many strange *friends*, none of them from school. In her on-line profile she listed her interests as 'goths, vampire stories, dark music and all things creepy'.

Tyler began typing quickly.

"What are you doing now?"

"I'm registering myself on the site. Well, not myself. I'm using a false name and your email address. I can't use mine."

"Hang on… You're using *my* email address?"

"You've got to have an email address to register."

"But…"

"Too late." Tyler hit return. A message popped up saying *your password has been sent to your email address.*

"I don't believe you!" said Melissa. "You've gone completely nuts…"

"You gonna help me or not?"

Melissa considered this.

"You're the only one who knows what's really going on except me. Oh, and Lucy. But then she can't really help right now on account of the fact that, well, she's been kidnapped."

"Alright. Move over." Melissa took the seat at her desk and went into her email inbox, found the password and then gave Tyler the seat again.

"I still think you're crazy."

Tyler was already busy entering fake details on her fake profile. Before long, a new member of Facebook, Becky Jones, was submitting friend requests to Lucy Denby and the Green Goddess.

"Now we wait," Tyler said, when she was done.

"Okay. What's next?"

"I'd best get back to my hideout before it gets too late."

"Okay. I'll let you know if Becky Jones gets any messages."

"Thanks. Thanks for all your help. Don't forget to use my new number if you want to call or text."

Tyler slipped out of the back door whilst Melissa's parents were in the lounge. She made her way back to the warehouse by a different route, just in case anyone was still trying to follow her and then she used her secret back way in. The warehouse was cold and unwelcoming but she was glad for it nonetheless. She crept her way up the stairs and was relieved to find no sign of anyone else being there. Her makeshift bedroom was just as she'd left it. Once the door was bolted and she was wrapped up in a coat and the sleeping bag, Tyler took out the red book and continued reading.

Zebedee's next chapter was *Necromancy and the Other Realm*. This began with an explanation of what necromancy was, for which Tyler was grateful, because she'd never heard of such a thing. It appeared that necromancy meant, basically, talking to the dead, but Zebedee went on to write about the various ways one might do that and these included some talk of magic, black magic and mediums, or as Zebedee explained, people who had a particular gifting, or ability, to communicate with ghosts. The chapter explained about ouija boards and séances and had a section with accounts of ghost stories in which people claimed to have spoken with ghosts. It was all pretty creepy. Tyler shivered and turned another page. She put the book down. She'd been so busy with everything else that she'd not managed to speak to Albert. She wondered if he'd found anything out for her, but peering into the ghost machine's mist and calling for him got her nowhere. He'd vanished. Tyler turned back to the book and scanned through the remaining pages.

Chapter Six was the missing one, with an odd page inserted. The following chapter was on *Practical Ghost Haunting* and the last section was entitled *Closing Comments by Orealia Stephensen.* This last chapter struck Tyler as an oddity. The little voice in her head was asking, *why did Zebedee Lieberman not write the last chapter himself?* It was strange. Tyler read on. It seemed that Orealia Stephensen had been a close friend of Zebedee and, upon his sudden death, she had taken it upon herself to complete his work. However, she did not appear to share Zebedee's enthusiasm for the subject, nor did she tend to agree with his opinions. She explained that his sudden demise was mysterious and that he had died whilst doing research for his book.

Tyler thought this very curious. The entire chapter had a sad feel about it and it closed with a plea from Orealia Stephensen to *keep away from anything to do with Ghost Haunting.* This seemed the oddest thing of all, as *that* was what the book was supposed to be about.

Shrugging this off as just one more peculiarity of the book, Tyler set *Ghost Haunting* to one side and peered into the ghost machine again. She called for Albert softly and was surprised when a moment later he appeared.

"Alright, Missy," he said with a grin. "Is it tomorrow already?"

"It is, Albert. It's good to see you. How are you?" Tyler kicked herself the moment she asked.

"I've been better, I suppose," replied Albert with a grin. "After all, I'm dead aint't I."

"Yes, of course. Sorry." Tyler swallowed, feeling uncomfortable. "Did you manage to find anyone? I mean, anyone who might know about the device?"

"I asked around, yeah. Not many on this side knows much about no device. But there was this one old maid. Said she'd seen some-fing like it before. Back when she were alive, she said. Seems she were a witch, ya' see. She were helpin' another old girl. They were tryin' t' trap a ghost. They had this thing, this device and the idea was to get the ghost to go into it so they could use its power for themselves. But some-fing went wrong and the old maid got sucked into the device instead. Says she's been dead ever since."

"So the device can trap the spirits of living people as well as ghosts?"

"I s'pose. That's what the old maid told me anyways. From what she said, it's easier that way. Ya' see, to trap a ghost, ya' first gotta find one. An' that ain't always so easy."

Tyler thought about this for a moment.

"Do you think she was tricked by the other witch? Perhaps it wasn't a mistake. Perhaps nothing really went wrong…"

"Who knows, Missy?"

"Can you get her to come and speak to me here?"

"Maybe. I'll see what I can do."

"Albert, when I came looking for you before, I met an old man, an old soldier. I think he was French. He was horrible. Do you know who he was?"

"Oh, that'll be old Travis. Gor-blimey, I should 'ave warned ya' 'bout 'im. You should stay away from 'im. 'E's a true rotter, so 'e is. 'E'll do ya' no good…"

"I will stay away from him if I can. I didn't exactly go looking for him."

"Good. Best ya' don't." Albert squinted at Tyler briefly.

"Did you find out anything else about the device?" she asked.

"You look different. What you done to ya 'air?"

"Oh, I dyed it and cut it short. Like it?"

"Yeah. Suits ya, don't it."

"The device, Albert?"

"Alright, alright. Yeah, I did find some-fing out. The old maid told me, if it's like the one she saw, it does many a marvellous fing. Many *magical* fings, she said – all using the power of the ghosts what's inside it."

"Magical things? Like what?"

"You can use it to tell the future. You can use it to look back into the past, too. She even said it can make you fly."

"Really?"

"Cross my 'art! Tha's what she said. She said it were called a con-trap, I fink. Yeah, that were it – as in con-trap-shun. It were called that 'cause to make it work you first 'ave to con ghosts into the trap, see?"

"A contraption. Yes, I see. Did she tell you anything specifically about the contrap?"

"There were one thing. Said it could look through stuff. You know, like solid walls. She said if you set it right, you could use it to look right through walls an' every-fing for miles around."

"Really?"

"Tha's what she said. Tha's all though. She didn't tell me no more about it. She went all quiet like. Like she were remembering' some-fing."

"Albert, have you ever heard of a man named Bagshot? Did Lucy ever mention him?"

"No, I don't reckon she did. Sorry, Missy."

"Don't worry, Albert. I'll look for you tomorrow. Thanks for your help." Tyler blew him a kiss and waved good bye.

"Bye for now, Missy."

A few minutes later, as Tyler was lying in her sleeping bag and trying to figure out the other symbols on the contrap, she thought of something else she wanted to ask Albert. She looked for him again but he had gone.

She flicked the switch to the symbol of the eye that was drawn as though it was looking directly at her. If her logic was correct, the eye facing the right was most likely for looking into the future. The eye facing to the left was probably for looking into the past. This left only the forward facing eye. She watched as the contrap rotated until the eye symbol took its place at the top where the chain was connected. She turned the contrap over and looked onto the glass. At first she saw nothing except the dark murky glass of the crystal, but as she gazed into it she began to make out small details. She discerned the room around her emerging slowly, as though the thing was waking up. Before long she could see the whole room through the glass as she turned her head to look about, always with the glass held before her eye. Yet Albert had said the contrap could look right through solid things. *That* was not happening. Not at all. It was just like looking through a small piece of glass and everything in the room appeared as solid as ever. Tyler puzzled over this for the next hour or so until, when testing it yet again, her little finger happened to snag on the chain accidentally. The small tug on the contrap sent her vision through the warehouse walls, the buildings opposite and into the next street. She looked again in disbelief. With her little finger now free of the chain, everything had morphed back to normal and the room was as it had been. So carefully taking hold of the silver chain, she grasped the contrap firmly and dragged the chain downwards, rotating the narrow middle collar slowly clockwise. It moved with a soft clicking sound.

"Wow!"

When she peered through the glass it was like the whole world morphed forwards, passing through solid material as though thin air, yet all the time she could see walls, shapes, objects, textures, every detail. Tyler was amazed. The further round the edge of the contrap she moved the chain's anchor point, the further away the image took her. Releasing the chain allowed the contrap to automatically drag the anchor point back to the top. She tried again, wondering how far the contrap could look, but released it when she, by chance, focused upon a naked backside in a shower, in a house she estimated was likely two or three miles away.

*

It was midmorning when the new mobile received a text from Melissa with a double bleep.

'Police in school again, asking about u now. No news on LD. It's in the newspapers. Hope ur ok. NVF when?'

Tyler hit reply.

'TONIGHT' she typed, hit send, turned over, went back to sleep.

Missing

An hour later she was awake and planning. There was much to do. She wished she had more time to work out what else the contrap did and how, as it would clearly come in handy when trying to break into a scientific research facility. But that could take weeks and, if Orealia Stephensen was to be believed, could prove very dangerous. In truth Tyler was worried that Lucy was in grave danger. If this device was as important as she thought it was, entire nations could be fighting to get hold of it. What was the life of a young girl when such things were at stake? The people chasing her would not consider murder an issue if it meant they'd get hold of the contrap. She wanted to get into the NVF building as soon as possible. If Lucy was there, they needed to get her out, make her safe. If she wasn't, they still needed to learn where she was.

Tyler sent another text to Melissa warning her that she'd be waiting in her bedroom after school as before. Then they could set out together and put phase one into action. Phase one was to enter the NVF building during the daytime when it was open and in use. This was their opportunity to learn what they needed to do to break in later on, after dark, when everyone had gone home. The break-in would be phase two.

Tyler stuffed a black outfit into her rucksack. She kept the contrap on its chain about her neck. *That* was small enough to hide in her shirt and too valuable to leave behind. She checked it was set to the skull symbol and tucked it away. She would need to travel light this time, so everything else would have to stay in her hideout.

She went into the other room where she'd blocked several of the windows up with old bits of board and carpet tiles she'd found lying around. From here the street below looked quiet. Clouds of slate were an army assaulting an ashen sky. It would get dark early today. Tyler hoped it would not rain and shivered at the thought of what lay ahead. She missed her mum and dad, wished she could go to them, go home, give it up. But every time she considered this, something stopped her. That small voice kept saying she could not. She *must* not. It would endanger them and herself *and* they would take the contrap to the police, the government, whoever. But *that* would be wrong and Tyler knew it. The contrap was dangerous. It needed to be destroyed, or buried forever, or locked away. Yet even now as she realised this fact, she could not allow that either. The contrap had people in it. Dead or alive, they were people, and they should be released, not held captive forever and forced to do another's bidding. This, then, became Tyler's secret goal. She would share it with no one, but aim to find a way of releasing the ghosts that were held captive inside. Then she planned to destroy the thing for good.

*

The newspaper article was brief and carried the same picture of Lucy as the poster. It ran under the title of 'MISSING: LUCY DENBY'.

Police are currently looking into the mysterious disappearance of local fourteen year old school girl, Lucy Denby. Lucy was last seen several days ago on Friday 12th December, around 3:45p.m. when she left Northwood Secondary School in Potter Street. Her usual walk home follows Potter Street, Hillside Road, Northwood Way and Gatehill Road.

Police are asking for anyone who thinks they might have seen Lucy after this time to call with details. It is feared Lucy has been abducted. Her case is the latest in a series of seven child disappearances in the area spanning the last year and a half. A substantial reward has been offered for information leading to Lucy's safe recovery.

Tyler folder the paper and tucked it into the top of the rucksack. *Seven child disappearances?* It was the first she'd heard of it, but then she didn't make a habit of reading the *Watford Observer*. All the same, the report left Tyler with a horrible feeling, an intangible fear she could not place. Were Lucy's disappearance and the previous six others connected in some way? She added another item to today's list.

Find out everything you can about the other six disappearances.

Melissa found Tyler reading one of Lucy's strange books under her bed after school.

"Any good?" she whispered.

"Interesting, I'll say that. Tell me, what kind of a person has books on actual vampires? I mean accounts of people who really think they're vampires, not just vampire stories…"

"Er, Lucy Denby…"

"Hmmm… Come on. We've got work to do."

Tyler told Melissa all she had discovered since they'd last met.

They printed a map off from the NVF website, even though they both thought they had a good idea of where the building was. They went over and over the plan.

"Leave nothing to chance," Tyler had said. It was something her dad had told her many times. *Always be prepared…*

Then it was a race to get there before the place closed up for the night. It was already dark. Street lamps were orange bugs frozen in ordered flight. It had not yet rained but the air had that heaviness Tyler recognised as a forewarning.

"What if someone recognises you?" Melissa asked as they walked briskly.

"You think they will?"

"I guess this Bagshot guy might. If he got a good look at you, I mean. He might see through your little makeover."

"Well, unless you want to go in alone…"

"Not really."

"Then we'll both have to keep an eye out for him. You'll know him when you see him. Grey beard, tall with thick rimmed glasses. If I see him coming I'll hide my face or something. I have a newspaper. I can pretend to be reading it. If you see him before I do, sneeze. If I hear you sneeze, I'll know he's coming our way."

"What if I sneeze because I just need to sneeze?"

Tyler shook her head despairingly.

"Then I'll probably be able to tell it was a real sneeze. And anyway, if he's not there, there won't be a problem."

"Alright. Bloody hell, I'm nervous."

"You should be. We're about to do something either very clever, or really stupid. But either way we'll be safer together. My dad says *two heads are better than one.*"

"Let's hope he's right," said Melissa.

The NVF building was in a corner of the town where other new-looking businesses clustered, an upmarket version of the industrial area where Tyler had found her hideout. The girls found it to be an intimidating place as they made their approach and Melissa would have turned back had Tyler not insisted that Lucy's life depended on their investigation.

Before they got too close, Tyler took out the contrap, set it to the eye symbol and viewed the building through it. She saw people working in rooms, walking corridors and sitting at desks. It was difficult to search in this way as she could never quite be sure if she'd been through every room, but she could not find any figure in there who could be Lucy.

"It's no good," she said, tucking the contrap out of sight. "We'll have to go in. Search it properly."

The building itself was large, but low; only two stories. They recognised it immediately as the one they'd seen on the website, only in real life it now seemed far more sinister. Melissa was shaking visibly.

"You gonna be alright?" Tyler asked.

"Yes, just give me a minute."

"Chill. Here, have one of these. It might take your mind off it." Tyler shook a Tic-Tac into Melissa's palm. "Well, here we go."

They pushed on the massive glass door and went in. Reception was an airy open plan space with three tropical pot plants and comfortable office furniture clustered around an unused coffee table. A severe faced woman with wavy red hair and a pinched nose peered over half-moon glasses from behind a desk. She put down a paper when the girls, looking around with interest, arrived before her. Tyler scanned the room for CCTV cameras but found none.

"Yes? May I help you?" the woman asked.

Tyler coughed nervously.

"My mum says there's a receptionist job going here. Is that right? She sent us to collect a form."

"That post is still being advertised, yes. You are aware you can download the application form directly from the website?" the woman explained, clearly irritated at the disturbance.

"Oh, yes. Yes we are," said Tyler nodding vigorously and smiling as best she could. "But my mum's printer broke the other day. We need a new one. So she asked us to pick up a form from here. Would that be okay? Do you have the form?"

"Very well," said the woman. "Just a minute…" She busied herself hunting through shelves of paperwork and paper trays of documents behind her desk. A moment later she returned to the desk empty handed.

"We're all out. You'll have to wait here while I copy some more. Please take a seat. I won't be a minute."

They sat briefly until the receptionist was out of sight. Tyler jumped up and used the contrap to check for approaching people. Melissa checked the stairs, peering through the safety glass of doors.

"All clear?" asked Tyler. Through the contrap she could see corridors, rooms, windows, chairs, desks and a few figures seated at computers but no one on the move.

"All clear," Melissa confirmed.

With a wink at Melissa, Tyler slipped through the closest door and hid behind it, listening in a long empty corridor. Ideally she'd wished for a key or a key card or some sure-fire way of getting back in once everyone else had gone, but this came with risks. A missing card or key would be noticed and suspicion aroused. Also a key card did not rule out the possibility of a code number being used on an entrance keypad. All *that* was just too much to hope for.

This plan gave her time to find exactly what she needed, whichever it was.

She heard the door open and close, back in the reception area. Through the door she heard the receptionist and Melissa talking.

"Oh, she's gone…"

"Oh, don't worry. She had a phone call. She had to go. Emergency… I told her I'd get the form for her and drop it round later."

"All right then. Here it is. Have it filled out and returned before next Friday. Interviews begin the following Thursday."

"Thanks. I'll be sure to pass that on. Bye."

In the corridor, Tyler viewed the rooms and corridors around her through the contrap. A moment passed and she guessed Melissa had left the building. Rooms either side of the passage appeared to be offices. She could see transparent figures working at transparent desks on transparent chairs. She needed to find a hiding place, somewhere to sit and wait. She headed deeper into the building, noting wall signs as she went. She passed the *Accountancy Department* and the *Human Resources Department* and a door labelled mysteriously *Documentation.* She was growing disappointed by the time she reached a lobby. The building seemed to have no scientific or experimental stuff in it at all. It was all offices, no laboratories or crazed professors. Still, she consoled herself, that did not mean that Lucy was not hidden away there somewhere. She still wanted to search the place properly, to be sure.

Before moving she checked the way was clear with the contrap and she noted the presence of motion sensors tucked away high up in corners and on walls. And they were active. She could see the little red LEDs flashing. There *was* an alarm then. That confirmed to her she would need to learn the code for the keypad on the door, or find out how it was operated if not with a code.

Tyler found a ladies' washroom, locked herself in a cubicle and waited.

It was already getting towards the end of the day, but Tyler had no way of knowing what time the workers at the NVF would leave and lock up. She hoped it would not be a long wait.

A woman came in and used the cubicle next door. When she was alone once more, Tyler slipped the rucksack from her back and changed clothes, stuffing her original outfit quickly into the bag. Now she was ready. She checked her watch.

4:55p.m.

There was movement in the contrap. She could see office workers packing things away, loading files into briefcases and tidying desks. A few minutes later they began to leave their places to make their way to the front doors. Tyler positioned herself so that she had a good view of the door's keypad. By adjusting the lever on the side of the contrap she could control her visual distance from the keypad. It took a few moments of fine control to get it just right, but then she could see the keypad clearly and was close enough to see the keys well. By the time the last person was leaving, Tyler was ready and waiting with Lucy's notebook to hand. She shifted focus slightly and moved up to find the face. The man was tall and although the contrap made him appear transparent, she could still make out a beard and those thick rimmed glasses.

"Bagshot," she said under breath.

She refocused, watched the ghostly hand select ALARM and LOCK from the key pad and then tap in a key code.

30011933

A translucent finger hit ENTER and a buzzer sounded from somewhere. Tyler guessed it came from the reception hall. She quickly jotted down the number as Bagshot let the door close behind him. Tyler didn't know much about alarm systems but she realised she would not have long before the alarm kicked in and trapped her inside the washroom unable to go anywhere without triggering motion sensors. She checked to see that everyone was leaving the building and not hanging around outside. A moment later she was in the corridor, sprinting to the front door, selecting DISARM and UNLOCK on the keypad and tapping in the number she'd copied. Finally she hit ENTER. A low tone sounded for several seconds, startling her. She ducked beneath the receptionist's desk in fear of being spotted by Bagshot or other workers who were now getting into cars or walking away. To her relief, no one returned to the building. She took a moment to text Melissa.

'PHASE 1 DONE. THE DOOR CODE IS 30011933. C U @ 9.'

The double bleep made her jump out of her skin when Melissa's reply reached her a minute later.

'Will b there. X'

Tyler set her mobile to vibrate and slipped it into the pocket of her black combats.

To search the place efficiently she really needed Melissa. Tyler was sorely tempted to get on with it now rather than face a tedious wait of four hours, but then what if someone had forgotten something? What if Bagshot, or one of his men, came back? It was too risky and her torchlight would be seen from outside the building. Better to wait until Melissa was there. Two could search the place in half the time. Two could warn each other if danger arose. Also she figured there would be fewer people about at that time of night, so less chance of getting caught. With little else to occupy her, Tyler took out the contrap, slipped the switch to the spiral symbol and called Albert's name softly.

Stars

Albert was not around. She waited in the dark watching the whirling fog in the contrap for what seemed like forever before switching to the *Tower of Doom*. The tower was building steadily. It was taller than she'd ever seen it before. She wondered if the tower showed her how she was doing, a kind of progress report. Every time she felt she might be getting somewhere, the tower grew taller; miniscule blocks of stone appearing and fitting into place. Whenever she was resting or getting nowhere with her mission, the tower crumbled.

She checked her list, risking a glance with the torchlight.

Pack bag
Buy newspaper
Meet Melissa

Break in to the NVF
FIND LUCY DENBY
Find out everything you can about the other six disappearances

She ticked off the first four items and felt good. Only a trivial two items left on today's list; relatively good going compared to the last few days.

A light flickered somewhere outside the dark glass of the NVF building. Tyler hurriedly switched off her torch and peeked over the reception desk. A man was out there, tall and in dark clothes sweeping around a long-handled torch. She glimpsed a peaked cap and a yellow badge at the top of his arm. A security guard. She ducked as the torch beam passed over the desk, held her breath, felt that old anxiety rising inside.

Not now… Please not now!

She crawled to the end of the desk and chanced another look. The man was still there, a hand to his brow, shielding eyes from reflections. He peered back at her but casually moved on, oblivious to her in the gloom.

It had been enough of a scare though. Tyler's heart was pounding, anxiety soaring uncontrollably. She fumbled for her mobile, fought to get it out of her pocket, hammered the keys until Melissa's number popped up. Her breathing was too fast and only getting faster.

Calm down, she told herself. *The danger has passed.* But it was too late. The panic attack was already triggered. Her chest felt compressed as though an elephant was sitting on it. However hard she breathed she couldn't get enough air.

Pick up, pick up. Pick up…

"Hello? Tyler?"

"Say, uh, the words… Uh, uh, uh. Say the words…"

"What? Who is this?" At the other end of the line the penny dropped. "Oh! Er, er, it will be okay. It will all be okay. Calm down, Tyler. Tell me what's happened."

Tyler's frantic breathing subsided. A moment later she was able to talk.

"Thanks, Mel. Better now. Sorry to give you a fright. I'm okay. I'm in the NVF and I'm waiting. It was just a security guard came by and made me jump. I'd best go. You still okay for later?"

"Yep."

"See you then. Bye."

"Okay. Bye."

Tyler pocketed the phone and tried to relax. There was no sign of the security guard. She took another look at the ghost machine, switched back to the spirit symbol.

"Albert?" She called softy. "Albert, are you there?"

A slight figure closed in from the haze.

"You looking for someone, girly?" The voice was a girl's, high and light. As the girl drew closer, Tyler could see she was about twelve, maybe thirteen years old. She was transparent like the others but she looked more ancient than any Tyler had seen so far. She wore a fine band of dark leather around her head like a narrow crown which held long mousy hair from her face. A simple drab dress hung from her slight form. Her face would have been pretty had it not been so drawn and dark eyed and pinched into such a scowl.

"I'm looking for Albert. Is he there?" asked Tyler.

"No."

"Is there any chance you might look for him for me?"

The girl mimicked Tyler mockingly.

"*Is there any chance you might look for him for me?* No. There isn't."

"Who are you? If you don't mind me asking?"

"My name is Claudia. And actually I *do* mind. Sticking your nose in here – acting like you own the place… Who do you think you are? "

"Well, my name is Tyler, since you asked so politely."

Claudia pulled a face, tongue out.

"What a horrid name."

"Who *are* you exactly?" Tyler wanted to know. "I mean, I know your name, but who are you? You look really old. And why are you so mean?"

"Mean?" said Claudia. "I thought I was being quite friendly."

"Yes, well… Never mind that. Who are you? Where do you come from?"

"I come from Londinium, of course. I was a slave when I was alive. A slave to a rich Roman nobleman. He didn't like me very much though…"

"Oh, I don't see why that would be," said Tyler. "So you lived in the time of the Romans? In London?"

"Yes of course. What a silly question."

"If you're Roman, then why don't you speak like a Roman? Shouldn't you be speaking in ancient Latin or something?"

"I'm dead aren't I. I can speak just how I want to. And in any case, you wouldn't understand a word I said if I spoke my old language. So what would be the point?"

"Oh I see. So you learned to speak English after you died?"

"You learn a lot of things when you die. Everything becomes clear. It's a shame really. People would live differently if they knew what we know."

"Yeah? What do the dead know?"

"We're forbidden to tell the living that kind of stuff. I *could* tell you, of course, but then I'd have to suck out your soul and shove you in the Shivering Pool…" Claudia chuckled to herself.

"Right… So what happened to you? How did you die?"

"Well, that's a very personal question, isn't it?"

"Yes. I suppose it is."

"Alright. I'll tell you, if you really want to know…"

"I do. Please tell."

"It all happened one night when Master had been drinking, as usual. He always used to hit me at the best of times. When he drank too much wine, it just got worse. One night I was pouring wine into a goblet for him. The very best wine, it was, and I spilled a drop on the floor. Well, old Master Titus didn't like that very much, did he. He stood up and wacked me on the head with his staff. I never got up after that. Still, serves him right, doesn't it. Silly old fool. He wasn't very pleased when I didn't get up. He got all cross. Really angry. I was quite frightened for a moment, thinking about what he might do to me. Then I realised I was dead. The old fool had already killed me when he hit me on the head. That'll teach him. If he carries on like that he'll not have any slaves at all in a month or two."

"What a horrible story. I'm sorry you were treated like that."

"Yes well… That's the life of a Roman slave. It always was the luck of the draw. I knew some girls who got *good* masters. Masters who treated them nice. Some even fell in love with their slave girls and married them.

Gave them freedom. Not me though. Oh well. It doesn't matter anymore. I'm dead now and that's the main thing."

"Is it?"

"Is *what*?"

"Is being dead the main thing?"

"Er… Yes. Isn't it?"

"I don't know… So you became a ghost because…"

"Slaves don't get treated that well, you know. Not in life. Not in death. He couldn't be bothered to bury me, or to pay for a funeral. He rolled me into a ditch at the edge of town and went about his business."

"I'm sorry," said Tyler and she meant it.

"Doesn't matter really…"

"I know. Because you're…"

"…*Dead*. Yes. Well anyway. I have to go now. Do you know? You're really very ugly."

"Okay. Thanks for that, Claudia."

"You're welcome. Good bye." Claudia froze in mid-air where she was hovering and then shot off into the distant fog.

"That was weird," said Tyler to herself. She checked her watch. Less than half an hour had passed. She wished she'd brought Zebedee's little red book so she could read the chapter she'd saved until last, the one on *Practical Ghost Haunting*. She had high hopes that, of all the sections of the book, this one would prove to be the most useful to her. However, she'd packed as light as she could so that she could sneak about easily and run quickly if need be. The red book was now sitting by her sleeping bag back in the warehouse.

Tyler tried the contrap again.

"Albert. Come on, Albert."

From way off in the distance, she heard a faint whistling. It grew louder. Someone else was coming through the drifting fog and she heard a high trill, a sad violin melody accompanying the whistle. Two figures emerged. One was Albert. The other was Marcus, or the *silent fiddler*, as Albert had called him. They came closer, Marcus letting the tune die when they noticed Tyler.

"Hi, Albert. I've been looking for you," said Tyler, relieved to see him. "Hello, Marcus."

"Alright, Missy?" said Albert.

"I'm alright. I wanted to ask you something else. Can you tell me, do you know anyone in there called Zebedee? Zebedee Lieberman?"

Albert considered this.

"I don't fink so. I can ask around though. 'E could be in 'ere. There's lots o' ghosts I don't know."

"Please do, Albert. It's important. If you find him, try and bring him to me. I'd like to meet him."

"I will, Missy. I will. By the way, Marcus 'ere wanted to speak with ya'."

"But he doesn't talk, does he?"

"Not normally, like, but it's different when you's a ghost. You can speak in different ways, see? I can 'ear what 'e's finkin', so I can tell ya' what 'e wants to say."

"Why's he want to speak to *me*?"

"I ain't a clue."

"Alright, Marcus, Albert… I'm listening…"

Albert closed his eyes and began to explain what the sad silent boy wanted to say.

"'E says he wants to tell ya 'is story, you know… To tell ya what happened to 'im and 'is family…"

"Okay."

"'E says it were in the war. The big war. The second big war. You know the one?"

"He means World War Two?"

"Tha's the one. 'E says 'im and 'is folks was livin' quite happy-like before it all begun. Then stuff started 'appenin'. Bad stuff. Soldiers came and took 'em away. 'E was with 'is family at first. They was all kept together in one great big village where everyone 'ad to wear a yellow star. It weren't a nice place. They took away every-fink they owned. They wouldn't let none of 'em work or nuffing. Then a bit later they took 'im away with the other kids an'e never saw his mum or dad again. Or any of 'is family. Then fings just got worse and worse."

"That's dreadful," said Tyler. She watched as a tear streaked its way down Marcus's grubby cheek. She wanted to give the boy a hug, yet there was no way to reach him.

"He saw some 'orrible fings in that place where they took 'im. The soldiers were killin' people. They'd shoot 'em just like that." Albert snapped his fingers. "For no reason at all. Everyone was livin' in fear for their lives. Marcus was made to work like the older ones, makin' bombs an' stuff for the soldiers.

"Them soldiers let 'im keep 'old of just one fing. 'Is violin. They used to make 'im play it for 'em. Then one day he broke a string whilst 'e were a'fiddlin'. 'E don't remember nuffink after that. 'E's been a ghost ever since. There's a few others 'ere with the same story to tell ya'. *Stars* I calls 'em. Not 'cause of the yellow stars they all 'ave, but 'cause it's like lookin' up at the night sky. They was all killed by the bad soldiers. They was all murdered, one way or another..."

Marcus wiped his eyes on his torn shirt sleeve and then turned to look behind him. Tyler found herself squinting into the mist beyond the two boys, trying to see what Marcus was looking at. Out of the haze she began to make out figures. Thin, grey figures with dark hollow-looking eyes. There were women and men, as well as children, and there were not a few of them. There were thousands and millions. The mist retreated leaving in its wake an ocean of wronged people, an entire nation filled her view, disappearing into the distance. Tyler wiped her eyes. Her face was streaming with tears because she'd never seen anything so sad. Her heart felt like it was tearing.

"Why... *Why* does he want to show me this?" she sniffed at Albert.

"'E thinks you should know, I suppose. Don't cry, Missy. It's alright."

"No, Albert. It's not alright. *This* will never be alright."

As she watched, the boys and the many were engulfed by the churning vapour and soon they were gone and she was alone.

Tyler sobbed uncontrollably for a long time.

Fire

A noise woke Tyler. She was in darkness. She hadn't meant to fall asleep. Now someone was coming into the building. A sudden bolt of nerves turned her stomach. She shuffled to the edge of the desk and stole a quick glance around its end. Melissa was tentatively crossing the reception area. Tyler relaxed.

"Pssssst. Over here," she whispered. "What's the time? I fell asleep."

"Five to nine. I'm early."

"Right. Did you see anyone around on your way in? Do you think you were followed?"

"No. No one around. It's pretty dark out there now and there aren't many street lights. Can't see why anyone would be hanging around in a place like this after dark. It's pretty creepy. I nearly bottled it on the way over."

"I'm glad you made it. Thanks for coming."

"Well, thanks for making me a part of this…" Melissa said looking around sceptically. "Where do we start?"

"You bring a torch?"

"Right here."

"Okay, you take that corridor. I'll take this one. From what I can tell they've all got rooms running off them. Work your way around and look for anything that might help. I'm fairly sure Lucy's not in the building but the device is hard to use. I can't easily tell where I am whilst it's passing through walls and rooms. But maybe we can learn something. Maybe they're keeping her somewhere else. We need to be quick. There's a guard somewhere outside and our torches can be seen through all this glass, so we make a quick search and get out of here. Right?"

"Right. What's the signal if I see someone coming?"

"Er, just shout *run* as loud as you can."

"Okay. See you in a while."

The two girls split up. Tyler used the contrap to check for people outside, but she could see no one around. She made her way down her corridor and into the first room. Not much to look at. She searched empty desks and found a filing cabinet that was locked. She considered booting up a computer to see what kind of things were on it, but quickly gave up on the idea. The light from the screen was too risky. Finding nothing of interest she moved on to the next room. More of the same. Four rooms later she was beginning to think they were going to find nothing of any help.

Then she found a room that was locked. On the windowless door was a sign which read 'Restricted Personnel Only'.

This is more like it.

She focused the contrap through the door and into the room to look around. She saw banks of computers, several filing cabinets and a lot of other office equipment. Some of the objects she didn't recognise, but then it *was* very dark in the room and she had no way of shining a torch in. There was one area of desk where moonlight reached from a high window, illuminating the things there. She stood on tiptoes and positioned the contrap as best she could to examine papers on the desk. The angle was all wrong. It was impossible to read anything, but then she had an idea. If she was in the room directly above, she could look down through the floor and see the papers perfectly well. She counted the rooms down from the end of the corridor. It was the seventh room. She found the stairs and made short work of them, went straight into the seventh room, lay flat on the floor and focused the contrap until it had passed through the carpet and the flooring.

One page immediately drew her attention. It was sitting on top of a pile of other papers and it had an image at the top, an image that made her hackles rise. It was a swastika. The Nazi emblem was printed or stamped on an old letter. She couldn't discern colours as the contrap showed everything in shades of translucent blue, but she imagined the letter was yellowed with age. It had creases in various places as though it had been folded up time and time again. It was also strewn with marks and stains. She tried to read it but quickly realised it was not written in English. It looked German to her. That made perfect sense, considering the swastika. Tyler couldn't read much German, but Melissa could read some. She'd even been to Germany. Several minutes later Melissa was face down, studying the document through the floor.

"This is amazing," she said. It was the first time she'd really used the contrap.

"Can you read any of it? What's it about?" asked Tyler.

"It's definitely a letter. It's from someone called Dr. Josef Mengele. I can't read his signature, but his name is typed underneath. I can't read much of it... Wow, this thing's hard to focus."

"It gets easier the more you use it."

"I can read a few words here and there. It seems to be about some kind of experiments. It's addressed to Dr. Von Verschuer at some place called the Kaiser Wilhelm Institute in Munich, Germany. It's dated the twenty first of October 1943."

"It's old, then."

"Uh-huh. It's older than my Granddad. There's a line here... Something about children being ill or sick. Then it says something about another experiment, no, a previous experiment. And this line here - I can make out just one word. Geist."

"What? As in *polter-geist*?"

"Yes. It seems he's saying something about a ghost or perhaps a spirit."

Tyler fetched out Lucy's notebook and had Melissa read out the details again. Tyler jotted it all down on a new page.

"We'd best move on," she said when she had finished. "Let's stick together. This place is freaky."

"Alright, but we've been here a while now. I think we should get out soon."

"I agree. Let's keep moving. We'll make it quick. Did you find anything down your half of the ground floor?"

"Not much," said Melissa. "Just these." She held out a fist full of pages. "Don't worry. I didn't take the originals. Someone had left a photocopier turned on, so I used it."

"Well done. What are they?"

"Not sure. Figured we could take a closer look later on when we've finished breaking the law."

"Good plan. Let's look in here."

They approached another room which turned out to be a kitchen. Next door was a washroom and then a lounge area.

"Nothing here. Let's try the other side," Tyler suggested, but as they were leaving the lounge area, something flashed in the beam of Melissa's torch.

"What was that?" Melissa asked.

"I don't know. Take a step back. Shine your light over there again…"

The same flash blazed briefly from a corner of the room beyond the longest of several grey couches.

Tyler went to the place, swept her torch around. She bent to retrieve something that glimmered like a piece of glass. It was a silver earring in the shape of a snake.

"Recognise this, Melissa?" she asked, lifting the earring and shining her torch onto it.

"That's one of the earrings Lucy got into trouble for wearing on sports day. I remember it well."

"She was here!"

Melissa's attention was drawn to the windows overlooking the car park.

"What's that?" she asked with a jolt of nerves.

Tyler turned to see a light bobbing its way through the car park outside below.

"Someone's seen us. They're coming. Let's get the hell out!"

They scrambled down corridors and stairs, skidded across the reception area and burst through the front doors. Stealth was no longer an issue. They had nothing to gain by trying to hide, but needed only to get away as fast as possible. They had a head start on the approaching figure, now shouting and aiming a light at them. Tyler guessed it was the security guard but didn't hang around to find out.

They bolted into the street.

"Split up!" said Melissa. "He can't chase us both…"

They parted, Tyler taking a route which went closer to the oncoming threat. She was the fastest and stood the best chance of escaping. For this reason she also wanted to draw whoever it was, away from Melissa. It worked. The pursuer stood no chance. Tyler left him behind puffing and doubled over, red faced. She gave him a grin and a cheeky wave before disappearing into the night.

*

Back in Melissa's bedroom they studied the pages Melissa had copied.

"This one's a letter from another place asking for parts for a machine. I can't tell what the machine is. The parts all have weird names. Six *tap heads*, whatever they are, some sort of *belt drive*, an *extractor valve* and fourteen *hydro-coils*… What have you got?" asked Tyler, both unimpressed and disappointed.

"Another invoice. This one is for half a ton of A4 paper. Not much help really. This here's a receipt for car tyres."

"That's all we have? They're just receipts and invoices for stuff they've bought or ordered. It doesn't help us at all."

"Let's see that letter? The one with the strange parts they asked for."

Tyler passed the letter to Melissa.

"Look. Here, at the top. This is a letter sent to the NVF, but something is strange about it. It's also sent *from* the NVF."

"How can that be?" asked Tyler. "Why would you send a letter from one place to the same place?"

"Ah, but it's not the same place. That's my point. It's another NVF building. They have a different building somewhere else. The address is still in Watford though. Ducks Hill Road."

Tyler grabbed the page back, stared at the address.

"Where's that?"

"Give me a minute." Melissa typed the road name into Google maps. "Here. It's on the other side of town."

Tyler grinned.

"Oh no. Not again," said Melissa.

"Melissa, we have to," said Tyler nodding. "She's there. I bet you, she's there. They took her to the place we were at tonight and then they hid her away in this other building."

Melissa shook her head.

"Seriously? We just broke the law. We broke into somebody else's property. We stole information from them. We even tampered with evidence!" She held up Lucy's earring.

"Shhhush! Your mum and dad will hear… We *stole* evidence. We didn't tamper with it."

"What's the difference?"

Tyler didn't answer.

"Right. I'll go by myself then," she said.

"Right. You do that. What should I do with this, by the way?" Melissa swung Lucy's earring before Tyler's face, a gothic silver snake with fake diamonds for eyes.

"Keep hold of it for now. There may come a time when we, when *I*, need to take it to the police."

"Okay. I'll keep it safe for you."

"Thanks. I'd best get back," said Tyler. "I'll be here tomorrow after school as usual. We've got some research to do…"

She was exhausted. It had been a long night and the thought of settling down in her sleeping bag and falling asleep was compelling despite the knowledge it would be in a freezing cold, empty, abandoned warehouse.

*

Tyler made her usual winding approach to the street where the old warehouse stood. She was dragging her feet and desperate for bed when she reached it, but then something made her look up. She could smell smoke in the air and knew somewhere nearby something was burning. She saw a flickering light in the sky and began to run. The old warehouse was on fire.

Flames licked up into the night, a golden crown flowing from the upper levels. She squeezed through the gap in the door and pounded the stairs, came out to meet a barrage of heat where her bedroom used to be. Within the dancing flames she could see her things incinerating. The door was open and burning also. Someone had been there. Someone had been through her stuff. And someone had set a fire. Sent a message. Above her head black smoke billowed. Tyler sheltered her eyes and peered into the fire, trying to get closer. The book was there. She could see it, the edges of the red cover curling and the pages turning to living ashes.

"NO!" she screamed. She tried again to get closer, desperate to run in, to save the book somehow. But *Ghost Haunting by Zebedee Lieberman* was gone and there was nothing she could do about it.

Tyler turned away and found the room where Bagshot and his men had cornered her. Everything was just as it had been left that night, except for one detail. Lucy's bag and its scattered contents were gone.

She checked the *Tower of Doom* and saw it was crumbling disastrously. She swore.

She left the warehouse, saddened and angered, in search of a new place to hold up. Was she being followed? At this point in time, Tyler May no longer cared.

Ghost Haunting

Tyler slept rough, wearing almost everything she had, and looking like a vagrant. It was freezing during the night and she promised herself she would never do it again. She hardly slept at all but came to her senses as the sun rose, sitting on the ground with her knees drawn up to her chest and her arms wrapped around her legs, huddled against a wall. Above her, a crooked signpost told would-be cyclists to get off and walk. She shed her outer layer of clothes and felt marginally less tramp-like and threading the narrow alley she made her way into town where she knew there was a huge Waterstones.

"Yes?"

"I'm after a book called *Ghost Haunting*. It's by Zebedee Lieberman."

The young, trendy, yet rather geeky shop assistant raised his brows at Tyler cynically.

"I've never heard of it," he said.

"Neither had I. Look, just search for it will you? If you can order me a copy, I'll pay right now. I have the money." Tyler waved a twenty pound note at the geek.

There was a brief wait as thin, practised fingers rattled on the shop's networked computer's keyboard.

"Nope. Sorry. We don't have it. I also did a web search. I can't find any record of such a book ever being printed."

"No worries. Thanks anyway."

"Any time," the assistant shrugged.

Tyler left the shop.

*

"Do you think they're Nazis?" asked Melissa.

"Well what do *you* think? They have documents dating back to the Second World War all about some freaky experiments involving spirits. They nearly *killed* me. They have taken Lucy, and who knows how many other kids. They want this contrap and will stop at nothing to get it. They torched *my* warehouse…"

"It wasn't *your* warehouse."

"You know what I mean…" Tyler was flicking through Lucy's notebook, hoping to find more clues. Hoping to find something she'd missed so far. She opened it on the page where she'd scribbled down the door code for the NVF building's security keypad.

"Why did you write down that date?" asked Melissa, peering over Tyler's shoulder.

"It's not a date. It's the security code for the NVF building. It's the one you used to get in last night when we had our little adventure."

"Oh yeah, but it *is* also a date," said Melissa. "People often use dates for codes they need to remember. My computer user-password is my birthday, for example." She took the notebook from Tyler and read out the key code. "Three, zero, zero, double one, nine, double three. That's the thirtieth of January nineteen thirty three."

"Does that date mean anything to you?" asked Tyler, bemused and becoming disinterested. Melissa sat at her desk and began typing on her keyboard.

"No. But let's see if Google knows it…" She finished typing, hit enter and a list of search results popped up on the computer screen. "Here we are."

They both scanned down the results. There were two hits relating to various laws, a hit about *seasonal variation*, and then something that caused Tyler's jaw to drop.

"That one. Click on that one." She pointed to the fourth list item. It was a reference from an on-line history book. Melissa clicked. They waited for the page to load up and then read about Adolf Hitler and how on 30th January 1933 he seized political power of Germany.

"Still think I'm talking nonsense?" Tyler asked. "The key code to the NVF building just happens to be the date on which Hitler took control of Germany. His 'great' moment of glory…"

"No, no, no… This can't be right. We don't have Nazis in England! That's ridiculous."

"It might be ridiculous but it's happening. That's why they have Nazi papers, that letter we saw… Don't you see? Did you read the paper report about Lucy? She's not the only one. Six other kids have gone missing from this area in the last year and a half."

"What are you saying? That an underground group of Nazis are stealing kids off the streets of Watford to use them in secret experiments? Do you know how ridiculous that sounds?" But even as she said it, Melissa's conviction wavered. She met Tyler's gaze and they locked eyes for a long moment.

"Oh - my - gosh… Nazis are stealing kids off the streets of Watford to use in secret experiments!"

"You see. It might sound unbelievable but what if it's true?" asked Tyler.

"We are the only ones who know…"

"Exactly. We have to stop them."

"No, wait! We can't. We have to go to the police now, surely," Melissa stated.

"You think they'll believe us?"

"No, but…"

"In any case I think some of the police are involved."

"Why do you say that?"

"Have you seen any progress from them? The police I mean. I went to the library earlier today. Checked every local paper printed in the last two years. I even printed off copies. The police have not found anything. Not a single clue about the missing kids. Don't you think that's a bit strange?"

"I suppose it is a bit odd."

"Can we look up a few more things on the net?"

"Get under the bed," said Melissa in a quick whisper. Tyler looked quizzically at her. "I think Mum's coming up the stairs," Melissa explained.

Tyler hid.

Mrs Watts came in as Melissa threw her school jumper over Tyler's foot which was protruding from the bed.

"You alright, Love?" Mrs Watts asked, poking her head round the door. "Thought I heard voices…"

"I'm fine. Just listening to a news report on a website. It's for a school project."

"Right. Dad says you forgot to take your form into school for the geography trip. It was supposed to be in three days ago."

"Okay. I'll take it Monday. Promise."

Mrs Watts left with a nod and a flat smile.

When it was safe again Tyler came out and joined Melissa at the desk.

"You going on the geography field trip?" Melissa asked.

"If I live that long…"

"I'm going, though Tanya Fields says Mr Hennings is an old perv. I've got to go with Mum and Dad tomorrow, by the way. We're visiting my gran. I tried to get out of it, but without giving anything away it was impossible…"

"It's okay. I'll be alright."

"Ready when you are."

"Do a search for," Tyler flipped through pages of Lucy's notebook, "Dr. Josef Mengele."

Melissa did the search and then read aloud.

"Dr. Josef Rudolf Mengele, born March 16th 1911 - died February 7th 1979, was also known as the Angel of Death. He was a German officer of the SS and a physician at the concentration camp Auschwitz. He was a doctor of anthropology having studied at Munich University and a doctor of medicine having also studied at Frankfurt University. He became notorious for his role in deciding who would be selected for forced labour and who would be sent to their deaths, as prisoners arrived at Auschwitz. However, he is more infamous for the cruel and bizarre experiments he performed on prisoners, thereby earning his nickname, the *Angel of Death.*" Alongside the information was a grainy black and white photograph image of a man's head and shoulders. Josef Mengele was a smart looking man with a confident smile and neatly cut hair.

Melissa was looking pale.

"Nice bloke, then," said Tyler.

"Oh yeah. A real honey-bunny," agreed Melissa.

"What about the *Kaiser Wilhelm Institute* in Munich, Germany?"

Search results were soon on the screen. Melissa clicked through to a site and read.

"The Institute of Anthropology, Human genetics and Eugenics - whatever that means - is the third Kaiser Wilhelm institute thought to have been involved in the crimes of the Third Reich…"

"What's the Third Reich?" Tyler asked.

"That's just another name for the Germans when Hitler was in charge."

"Right."

"It goes on to talk about research the Institute did. It seems it was all about the racial differences in people. You know, like what makes one person look different from another. Like what makes your skin black and mine white. It was all science work for the government. I mean the Nazi government."

"So the Institute was helping the government? Helping Hitler?"

"Yep."

"One more. Try Dr. Von Verschuer…" Tyler spelled out the name.

Melissa read out the information from the search.

"Dr. Otmar Freiherr Von Verschuer - that's a bit of a mouthful - became secretary for the German Society for

Race Hygiene in 1924 and worked at the Kaiser Wilhelm Institute of Anthropology – blah, blah, blah - until the Institute's dissolution in 1945."

"That's when the war ended isn't it?"

"Yes. It goes on about other places Von-what's-his-name worked at. More science stuff… Then it says this – one of Von Verschuer's most well-known assistants was Josef Mengele, who later became known as the *Angel of Death*… Ah, this is interesting. It goes on to say that in 1945 when they knew they had lost the war and that they would soon be discovered, Von Verschuer had all the research files moved to his private home. They reckon only some of the files about their experiments were ever found."

"Pretty creepy, huh?"

"Yep. Makes sense of the letter we saw though. This guy worked for the other guy assisting him with Nazi experiments and research stuff.

"Oh, by the way – you got a reply from the Green Goddess, or should I say, *Becky Jones* did…"

"Really? Let's see," said Tyler.

Melissa opened a new browser window on the screen and went to Becky Jones' Facebook page. They were soon looking at a new message that had come from the person professing to be the Green Goddess.

'Welcome friend! Tell me what you are in to? I'm collecting ghost stories. Have you ever seen a ghost? What's your story?'

Melissa clicked onto the Green Goddess's profile. Now befriended, Tyler's fake personality had access to more information on the profile, including a list of friends.

"Her friends are just as weird as Lucy's," noted Melissa.

"…Or even weirder," Tyler agreed.

"She says in her blurb she's collecting strange stories and researching all things to do with ghosts. She's a member of something called the *Glastonbury Originals*, a group called *Save the Kittens* and another group called *Blue Solstice.* What do you think they are?"

"Not sure I want to know," said Tyler, "though *Save the Kittens* sounds pretty harmless…"

Melissa clicked on the first group.

"The Glastonbury Originals look like a bunch of old hippies and weirdoes. Nothing new there…"

"What about Blue Solstice?"

Melissa clicked the mouse.

"They all look a bit more normal. There are a few goths in there. Hang on a minute." Melissa clicked through several other profiles of members of Blue Solstice. "They're all witches. Every one of them. Blue Solstice is the name of a coven."

"And the Green Goddess is after the device, I bet," said Tyler.

"What should I answer to her question?"

"Say, *I have seen a ghost.* Then say, *is there something you are looking for?*"

"Okay. If you say so." Melissa typed the reply and hit send.

*

Tyler slept under Melissa's bed that night.

"Don't you think that's weird – about Zebedee Lieberman's book?" whispered Tyler in the claustrophobic darkness. "It's like the book never existed."

"Maybe the guy in the shop doesn't know what he's doing."

"He seemed pretty sure of himself. Quite cocky, I'd say. I don't think it's *him.* I think there's something strange going on."

"You're telling me. Listen, we should go to sleep. You can search the internet yourself in the morning. Just wait until Mum and Dad have gone to work before you go moving around too much."

"I can use your computer?"

"Be my guest. You know the user password."

"Thanks, Mel."

"You're welcome."

"Good night."

"Good night."

Tyler wanted to use the contrap to see if Albert was around but she dared not. If he was there she'd want to speak to him and that would be difficult to do in whispers. She also wanted to try a few ideas out with the contrap, but again, that would have to wait until she was alone. She made a list for the next day by torchlight and went to sleep.

*

Melissa shook Tyler awake and was soon leaving with Mr and Mrs Watts and Melissa's younger brother, John.

Tyler showered quickly and ate breakfast, feeling guilty for pilfering food from Mr and Mrs Watts.

Not really knowing what she would face at the second NVF building, she wanted to be as fully prepared as possible. There were, therefore, a few items of shopping on today's list.

When Tyler returned from the shops, she turned on Melissa's computer and searched for the red book on Google. Nothing about a book called *Ghost Haunting* or a man named Zebedee Lieberman featured on the search results. Tyler tried a few different combinations of the words just in case something came up. Nothing did. It felt like a dead end.

She took out the contrap and called for Albert. No one was home.

She studied the contrap, looking at each symbol in turn. She couldn't find out anything more about it through the red book or from Albert, at least not right now, so Tyler did the only thing left that she could do. She tested it. She was desperate to know how else she could use it, as it had proved so useful in the NVF building. The next thing on her list was to visit the other NVF location and work out a way of breaking into that too. If the contrap could help her in any way, she needed to know.

She tried the eye symbol which faced right, flicking the switch and watching the contrap rotate into position. Then she turned it over and looked into the viewing glass. The glass was dark and misty as before, almost black. But as she waited, the mist cleared and she found she was looking at Melissa's room. But it wasn't the future. It was now.

Tyler held her hand up in front of the contrap and she could see it clearly. Then she tested a theory. She took hold of the chain and pulled it ever so slowly downwards, rotating the central section clockwise with a series of clicks. Light from the bedroom window began creeping across the room at an accelerated rate. She saw other shadows moving and then realised someone else was there moving about only it was like a speeded-up film. The figure was dashing about like lightning. Easing back on the lever she was able to slow the speed of the image she was watching and only then could she tell that the figure was her double. It was odd watching herself. Melissa appeared in the room with her other self and there was lots of movement. After a minute or two she saw the two girls leave the room and noticed the sky beyond the window had darkened. Tyler considered stopping and trying another of the symbols then, but having gone this far she now wondered if they would both return safely. She was concerned when only one figure came back into the room and went to bed. Before the light went off, Tyler thought she could see Melissa crying. So where was the other Tyler? What had happened to her?

Tyler shivered and released the chain. The contrap purred back to its original position. She was shaking. Perhaps this wasn't such a good idea. The red book had warned her about using a *ghost haunting* device. Still, she was determined to learn more.

She flicked the switch to the symbol which looked like a tiny pair of wings.

This should be interesting, she thought.

Taking a deep breath, she steeled herself and gripped the contrap firmly in her left hand. With her right hand she wrapped the chain twice around her fingers and pulled downwards to gently rotate the central ring of the contrap clockwise. It clicked softly as before. Tyler felt a strange sensation. Her limbs felt light and then her whole body was weightless. Suddenly she was lifted off the ground and rising. Her head met with the ceiling of Melissa's bedroom and everything went black.

Zone 41

Tyler came round with a headache and a stiff neck.

"Well that was pretty dumb," she told herself. She checked her watch, wondering how long she'd been out.

3:00p.m.

Tyler had an idea. Again the afternoon was growing dark early outside Melissa's window. Tyler needed more space. It would not be without risks but she decided it would be worth it. She stripped and redressed in all black. Next she left the house and walked to the bottom of the back garden. Melissa's garden was large and now shadowed by trees. Tyler tried the contrap once more, this time knowing exactly what to expect. She took off from the cold dewed grass, leaving her stomach behind, and was soon passing the tops of the trees. She quickly lost her nerve and wished for solid ground again so, easing off the pressure on the chain, she descended.

Her landing could have been more refined. She bruised an ankle and toppled onto her backside. All the same, it was amazing. Tyler sat there in the damp gloom grinning at the contrap for several minutes wondering if she was dreaming. Things like *this* didn't happen. She'd wake up soon. She knew it.

But before that happened she intended to have another go.

She knew how to go up and down. That was all governed by the rotation of the central collar, but how was she to tell the contrap what horizontal direction she wished to move in? There had to be a way. She examined the device again, thinking that she'd perhaps missed some small detail, a tiny lever, a miniscule button. Yet there was nothing she hadn't already seen and used. This left her puzzled for a few minutes until she decided to try it again, just to see what happened.

Tyler took off as before but went higher this time. She was temporarily distracted by the view. In a few seconds she'd flown high enough to see the whole of Watford spread out beneath her. It glimmered with a thousand streetlights. Tyler had never seen it like this before. She looked down at the contrap when she saw that she was moving forwards, drifting over houses. Panic shook her as she struggled to locate Melissa's house below. She didn't want to come down in someone else's garden but then she saw why she was drifting. She had tilted the contrap. It was leaning forwards in her hand. Immediately she righted it and her forward motion ceased. She tilted the contrap back the other way and found she floated backwards.

A grin hit her again. She couldn't help it.

She turned the contrap cautiously to the right. She moved to the right. When she turned the contrap to her left she moved left. It was simple.

Simply brilliant. But what else could it do?

No time. Below her on the road Mr Watts' car was approaching the house. Tyler manoeuvred her way back to the garden and then to Melissa's bedroom window where she hovered. She slipped her hand into the small gap in the top window which had been left open, and flipped up the catch.

*

"Melissa you gotta see this. You gotta see what this thing can do!" Tyler showed Melissa her latest discovery, this time careful to avoid a collision with the bedroom ceiling. Melissa was also amazed.

"You're in the papers today," Melissa explained a short while later. "I bought you a copy."

The Watford Observer's article on the disappearance of Tyler May was almost a word-for-word copy of the Lucy Denby story she'd read the day before.

"Your mum and dad are really upset. They think you're dead or something," Melissa went on to say. "You should really go home, you know. They came into school today. They wanted to talk to all your friends. I had to lie to them. I didn't like doing it very much. Promise me you'll go home soon."

Tyler promised she would.

"But not yet," she added. "I'll go home once Lucy is safe."

*

When they reached the small, scattered industrial estate at the end of Duck's Hill Road, they could find no building names anywhere. They had planned as best they could for the coming night, although they had found no reference to the second NVF building on the internet and so did not know what to expect. There was, however, one large building with its lights still on. Apart from this, the whole area was in darkness. Behind the illuminated building, woods rolled away into the night. It was a dry evening, but bitterly cold. They crept closer, their black clothes helping them to blend with shadows.

"That's the one," said Melissa with sudden conviction. "It's a research facility. They probably keep it open all day and all night. Run it in shifts, so it never closes."

Tucking themselves behind a wall a short distance away, they huddled in shadows where Tyler scoped the building out with the contrap. Beyond its shell she saw workers in lab coats, glass chambers and banks of computers. There were men in strange protective outfits complete with head gear, unrecognisable machines with funnels and control consoles, and figures making copious notes on clipboards.

"You're right," said Tyler. "This must be it. It's like one great big science lab."

"Can you see Lucy anywhere?"

"I'll have a look for her."

A few minutes passed as Tyler searched. Melissa shivered, teeth chattering.

"I can't see her anywhere," said Tyler, disappointed. She continued to scan the building with the contrap.

"Do you still want to go in?"

"Yes. We might find a clue that tells us where they're holding her. But it's not going to be easy. I can see CCTV cameras. There are three security guards watching a bank of TVs and about ten other people still working in the labs."

"It's impossible then. We can't go in now. We wouldn't stand a chance." Melissa sounded ready to go home.

"It'll be easier to get in with it open like this. I'm guessing there are all manner of alarm systems when it's locked up. If it ever is… Wait a minute…" Through the contrap, Tyler had found a section of the building that appeared to be unoccupied. "I wonder what's in there," she said. "Looks like there's a part that's all shut off…"

"Can you see anything in there?"

Tyler adjusted the contrap.

"Yeah. There's some kind of machine in there. A big one."

"Any ideas, then? It's freezing out here," said Melissa, looking around nervously.

"I know exactly what to do with these guys," said Tyler raising her brows twice in quick succession. She had come prepared, as usual. In her backpack was a rope, two torches, two cigarette lighters, the notebook and a pen, her old mobile phone, a Swiss army knife, Mace UV Defence Spray and five packets of joke shop smoke bombs.

"This is going to be an interesting evening," said Melissa, peering into the bag.

Tyler took out her old phone and switched it on. If the police wanted to trace her to this place, so much the better. In the meantime she wanted her camera phone at the ready. She briefed Melissa and gave her two packs of smoke bombs and a lighter. She focused in on the two outer doors of the NVF building using the contrap. The front door was covered by two CCTV cameras, one fixed high up on the wall at each end of the front of the building. The back door was only covered by a single camera.

"You take the front," said Tyler. "Your mobile on vibrate?"

"Yep."

"Good. Wait for my call. I'll let you know when I'm in."

"Right. Tyler…"

"Yes?"

"Good luck."

"Thanks. You too. Ready?"

"Yep."

Tyler checked the *Tower of Doom.* It was higher than ever before and still building.

"Then let's do it."

Tyler set the contrap to the winged symbol and left the ground. She flew over the NVF building high enough not to be seen and then lowered herself gently down into a shadowy spot between two trees on the other side. She lit a smoke bomb and tossed it over towards the back of the building. She followed it with several others and soon there was a dense smoke hanging about the place. She knew that round the front Melissa was doing the same thing. Tyler hoped any security guards watching the door monitors would see a fog developing and not two girls playing with smoke bombs. When it was as thick as she figured it was going to get and providing good cover, she took off into the air and lowered herself down in front of the back door. She posted a couple of lit smoke bombs through the letter box and flew up over the building again.

She hovered there until she heard the fire alarm ringing from below. Tyler brought herself down in the sheltering treeline and hid in time to see the first of the scientists leaving the building. They streamed out of the back door to file their way around the side to the front of the building. By this time the smoke bombs were burned out completely but the night air was still and a believable mist now hung about, although it smelt quite unnatural.

The way was now clear. She waited a moment longer, just in case a latecomer left the building, but no one else came. Cautiously, Tyler left her cover, dashing to the door. Once inside she phoned Melissa. Moments later Melissa used the back door to join Tyler in the building.

The *New Vision Frontiers* research building was very different from the office block they had encountered the previous night. It was glossy and much more futuristic. Safety doors truncated corridors every two metres and every room was a glass-walled laboratory. Tyler was not interested in any of these labs. She made a running beeline for the central section of the building, which had appeared devoid of workers.

"Worked a treat!" shouted Melissa over the ongoing alarm, utterly surprised by their success.

"Of course…"

"Where are we going?"

"The rooms where no one was working. I've a feeling it's all locked off. Like an area only the most important people are allowed."

"Then how will *we* get in?"

"Do I have to think of everything?"

"Pretty much."

Melissa received a dark look but followed nonetheless.

"Here it is," said Tyler when they came to a door different from the rest. It had a hefty locking mechanism that crossed its entire width and a slot for a key card set into a wall-mounted unit with a flashing red LED. Above the door was written in huge letters ZONE 41. "We need a card. See what you can find…"

Melissa doubled back and began searching labs.

Tyler set the contrap to the eye symbol and searched through solid walls. Up ahead, beyond a corridor, she could see an elevator. She clocked the arrows above and below the lift's service button. She swept the contrap downwards and saw more rooms on a lower level through the floor at her feet.

Melissa returned, key card in hand.

"I found this in a drawer three rooms back."

"There's a whole other level below ground! I didn't notice it from outside. I bet she's in there! Try the card," said Tyler, checking her watch. "I reckon we have about ten minutes max. before they come back in and figure out they've been conned."

Melissa shoved the card into the wall slot. Nothing.

"Other way up?" suggested Tyler.

Melissa turned it, reinserted it. There was a beep. The door slid sideways, vanishing into the wall with a *swoosh.*

"Bingo," said Melissa.

Tyler was just about to launch herself down the now open corridor when Melissa caught her arm.

"Wait! Something's not right…" Melissa peered into the gloomily lit passage where an orange safety light blinked. She looked at the little red LED still flashing away on the key card unit. "Why didn't the lights come on? I mean, you'd expect the lights to come on automatically wouldn't you – when the door opens... In a space-age place like this?"

"You've been watching too much TV," said Tyler and she tried again to enter the corridor.

"Hang on!" said Melissa, and taking a smoke bomb, she lit it and tossed it into the corridor. A moment later they were staring at a network of crisscrossing infrared beams, shown up by a haze of smoke. "See what I mean? I was right. The area has its own security system."

Tyler weighed the new challenge briefly.

"I can get through this. I mean, not normally I couldn't. But with the contrap, I can. I'm pretty sure I can," she said, as though to convince herself. She readied herself with the contrap and gently left the ground.

Melissa watched as Tyler performed a silent acrobatic display in slow motion. She passed between red beams gracefully, ducked and twisted her way over crossing red lines.

Melissa checked over her shoulder nervously.

Gliding and spinning, Tyler made her careful route to the other end of the corridor where she alighted triumphantly without triggering the alarm. On the wall by another closed door was a green button and, beneath that, a red one. She hit the green. Lights blinked on. The infrared beams were instantly shut off and the second door slid open. Somewhere an electronic beep sounded the *all clear.*

"Come on," said Tyler.

Melissa dashed down the corridor and together they ventured further into Zone 41. When they reached the elevator, Tyler thumped the down arrow button to summon the lift.

"What about this level?" asked Melissa. "Should we search it first?"

"No time. If Lucy's here, she's below us. We'll start there and then come back up if we don't find anything." Tyler was searching with the contrap again as the lift arrived and doors opened. "I can see somebody. Somebody's curled up on the ground. It could be her!" she said.

They took the lift to the basement level and exited into a junction of three passageways.

"This way," said Tyler, heading off. They found the room where Tyler had seen the lone figure, but it was locked.

"We don't have time for this," said Tyler. "They'll be back inside any minute."

Then Melissa noticed a fire axe set into a wall recess, along with a coiled hose.

"The axe!" she shouted.

Tyler grabbed the heavy axe and aimed it as best she could at the door lock. She hit the wall, jarring her shoulder with the shock of impact. She swung again, this time embedding the axe blade in the solid door. It took all her might to pry it loose.

"Let me try," said Melissa. She surprised herself when she hit the lock square on, smashing it to pieces.

Tyler shot her an approving look, nodding with respect before kicking the door open to enter.

They found Lucy Denby with hands cuffed behind her back and thick black tape across her mouth. The cuffs were tethered to a wall plate by a short length of thick chain. She was in a dishevelled school uniform and had obviously been crying. Stale eye makeup was smudges of black around reddened eyes.

Lucy saw the girls and her eyes widened as she struggled to get up off the floor.

Melissa still had the fire axe. She aimed it at the chain, severing it mid-length with one blow.

"You're pretty good with that thing," said Tyler, peeling off the tape so that Lucy could speak.

"You found me! How the…"

"No time. We have to go," said Tyler.

They were getting out of the elevator in Zone 41 on ground level when Lucy suddenly stopped.

"Wait! I have to know what's in there…" she said, nodding to a closed door to her left.

"Lucy, we haven't…" Tyler began to object, but Lucy wasn't listening. She shouldered open the door and went in, her tail of broken chain dragging along behind.

Tyler and Melissa followed.

GAUNT

In this chamber was a large, complex machine. Strange looking lobes edged a shimmering doorway at one end. At its centre gleamed a control panel the size of a Rolls Royce. Along the length of the construction one word was etched into the sheet metal.

GAUNT

The machine was strange enough, but what really focused their attention was a gaping, blackened hole in the metal where it appeared some kind of explosion had occurred. Metal casing was torn and warped. The ceiling above was also blackened with soot.

Along two sides of the room ran steel desks with microscopes, flasks and other lab gear.

The fire alarm suddenly stopped ringing.

The girls looked at each other, knowing their time was up.

"Happy?" shouted Tyler. "We've got to go. RIGHT NOW!"

Lucy wasn't interested. She was frantically searching the desk surfaces for something, hands still cuffed at her back, broken chain skittering on the hard floor.

"Here! Over here! Grab that file. Anyone got a camera?" she asked.

"I have," confessed Tyler, rolling her eyes.

"Get a shot of that monstrosity and I'll come with you," Lucy stated.

Tyler took out her mobile and snapped the GAUNT machine while Melissa snatched the file from the desk.

"Right. Can we go, PLEASE?"

"What are we waiting for? Christmas?" said Lucy as she ran out. The others followed. Their path was clear until they reached the back door but a tall silhouette loomed before them as they went outside. Tyler knew who it was at one glance.

"Bagshot," she said.

"Well, well, well. Look what we have here…" said Bagshot, towering over them and straightening his glasses. Tyler had her Defence Spray ready.

Lucy wasn't interested in conversation. She glared at Bagshot with accumulated loathing.

"I was hoping we'd bump into you," she spat. She span on her heel, launching the chain at him like a whip. It wrapped itself around his head, bloodying his nose and sending his glasses flying. It was enough. The girls made a dash for the woods and were hidden by the trees long before he recovered and his cries of pain subsided.

"I like your work," said Tyler to Lucy as they ran, dodging branches and trunks.

"You'd do the same if he'd locked you away for the best part of a week. I thought he was going to kill me. Anyone got anything to eat? I'm starving."

"Nothing on me," panted Melissa. "Sorry."

Tyler shook her head.

Melissa was beginning to lag behind.

"Wait! I can't keep up!"

Tyler slowed. Lucy *tutted* impatiently and dropped back.

"Grab my arm," she said. "I'll help you." Melissa linked arms with Lucy.

"Come on!" Lucy cried.

They heard Bagshot calling after them, warning them they wouldn't get away and had nowhere to run. They could hear him barking orders to others who had joined him.

Five minutes later the girls were breathless and lost in a sea of trees.

"Anyone know where we are?" asked Lucy.

Tyler took out her old mobile and switched it off.

"Not really. This wasn't part of the plan," she said.

"What *was* the plan?" Lucy wanted to know.

"Well we were kind of winging it really," explained Melissa.

"Right," said Lucy, glaring at them. "So what now?"

"Are they still following?" asked Tyler, peering back the way they'd come.

"Over there," Melissa pointed. "I can see lights."

"They're coming," said Lucy.

"Can't you do something with that silver gadget of yours?" asked Melissa.

Tyler drew out the contrap and took off vertically through the trees. She soon returned to the forest floor. She began to say something.

"This…"

"Can you fly us all out?" asked Melissa.

"Try," said Tyler. "Grab hold of me!"

Melissa and Lucy threw their arms around Tyler. A moment later they were still on the ground and going nowhere.

"I guess it doesn't work like that. This way," Tyler said. She set off again and the others followed. "There's a lake off to our left. If we keep in a straight line we'll eventually hit a road. I think we'll come out somewhere near our school."

Tyler ran at Melissa's side for a while.

"We just saved her life. You'd think she'd be grateful…" said Melissa.

"I know!" Tyler agreed.

Melissa suddenly stopped.

"What's that?" She pointed. The others stopped to look.

A light was gliding through the trees some way off. It didn't look like the jostling lights of their pursuers' torches. This light was different. They watched it move, a ghostly shape, shivering in the dark.

"It looks like a ghost," said Lucy, matter-of-factly.

Tyler didn't like the thought, but she had to agree.

"Well, we've got to go somewhere or they'll catch up with us," Lucy said.

"Follow me," said Tyler, changing course and setting off again.

The others followed, Lucy at Melissa's shoulder.

"Look, I don't mean to be rude," began Lucy. "But who's in charge here?"

"I am," said Tyler whilst at the same time Melissa said, "She is."

"Right," said Lucy. "Then I think you should know – we're actually running towards some more ghosts. Perhaps they've moved…"

Tyler looked up and saw that Lucy was right. There were three silent, spectral figures drifting between trees up ahead.

"As I said, this way." Tyler changed direction and upped the pace. They passed close by one of the eerie forms and Tyler found herself blinking and looking twice. She tried to shake off the uncanny notion that she recognized the translucent face that had smiled back at her.

The girls left the phantoms behind and ran at full pelt until they could no longer see any lights. Melissa collapsed in a heap on the forest floor.

"I can't go on," she puffed.

"I think we lost them anyway," said Lucy.

"Have you seen them before?" asked Tyler.

"What, the ghosts?" said Lucy. "No, it's just that nothing really surprises me anymore. Not since I got hold of that *thing* you have."

"Do you want it back?" Tyler asked Lucy tentatively. She was not sure if she was ready to give the contrap up just yet.

"No. Bloody hell, no! That thing's only ever caused me trouble. It nearly got me killed… Well, I guess you know all about that now."

"What now?" asked Melissa, beginning to recover.

"McDonalds," said Lucy. "I gotta eat or I really will die. But first, can somebody *please* get me out of these handcuffs?"

Tyler checked the *Tower of Doom.* It was complete. For the first time she could see the entire tower complete with battlements before a glowing full moon and a moody night sky.

*

As usual, McDonald's was empty at this time of night. A few older kids were fooling around outside, but inside, the three girls had the place to themselves. Out on the road police cars screamed.

"I guess we made an impact," said Melissa watching blue and red lights flash by. "Would someone like to tell me what is going on?"

Tyler and Lucy looked up from their meals, mouths full of fries and burger. They looked at each other and couldn't subdue laughter.

"Honestly…" Melissa dipped a French fry in ketchup and bit.

Tyler swallowed.

"You got to admit. It's pretty funny really…"

"If by *funny* you mean completely *weird*, then yes, I admit it is." Melissa remained un-amused. "This is serious!"

Tyler straightened her face with some effort.

"Yes, of course. You're right. You always are. I guess I'm just… I'm just glad we made it out of there alive. Did you see Bagshot's face when Lucy got him with the chain? That was great!" The chain was now on the ground where they'd left it, having smashed some links of the handcuffs with a brick. It had been a tricky operation and the separated cuffs themselves were still around Lucy's wrists, but at least she was free to move her hands once more.

"Actually I don't approve of violence," Melissa stated. "It never solves anything."

"So you would rather we'd sat down and had a nice chat with Bagshot, would you?" asked Tyler.

"Well, perhaps there are exceptions," Melissa had to admit in a moment of self-doubt.

Lucy finished her food and looked at them both, waiting. When she was sure they were listening, she began.

"I don't know if I can tell you exactly what is going on, but I'll tell you what I know." When she was being serious like this, her eyes became extremely focused in a captivating way. Even with the smudged black eyeliner and the tired look she now wore, they were piercing. The girls listened.

"I don't really know where to start. I was… I got into some stuff I shouldn't have got into. Made friends with, you know, *the wrong type*… Along the way I found out from this guy about this book. He said he'd had it stolen and he wanted it back. He said it was very rare and worth a lot of money. He said he knew who had stolen it from him and so, being a complete idiot, I thought I'd help him get it back. His name was William Blake…"

"What, like the famous poet?" asked Melissa.

Lucy gave her a blank look.

"I'm not really into poetry… Unless you count Marilyn Manson."

"It's just that… Well, it sounds like a fake name to me."

"Probably is. Who knows? The point is I ended up helping this *William Blake* guy to get back his book. I think he might have set me up, but I can't be sure. In any case, I was supposed to break into this other guy's house and get the book for William. I guess I did it 'cause I fancied him…"

"Was it a small, red book called *Ghost Haunting*, by any chance?" asked Tyler.

"You found it then… Do you still have it?"

"No. It… It got burnt. Bagshot and his friends... Sorry."

"Oh well. Anyway, we made this plan where I was to help William get the book. He was going to create a diversion so I'd have the house to myself - you know - the house of the man who he'd said took his book - so I could search for it without getting caught. It worked. I got the book. But when I went to meet William where we'd agreed to meet afterwards, he never showed up. I haven't seen him since. Next thing I know, this guy is following me in the streets. It was dark and I was scared. I was up on Hogs Back – the little hill with the trees… I wouldn't have gone up there, but I was trying to lose him.

"Well, I thought I *had* lost him. But then he was suddenly there in front of me. It was like he appeared out of nowhere. I expect he used the device. He tried to take my bag from me, was going on about the book and how I had no right to take it and all that. I fought back and gave him a big shove. He tripped on a root or something and fell backwards, rolled away down a bank. But his coat got caught on a branch and it came right off him. I was going to make a run for it when I saw the silver thing, the device."

"So you took it," said Tyler.

"Yes. It fell from his pocket. There were some letters and stuff too, all folded up in the inside of his coat pocket. I grabbed the lot."

"And the man was…"

"…Bagshot. Yes. I think you pretty much know the rest. I realised something creepy was going on and I started poking around to see what I could learn. Something about it all just didn't feel right. I saw Bagshot a couple of times and followed him. I made notes and sketched him and others I saw him meet up with. I kept hold of the device and tried to work out what it did – what all the little symbols meant. The last time I followed Bagshot he must have seen me. I knew I was being followed after that. I kept seeing men in long coats everywhere I went. I'm sure they were watching me. I kept the device in my bag and went to school the next day as usual, but by lunch time I'd convinced myself they were going to try and get me. They got me on the way home, but by then I'd already swapped bags with you before I left school. It was a spur of the moment kind of a thing. I thought that way, at least, they wouldn't get the device back."

"Well thanks for dragging me into all this," said Tyler.

Lucy glared at Tyler, stood up and headed for the door.

"Wait," called Melissa. "Where are you going?" She got up and caught Lucy by the arm. Lucy broke free.

"I didn't ask to be rescued. If you ladies don't want to help, I'll be on my way."

"Please! Sit down," begged Melissa. "We *do* want to help. And anyway, we need to stick together now. After tonight they'll be after all of us. Not just you."

"Whatever." Lucy scowled. She sat back down, crossed her arms. "Anyone got any gum?"

The others shook heads. Lucy stared out of the window.

"Now, where were we?" said Melissa.

"She was just having a go at me about how I dragged you all into this…"

"Yes. Right. Thanks."

"So when they caught you, you'd already put the book in your desk at school," said Tyler.

"Uh-huh. I'd put the book in my desk days before. To be honest, I'd almost forgotten about the book since I got the device. Anyway, it seemed the safest place for a book. I knew they probably wouldn't risk actually going into the school and I didn't see why anyone else would go poking around in my desk. If they did, I figured all they'd see is another book and it would go unnoticed."

"Again – sorry," said Tyler.

"So what was that big machine we saw in the NVF lab?" asked Melissa.

"A very good question," said Lucy. "Let's see that file first. I'm hoping it will tell us something. Then I'll tell you what *I* think."

Melissa cleared a spot on the small table and put the file down. It was a reddish brown cardboard folder with an elastic fixing to hold it closed. On the cover was the word *GAUNT* in bold letters and beneath it in smaller text was printed *Guided Analytic Utility Necro Transducer*.

Melissa read the title aloud.

"What the heck does that mean?" she asked.

"Well if *you* don't know, we're stuffed," commented Tyler.

Melissa swallowed and met their expectant faces.

"Alright. I'll have a go," she said, tentatively. "Guided means, well, *guided*, I guess. Like a guided missile. Analytic must mean it has something to do with analysing something, like when someone analyses data, and Utility means the thing is useful for something. But probably something specific, I think."

"And *Necro Transducer*?" said Tyler.

Lucy stepped in.

"*Necro* usually means to do with the dead. I mean dead people. Like *necromancer* means someone who speaks to the dead."

"Why am I not surprised that you know that?" asked Tyler. Lucy shrugged.

Melissa continued. "I'd have to look up transducer, but it sounds like something electrical to me? Don't you think?"

"Who knows?" said Tyler. "We'll look it up later."

"It's a ghost machine," said Lucy with conviction. "Like the one around Tyler's neck. Only bigger."

"Much bigger," said Melissa.

"I heard them talking about it," Lucy continued. "It's something they've been working on for years. For decades. They've been trying to get it to work for ages, but with little success. Then about three days ago they did something to it. Found the key. Solved the problem. They started locating ghosts and bringing them back…"

"Back from where?" asked Tyler.

"I don't know. The *other side*? The place where ghosts normally hang out?" Lucy suggested. "Only, I think something has gone wrong. Somehow they lost control of it. I couldn't hear much when it happened but the other day there was an explosion from somewhere above me - I mean above where they had me chained up.

Bagshot had been visiting every day to question me. It happened when he was right there with me. He wasn't too pleased when it happened. He stormed off looking like he was about to kill someone."

The File

Tyler studied the file's cover. "There's something else," she said. The symbol was faint, but now they could study the file properly, it was clear enough. Behind the lettering was a large swastika, printed like a watermark in the card. "It's not just that letter we saw, Melissa. They *are* Nazis. I don't want to say *I told you so*, but - I told you so."

"That explains a lot," said Lucy.

Melissa couldn't argue.

"Okay, so we've got Nazis in Watford. What are we going to do about it?"

Tyler sipped iced cola through a straw and opened the GAUNT file.

"We're going to stop them."

Inside was an assortment of loose A4 pages. Some were pages of writing, both typed and printed sheets. Others were diagrams and schematics, illustrations of complex machine parts. There were pages and pages of reports about experimental results and conclusions. They understood very little of the file's contents and much of the writing was in German. Most of what was in English was pencil scrawled in a terribly illegible hand.

"This isn't much use to us," said Tyler disappointed. "Not with all this stuff written in German."

"My dad says the Germans are the best engineers in the world," stated Melissa.

"It's evidence. Proves what they're doing," said Lucy. "It might not mean much to us, but it could prove they're doing stuff they shouldn't be doing. I expect an engineer would understand it all. Well, maybe a German engineer…"

Tyler told Lucy her story and offered her theories about the NVF and the missing kids.

"I think you're right," said Lucy, when Tyler had finished.

"Not another one," said Melissa despairingly.

"And what about the things we saw in the forest?" Tyler wanted to know.

"I have a theory of my own," began Lucy, pawing through pages of the open file. "Only a theory, mind. You saw that machine. And we know that Bagshot had the device – *your* device," she nodded to Tyler. "It's obviously pretty precious to them if they're prepared to go to these lengths to get it back. I think they're trying to make more of them, or at least, learn how to make them. I think the GAUNT machine is something to do with it. Only, it went wrong and instead of trapping ghosts into the machine, they've released them. I think that's what we saw in the woods."

Tyler remembered the haunting face she'd seen in the forest, although she didn't mention it to the others. She couldn't put a name to the face, yet it was somehow very familiar and this continued to bother her.

"Why would they want to make more of them?" asked Melissa.

Lucy met her gaze brutally.

"It's just a thought, but can you imagine a whole army of soldiers armed with these things?" Lucy asked.

"That's it!" said Tyler. "That's what they want it for. Of course. They want to mass-produce the device, or something like it, and then sell them to the highest bidder."

"Uh-hu," said Lucy with a knowing nod. "Or they want it for their own Nazi army."

"That's kind of scary," said Melissa. "Any army with that kind of power would be completely unbeatable."

Lucy nodded again.

"Look at this," said Tyler then, plucking out a single page from the file. "It's another letter addressed to the NVF, only this time it doesn't say *New Vision Frontiers* under their NVF logo. It says Necro Visionistic Facilities."

"Sounds about right," Lucy said. "In other words, laboratories where they're looking into ways of raising the dead and harnessing their powers…"

"So New Vision Frontiers is a cover?" concluded Melissa.

Tyler nodded.

"Looks that way to me. It's just a name that would draw less attention to what they're really doing in these labs. Necro Visionistic Facilities is their real name."

Tyler drew out the contrap from her shirt and switched it to the spiral symbol. She wanted to speak to Albert. She was thrilled when he appeared in the viewing glass a few seconds later, waving his cloth cap.

"Albert, good news. We've found Lucy."

"Oh, that's great. Say 'ello to Lucy Loo from me, won't ya." Albert grinned merrily.

"You can say it yourself in a minute. Albert, can you do something for me? Can you fetch Marcus again? Can you get him to tell his story, just like he told me? I think it's important."

"I'll see what I can do, Missy. You wait there." Albert disappeared but was back a moment later with Marcus at his side.

Tyler spoke to the girls across the table.

"I've got something to show you. Someone I met. I think you should hear his story."

Suddenly she knew why she'd seen Melissa crying when she'd looked into the future using the contrap. Melissa was about to hear the story of the many and then she was to go back home and go to bed weeping. Marcus' story had even brought tears to Lucy's stony eyes.

*

They parted ways outside the restaurant, Melissa heading for home still in tears, Tyler and Lucy trudging wearily to Lucy's back garden where her parent's summerhouse awaited them.

"It's not perfect, but it will have to do for now," she'd said. "When my parents are out we can use the house as long as we don't leave any signs that we've been there. But we'll be safe in the summerhouse and it's pretty much screened off from the main house by some trees. No one will see us and nobody uses it in the winter. We'll just have to be careful how we come and go."

They'd had that old discussion again. Do we go to the police? Shouldn't we all just go home? But in the end the three of them had agreed it was still too dangerous. They knew they'd angered Bagshot and his people, and that he was not only still after the contrap, but now also probably seeking revenge. The only one of them who had not been tracked down and followed already was Melissa.

"Just as well," Tyler had said. "We need you and your computer. Are you sure Bagshot didn't get a good look at you when we left the lab?"

"He only saw me for a split second before he got a chain in the face," Melissa had said. "I'll be alright. I'll see you tomorrow…"

Lucy kicked a stone. They watched it skitter across the street as they walked. Lucy's eyes were watery.

"So it's just *us* against the Nazis, then," she said.

"Until we know it's safe. Until Bagshot is in prison," said Tyler.

"Listen, about the device…"

"Apparently its proper name is a *contrap*. Like contraption."

"Right. About the contrap; I don't think it's really safe to use. That book had this weird page added…"

"I read it. The warning. The missing chapter on *The Dangers of Ghost Haunting*. Very strange, I agree."

"I'm just saying. I think you should only use it when you really need to. There's something… There's something wrong…"

"Yes. I think you're right. There's something very wrong with trapping people inside a metal box that forces them to do stuff for you. Ghosts or not."

"I'm glad you understand."

"Oh, I forgot!" said Tyler suddenly. "Your notebook. Here..." She took out the little black notebook she'd added her own notes to, and offered it to Lucy.

"Thanks." Lucy took it and put it in her coat pocket.

*

The summerhouse was cold but warmer than the night outside. If nothing else it was a good shelter from the wind and rain. They used quilted summer loungers for beds and joked about getting sunburned whilst they slept.

"So what's with the goth thing?" Tyler asked Lucy as they stared up at the summerhouse's pine lap ceiling.

"Oh, I don't know," confessed Lucy. "I just like being different I guess. Sometimes it's just easier to play at being bad rather than go along with all this *goody-goody* stuff. Know what I mean?"

"I guess."

"I suppose what I mean is, Mum and Dad think I'm this perfect little princess. Goody-two-shoes... I don't feel like that. I don't think I am that."

"Right."

"And you? You seem to be pretty angry at the world..."

"Oh, I just don't like being pushed around."

"Me neither," said Lucy. They high-fived. "You warm enough?"

"Yeah. Slept on the street last night. Believe me, this is luxury."

Tyler found her list and, for the first time in days, ticked off every item. It felt good.

She lay in the quiet after that, trying to sleep, yet she couldn't resist taking out the contrap one more time and checking the *Tower of Doom*. She lost her smile when she saw the tower was low once more and slowly crumbling. But then again, it made perfect sense. She'd completed one task. She'd saved Lucy. Now she had a new mission, a bigger one, a more dangerous one. She took out a fresh piece of paper and began a new list, staring at what she'd written.

Find the missing kids
Stop the Nazis

*

Albert wasn't there. She'd looked for him all morning but Tyler could see no sign of him. Lucy had made them bacon and eggs for breakfast, so those were also on today's shopping list as they needed to replace what they used from the fridge. It was Sunday. Mr and Mrs Denby were at church and weren't expected back for another two hours. Lucy was in the shower and Tyler was sitting in Lucy's kitchen with her eye pressed to the contrap. To her dismay the old French knight appeared, picking his nose, chainmail rattling.

"Gross," said Tyler.

"Ah, mon amie! It is good to see you again," the old soldier clapped gauntleted hands and opened arms wide.

"Hello, Travis."

"Bonjour, bonjour. And how can I 'elp you today? Perhaps we can make a little trade, no?"

"I'm not trading anything with you, Travis. Is Albert there? Can you find him for me?"

"But of course, of course! I will find Albert and bring him to you... Then you will 'elp me with a little something, no?"

"Help you with what?"

"Ah! It is but a trifle. A very little thing, really. All I want you to do in return is to say but two words."

Tyler could think of two words.

"That's it? I just have to say two words?"

Someone else was approaching out of the swirling mist.

"But yes! That is all..." said Travis.

"Oi! Travis! You leave 'er alone. You 'ear me?" Albert shouted.

Travis raised hands in submission and backed away.

"Alright, alright. I have done nothing. I will go away. Au revoir, mademoiselle. Until the next time." Then he was gone.

"You all right, Missy?" said Albert. "Was 'e botherin' ya?"

"Not really. How are you Albert? It's good to see you."

"You too, Missy. I can't complain, I suppose. It's a bit cold in 'ere sometimes, but it's alright."

"Did you have any luck finding Zebedee Lieberman?"

"Oh, yeah. I was lookin' for a Mr Zebedee Lieberman. Sorry, I ain't found 'im yet. I'll keep tryin' though. Don't you worry. What you want 'im for?"

"I want to talk to him about a book he wrote."

"Right."

"It's important, Albert."

"Tell ya' what, you stay 'ere and I'll take a quick look 'round. See if I can't track 'im down right now..."

Tyler promised to wait.

Albert disappeared into the mist and Tyler was left alone for several minutes. Another figure materialized, this one a crazy-looking woman. Tyler judged she was about thirty years old, but by her dress she must have lived a long time ago. She looked like a Tudor.

"Hello, Deary!" the woman greeted Tyler with a mocking bow. There were too many gaps in her mouth where teeth used to be; eyes were sunken; hair was a straggled thatch of grey, supporting a white bonnet at its peak; her loose shirt, once white, was now a grimy shade of grey, over which she wore a tightly laced bodice. Below all this, grey skirts fell to the shifting fog at her feet.

"Hello," said Tyler, though the woman did not appear to be looking back at her now, but rather, off to Tyler's left, and so Tyler wondered who the woman was actually addressing.

"What you doing here?" the woman asked sounding mildly surprised.

When nobody else appeared or replied, Tyler said, "I'm just looking for someone. My name's Tyler. What's yours?"

"They call me..." mumbled the woman, whose demeanour had changed into that of a small timid child. Tyler strained her ears trying to make out a name and was left unsure if any name was even spoken.

"Pardon?"

"They call me..." again the woman muttered as if talking to herself.

"Sorry?"

"VIOLET!" the woman screamed at her violently, clutching her head as though it hurt. "I said they call me VIOLET CORPE!"

Tyler was beginning to wish Albert had not asked her to wait around. The contrap was an amazing thing, but it seemed as equally sinister and was filled with some very bizarre elements. She had known Violet Corpe for a total of twelve seconds but already knew she was clearly one of the strangest.

"Well okay…" said Tyler, unsure of how to respond.

Violet beckoned for Tyler to come to her, drew closer and cupped hands about her mouth as though she wished to impart a secret.

"Can you get me out?" she whispered, her face pleading, eyes bulging from sockets. "I'd… I'd really like to get out…"

"Er, no. I don't think I can," said Tyler, wondering if this were true. "I don't know how I would do that."

Violet checked about either side of her to be sure no one else was listening.

"Go on. You can find a way. I know you can." She smiled. Tyler wished she'd stop. The smile made Violet even creepier than before. Tyler found herself torn. She wanted to switch off the ghost portal but she'd promised Albert she'd wait.

The next moment Violet procured a huge carving knife from somewhere and was pointing it at Tyler.

"You just get me out or I'll cut you up!" she said. "I dunnit before…"

Tyler switched back to the skull symbol, tucked the contrap away and took a gulp of hot chocolate. She needed a distraction so she grabbed a remote and turned on the small kitchen TV. A cookery program flashed up onto the screen. She could hear Lucy using a hair drier upstairs.

Ten minutes later she lowered the TV's volume and switched the contrap back to the spiral symbol. Violet Corpe had gone. Tyler was relieved. She called Albert's name hesitantly. A distant voice greeted her from beyond the vaporous haze.

"I found 'im! I found 'im Missy... 'Ere 'e is."

Albert came out of the mist. Tyler thought he was playing some kind of trick on her until a second taller figure followed.

Zebedee Lieberman

Zebedee Lieberman was a thin, spidery man with a top hat and black tailcoat. Tyler thought he looked a little like a malnourished funeral director. In other ways, however, he was very different. His face was one big smile, his eyes bright and jovial, if not mischievous, and his gait was not a slow respectful funeral march, but spritely and quick. She caught a glimpse of a shiny gold pocket watch protruding from his waistcoat. His beard was long and grey and on his right eye he wore a monocle. As he came closer he tapped the intangible ground at his feet with a smart black brass-handled cane, though he appeared to have no need of a walking stick. Firmly clamped in his mouth was a long, curved smoking pipe which he removed whenever he spoke.

"Yes, yes, yes, young lady, what is all this about? This fine fellow, here, tells me you wish to speak with me?" he said, gesturing at Albert with the stem of the pipe.

"He's right," said Tyler. "I do. It's about a book you wrote."

Zebedee was suddenly more interested.

"My book? Do you mean *the* book?"

"I guess so. Did you only write the one?"

"Well I never! How do you know about my book? Yes, I only wrote one and I didn't even get to finish that... Don't suppose it matters really. Most of it was a load of old tripe. I'm surprised anyone anywhere knows anything about it. Good heavens! I could fill a few books with what I know now, of course. You learn an awful lot when you die. Yes, I could write a thing or two now..."

"I know you didn't get to finish it, but someone finished it for you."

"Who?" Zebedee asked at once.

"Someone called Orealia Stephensen."

"Really? Good old Orealia! Did she do a good job?"

"I don't really know. She didn't really seem to agree with some of your ideas..."

"Dear me. That's too bad. Oh well, never mind. I don't suppose it matters anymore..."

"I guess not. Zebedee, can you help me with some things? I have this contraption, this device... I think you called it a ghost machine in your book. But the thing is I still don't know what half of it does. And I need to know everything about ghost haunting that you can tell me. I'm guessing it's because of the book, and what you were researching, that you ended up inside the device..."

"Smart girl, smart girl! Right you are! That is exactly what happened. But I'd best tell you the tale from the beginning.

"It all began with an inheritance. My Great Uncle Hemmings died and left me a few bits and pieces. He was a bit of a recluse, you know. He didn't mix with others very much. I rather think he liked his own company. Anyway, one thing he *did* like was travelling. When he visited different lands he would always bring back a few mementoes. By the time he died he must have travelled all over the world, I should think. In any case, some of the things he left behind were, well frankly, a bit strange. I considered I'd received a good haul compared with my brother, Isaac. But that's by the by.

"Amongst the few things he left to me was a rather splendid piece of furniture, an antique walnut cabinet from Tuscany. A fine thing it was, made in the fifteenth century and covered with intricate carvings. It had drawers here and there and little cupboards cunningly tucked behind the panelling. At the top, in the centre, it had two little doors which covered two drawers. The doors could be locked shut with a little key and so, as I didn't have the key, they remained closed for the first five years after it became mine. Then I found a key tucked away at the back of one of the other drawers. It fitted the lock and opened the top doors. I found the two little drawers inside empty. Another twenty five years passed before I noticed, one day, the secret compartment behind those little drawers, a narrow walnut box about so big." Here Zebedee held his index fingers about ten centimetres apart.

"Inside the compartment was the device, the one you are holding now, I suspect. I haven't a clue where it came from originally, when it was made, or who created it, but I guessed it was quite ancient. There was an old piece of folded paper with it, a note from somebody named Eucrates Onuris the Fourth. The note said, *My dearest Ramla, please keep this trinket safe until my return. If anybody comes looking for me, you must deny all knowledge of me for your own sake.* There was no date. In hindsight, I speculated whether Onuris' disappearance had something to do with the device. Perhaps he was being hounded by somebody who wanted it. If so, he may have left it in safe hands whilst he went to broker a deal. For some reason he clearly never returned to his sweetheart and I presume the device lay hidden and forgotten for many years.

"I played around a bit with the device, much as you must have done, I imagine, and discovered some of its capabilities."

"Yes," said Tyler. "I know some of the things it can do, but I need to know what else it does. Can you tell me?" Tyler went on to explain her situation and all about the Nazis and Bagshot. "So you see we really need all the help we can get."

"Right, right. Of course. I will help you all I can, dear girl. And I will tell you how I ended up in here, so that you do not end up the same way!"

"Yes. I'd like that," said Tyler.

"Well, where was I," said Zebedee tapping out his pipe and refilling it with ghostly tobacco.

"You were finding out what the ghost machine did."

"Ah yes… The ghost machine… Well, I learned through trial and error at the beginning. That's when I didn't truly appreciate what it was and the power it held. As I learned more, I realized I needed to do some research to help me, and I began making copious amounts of notes. That's what made me think of writing a book on the subject. In the end I decided to work on the book, but only to put in some of what I'd learned. I didn't want to let people know that I *had* such a thing, and just how powerful it could be, because I feared they would try to take it from me. And anyway, by keeping it secret I could continue to grow rich using it and nobody would know the secret of my wealth.

"Now, to the ghost machine itself… I quickly found the dark tower, and as I endeavoured to learn more, so the tower seemed to grow and build. It became plain to me that the tower showed me how well I was doing in the things I was trying to achieve."

"Yes, I found the same thing!"

Zebedee struck a match and lit his pipe.

"Ah, but have you realized *this*? Hold the glass to your eye and walk in one direction, the tower will fall. Walk in another and it will rise. Simple, yet brilliant. If you are lost it will show you the way home. If you seek something that is lost, the tower will show you where it is."

"I see. And the other symbols?"

"The spiral, you clearly already understand. It is a communication portal to the inside of the ghost machine where we ghosts abide."

"What about the eye symbols?"

"The future and the past, naturally… The central eye can show you anything anywhere in the present. You simply point the device and move the lever at the edge clockwise. I should warn you though. The present is present and cannot be altered by the machine. The past has passed and so likewise cannot be changed. The *future*, however, is yet to take place. Tell me, child, what is your understanding of the power within the device?" He sucked on his pipe and blew smoke rings.

"If what I read in your book is true, then the power comes from the ghosts, the ghosts trapped within it, or at least, bound to it…"

"That is true. You must remember, then, that the future can never really be seen by ghosts or man. The difference is, cumulatively, as ghosts, we know so much, and have access to so much more information than living people, that we can often take a fair stab at what the future holds. It is not the work of a single ghost, you understand, yet it could be influenced by individual ghosts."

"So what the device shows you is the ghosts' guesswork?"

"Er, sort of. Something like that. Yes. So you should remember it cannot always be trusted. It could lead you astray - make you think something is going to happen that does not come to pass."

"How did you learn that?"

"It's a long story, but again, after a while I realised that what the device was showing me wasn't exactly what then followed. The rest was purely a step of logic. The point is, it's not to be trusted."

"I see. Right. The skull symbol saved me one time. I was falling and I stopped before I hit the ground."

"Yes, the symbol for death can save you from death. But be warned, it does not stop you from getting hurt all the time. If you walk into a fire you will still burn. The difference is you'll not die from it. I learned this the hard way when I put my hand into a fire to test it out. The fire burned me just as normal. But set the switch to the skull symbol and water will not drown you as long as you're wearing the device. Receive a lethal wound and you'll not bleed to death – as long as you are wearing the device. Fall from a building and you will never hit the ground. But take the device off, or switch to another symbol before you have healed and you will surely die."

"Okay. I've used the symbol for flight - the little pair of wings - so that leaves the symbols for fire, the heart and the tree."

"Ah. Then you have learned almost as much as I had, before I was trapped in here. I can only tell you about one of those remaining symbols and that, again, comes with a warning."

"Which symbol is that?"

"It's the tree symbol. Can you guess what the symbol signifies?"

Tyler thought back to the notes in Lucy's notebook.

"Is it knowledge? As in the *tree of knowledge*?"

"Very good, very good! It is indeed. I stumbled upon the power of the tree symbol one evening almost by accident. It was one of the last three symbols I had yet to understand. So, I was sitting at my desk in my study, switching back and forth between the last three symbols, pondering what they were for. Then, by pure chance, I mumbled to myself whilst the tree symbol was selected. I said, 'What in heaven's name are you for?', or something like that. To my amazement the very words I'd spoken suddenly appeared within the device. It was as though someone had typed them and thrown them into the viewing glass. The words drifted off into the mist and disappeared. I thought it most peculiar, so I sat and waited. The next minute words began to come back out of the mist. Can you guess what they said?"

"Was it an answer to your question?"

"Clever girl! Clever girl! It was. The words drifted about in the mist and I was able to read them. Three succinct words… It said 'I answer questions'."

"I see," said Tyler. "But I can speak to ghosts in the ghost portal. Why would I use the tree of knowledge rather than ask a ghost a question?"

"My dear girl, haven't you met any of the others in here? They're about as helpful as a felt bicycle. The thing is; you can ask the device a question using the tree of knowledge and the device is honour bound to give you an answer.

"A word of warning though: as with foreseeing the future, ultimately, you are dealing with ghosts. The device will force them to answer any question you ask, but their answer might not be entirely true, or entirely helpful."

"I understand, I think," said Tyler. "So I think that's all the symbols…"

"Yes, I think so. I set the device to the tree symbol and asked what the remaining symbols were for, but I only ever received nonsense riddles from the mist. Evidently the device did not wish me to know. I never did discover what the last two symbols were for."

"Thank you for your help, Zebedee. I think I'd best go now, but I expect I'll see you again."

"I do hope so. Oh, before you go, just one further cautionary note… I didn't tell you how I came to be in here, did I?"

"No, not yet."

"Well, as I said before, I used to sit at my desk, trying to work out the ghost machine and all its intricacies. I used to talk to the ghosts and try to find out from them what the thing did. There is one ghost I really should warn you about. He's a Norman knight who was murdered by Saxons shortly after the Battle of Hastings. You know, 1066 and all that… His name is Travis. I don't know how he found out, but he knows some things about the ghost machine that most others don't; things about how it works. It was Travis who tricked me into the ghost machine."

"...The *con trap*," said Tyler.

"Excuse me?"

"Oh, nothing... Do go on."

"Right. Well, Travis was always trying to get me to go into the machine. Most of what he tried didn't work. For one thing, I never had any intention of doing what *he* said I should do. But I was talking to Travis one time when he told me about how to use the lever with the spiral setting. He said if you pull down the lever anticlockwise and say the correct words, you open the portal *into* the ghost machine. If you pull the little lever clockwise with the same words, you open the portal *out* of the ghost machine. I tested the ghost machine, just this once, foolishly trusting his words. Of course, he'd tricked me by giving me the wrong directions. I had grown fond of a certain lady ghost and I wished to set her free from the machine. I pulled the lever, said the words he told me to say. The next thing I knew, my very living soul was sucked out of my body and into the ghost machine."

"And what are the words? Can you still remember them?"

"I shall never forget them. The words are *Phasmatis licentia.* But promise me you'll use this knowledge with care. The ghost machine is a finely balanced tool. Changing the balance would not be without its dangers..."

"How do you mean?" asked Tyler, finding a pen and quickly noting down the secret words.

"I mean, if you put one ghost into the machine, you should probably let another ghost go out. And vice versa. But then, that's just my theory..."

"I'll remember that."

Zebedee sucked on his pipe.

"You can probably guess what happened next. At that time I had a housekeeper, a Scandinavian woman called Orealia Stephensen who had her own key to my house. She must have come in the next day and found my dead body, slumped over my desk. She also found…"

"The ghost machine," said Tyler. "And she tried to find out what it does, just like everyone else who has ever found it."

"And there you have it. The only difference with Orealia was that she also had access to all my notes. She would have had a head start."

"Do you think she's in there too?"

"Who knows?" said Zebedee. "There are a lot of us in here…"

"Is there anything else I should know about the ghost machine?" asked Tyler.

Zebedee puffed on his pipe and consulted his pocket watch briefly.

"I don't think so. Tell you what, I'll let you know if I think of anything."

"Thanks," said Tyler.

Zebedee examined the watch more closely.

"Do you have the time? My watch appears to have stopped…"

Tyler checked her own watch. "It's five past ten," she said.

"Is it really?" said Zebedee, sounding quite bewildered.

The List

Tyler switched to the tree symbol.

"What does the fire symbol do?" The words formed inside the contrap lens and then drifted away into the murk. A moment later new words appeared, bobbing into view.

The fire symbol denotes the meaning of the fire setting.

"Great. Thanks." She tried again.

"What is the meaning of the fire setting?"

The meaning of the fire setting is denoted by the fire symbol.

"Answer the bloody question, you stupid machine!"

No reply.

"What about the heart?"

The heart is a muscle that pumps blood around the body.

"I know that! I mean the heart symbol on the device. What is it for?"

The heart symbol denotes the meaning of the heart setting.

"Oh forget it…"

Lucy came down the stairs having finished drying her hair and went into the kitchen.

"That's the first shower I've had for nearly a week."

"I'll go next, if that's okay," said Tyler.

Lucy wasn't listening.

"Lucy?" said Tyler. Lucy was glued to the TV screen.

"Turn it up," Lucy said. "Now!"

Tyler hit the TV remote and looked at the screen. What she saw was shocking. The news program was showing CCTV pictures of a break-in, Tyler running down a corridor followed by Lucy and then Melissa, cradling a huge fire-axe.

'…happened last night at around nine-thirty in a suburb of Watford…' the newsreader said. The CCTV sequence was replaced with three still images, blurry close-ups of Tyler, Melissa and Lucy. 'Police are now searching for three suspects caught here on closed circuit television images taken during the raid on the damaged property.' The newsreader moved on to a new story about Christmas shopping.

The girls looked at each other.

"Melissa!" said Tyler. "We have to get to her before the police do."

"Bummer…"

"We'll wear masks next time."

"What do you mean, *next time*?"

"Well, you never know…" Tyler hit keys on her new mobile phone. "We'll be alright as long as she answers her phone."

"Unless her parents have just watched that."

"Melissa… Melissa! It's Tyler. The police are after us all. You have to get some things together and get out of your house. Get packed and get yourself over here as fast as you can. Bring all the money you can get your hands on."

"We can't stay here anymore," said Lucy when Tyler was finished on the phone.

"You're right. The police will be crawling all over this place any minute. We need to get away."

Tyler gathered her belongings while Lucy threw a bag together. Lucy was back downstairs five minutes later. She went to a kitchen drawer and lifted out a tray of cutlery. She took out a credit card from the bottom of the drawer, slipped it into the back pocket of her black jeans and replaced the tray.

"Mum and Dad keep it in there for emergencies. I'd say this counts… Wouldn't you?" Then, snatching a key from a row of hooks by the door, she headed out. "Come on."

Tyler called Melissa back and told her the new meeting place. Fifteen minutes later the three girls had all reached Hogs Back. The little hill was well sheltered from view by trees and bushes.

"So where do we go now?" asked Tyler breathlessly. "I'm all out of ideas."

"That key I took – it's a key to my Aunt's house," said Lucy. "She left to spend Christmas with relatives in America three days ago. Mum and Dad are supposed to be watching the house, but I doubt they'll notice the key's gone for a few days. I think they only plan to go in once a week to water the house plants."

"Sounds like a plan."

"Is it far?"

"About half an hour on foot."

Melissa took the GAUNT file out of her bag.

"Guys, I think I found something. It might be important." She passed around a loose page from the file.

"It's just a list of weird names and stuff," said Lucy, unimpressed. "We should go. We should get off the streets."

"It's not just a list of names. Look, Adolf Hitler! They're all German names," explained Melissa. "I mean, they are all German Nazis. Infamous Nazis."

"Infamous for what?" asked Tyler.

"Infamous for their part in Hitler's war. I looked them all up. They're all responsible for their part in the mass murder of millions of people. And look," Melissa pointed to a name on the list. "Remember this one, Tyler?"

Tyler read the name.

"Josef Mengele. Yes." Then she stared at Melissa and a chill ran through her. She not only recognised the name but she remembered the face as well; the spectral face she'd seen smiling back at her in the woods. She'd seen the same face on a page when they'd searched the internet. "It was Josef Mengele," she whispered to herself.

"Who was?" asked Lucy. "What are you talking about?"

"The ghost I passed in the woods was Josef Mengele. I swear it. Somehow they've brought back Josef Mengele from the dead."

"Then the rest of the list…"

"Adolf Hitler? You are joking…"

But Tyler wasn't joking.

"I think it's safe to assume he was probably the first one they would want to bring back. They are Nazis after all…"

"How many names are on the list?" asked Lucy. "Perhaps the machine went wrong before they could bring many of them back."

Lucy counted. "Fifteen."

"How many did we see in the woods?"

"I saw three, maybe four of them, I think," said Tyler. "But I guess they could have gone anywhere. I mean, just because we only saw three or four, it doesn't mean…"

"Wait, the page has information on each of them, when they were born, when they died and other stuff. But look here," Melissa tapped the page, "at the end of the line for each name – some of them are ticked off. Six of them."

"Is Mengele ticked off?" asked Tyler.

"Yes."

"Who else?" said Lucy.

Melissa read out those with ticks by their names.

"Heinrich Himmler, Reinhard Heydrich, Adolf Eichmann, Herman Goering and… Adolf Hitler."

*

Aunt Abigail's place was a small terraced house, well furnished with comfortable couches and rugs. It was surprisingly warm considering the heating had been turned off for three days. Lucy used the front door key to let herself in and quickly found another key in a kitchen cupboard.

"We'll use the back door from now on. Less conspicuous."

The three girls made themselves comfortable, peeking through lace curtains to see if anyone had spotted them or followed them. When ten minutes had passed and no one had shown any interest in their arrival, they began to relax. They sat in Aunt Abigail's cosy lounge and began to plan. They decided they would need to get some shopping, food mainly. Lucy drew the short straw on that one as she looked so different from the TV clip in which she was still wearing school uniform. Now she was fully gothed-up: all black clothes, thick black eyeliner and a deep red lipstick, eye-shadow that any vampire would have been proud of, all this capped off with the biggest a pair of boots Tyler had ever seen: black knee-high platforms, five buckles per shin.

Tyler told her companions about Zebedee Lieberman and the other uses for the contrap.

"I say we take a vote," suggested Melissa.

"Alright. What exactly are we voting on?" asked Lucy, chewing gum.

"What we're gonna do, I suppose," said Tyler. "Anyone got any ideas?"

Lucy cracked a can of Coke. "I say we lay low for a few days. Give the police some time to forget about us and give us some time to think things through…"

They all thought about that for a moment.

It was Tyler who broke the silence.

"Problem is - if we're right and, believe me when I say I wish we were wrong, Bagshot and his Nazi followers have released six dead Nazis from the grave and they are, as we speak, roaming Watford. Who knows what they're up to? Can we really afford to wait around much longer?"

"We should go to the government or the Prime Minister or something," said Melissa. "We can't deal with this all by ourselves. It's too big."

"Yes, you're right," said Tyler. Lucy shrugged and then nodded.

"Right then," said Melissa. "We agree. But how do we do that?"

The three girls looked at each other blankly. After a long moment Lucy said, "I guess we start by going to the police…"

"Okay. We'll take a vote. Who thinks we should go to the police?" said Tyler, arms folded.

Nobody responded. The only sound was Lucy's gum smacking.

"So plan B is?"

"We'll do something about it ourselves," Lucy said.

"I suppose we have to, really," Melissa agreed reluctantly. "We're the only ones who know what's really going on."

"And the safety of the country is down to us. Who knows what these Nazis are gonna do next," said Tyler.

"We should try and find out," said Melissa.

"I agree."

"Yes, we should."

"Then that's what we'll do. That's plan B. For the meantime, anyway."

"But what exactly can a ghost *do*? I mean, I know Bagshot could be up to something else that's threatening, but exactly how worried about these Nazi ghosts should we be?"

"I don't know," admitted Tyler. Something was bugging her about the number. For some reason the number six, the number of Nazis Bagshot had erroneously released upon the unsuspecting world, was on her mind. "We can track them. Well, maybe not all of them at once. But we can certainly track them one at a time using the ghost machine. It's strange though. They didn't really look the same as the ghosts I've seen in the device. They were - I don't know - more solid..."

"Okay," said Melissa. "But we don't want to get caught. Let's get some supplies in and take another look at that file, holdup here for the afternoon. Then we can go out when it's dark – we could be out and about by five o'clock – and we'll try to find out what they're doing."

"All we need do, is agree who we're looking for and the ghost machine will eventually lead us to them," explained Tyler.

"Then we should begin with Adolf Hitler. He was the most important of them all. Probably the most evil and certainly the most important..." said Melissa. "And if any of them are getting organized, it's probably him."

"Agreed."

"Yes. Right then," said Tyler in summation. "Lucy will get the shopping before the shops close. Melissa and I will go through the GAUNT file to see what else it can tell us."

"Oh," said Melissa. "That reminds me. This morning I looked up *transducer*." She took out a folded A4 sheet of paper and read from it. 'A transducer is a device that converts one form of energy into another. Energy types they can work with are things like electrical energy, mechanical, electromagnetic, light, chemical, acoustic or thermal.' The info. suggested there were probably other types not in their list. It said transducers are commonly used in measuring instruments."

"I'm not sure that helps us much," said Tyler.

"Well, it's hard to explain, but I think it makes sense with the GAUNT machine. The Necro Transducer… It finds ghosts, seeks out individuals, their *spirit* if you like, and then transforms it into something else, a physical form - like what we saw in the woods."

"So Bagshot, or his scientists, programmed the machine to find certain ghosts and bring them back to life?" asked Lucy.

"Something like that," Melissa confirmed.

"How else could they be sure who they were bringing back?" said Tyler. "Now tell me, if you were Adolf Hitler and you'd just been brought back from the dead to find yourself in the middle of Watford, England, what would you do?"

The Tower of Doom

It seemed to take an age for darkness to fall that day. Tyler peered out of Aunt Abigail's net curtains to assess the gloom beyond the window. She surveyed her list again.

Find the missing kids
Stop the Nazis
Track down Adolf Hitler's ghost
Spy on Hitler
Stop the Nazi ghosts from doing whatever it is they are planning to do
Have Bagshot and his Nazis arrested and put in prison
Clear your name

Not the longest list she'd ever made, but surely the craziest. She recalled times when her mum had found lists in the back pocket of jeans when she'd been loading the washing machine, and she wondered what kind of a reaction this one would have induced. She checked her watch.

4:35p.m.

Lucy peeked over Tyler's shoulder to cast her eye down the list.

"Should be a stroll in the park. Come on. I reckon it's dark enough now. Don't you?"

"I don't know, but I can't wait any longer. Is Melissa ready?"

"She's still going through the file. Do you always write lists?"

"I write a list for every day. If I don't, I feel kind of, well… I just don't feel right."

"I think I've found something," said Melissa from across the room.

"What is it?" asked Tyler.

"It's to do with these experiments' results and conclusions. I'm not quite sure what it means." Melissa shuffled papers, seeking clarification. "It seems to me they tried various different things to get the GAUNT machine to work. They had mixed results as far as I can tell. One time there was an accident involving one of the scientists who was conducting the experiment. The experiment is dated 5th October, a little over two years ago."

"What happened?" said Lucy.

"Apparently he died from…" Melissa squinted at bad handwriting. "…*injuries sustained due to escaped essences* – whatever they are – during the course of the experiment… It mentions something about a displaced cathode ray."

"What's that?"

"Haven't a clue."

Melissa continued. "The thing is, something about *that* event made them change their approach. They started putting something into the machine every time they tested it."

"What?"

"I don't know. The references are vague. It's like they've used code words or something. I'll keep looking. Maybe it's here somewhere."

"We need to get going," said Lucy. "It's dark now."

"She's right. Let's go."

"Okay. I'll get my coat."

They went out into an icy night, heads covered by hoodies, and Tyler set the contrap to the *Tower of Doom* and looked into the crystal lens. She turned right into the street and took a few steps. It was a bit strange, walking with one eye on the tower and the other trying to see where she was going, but she soon became used to it. This way the tower crumbled. She turned and walked in the opposite direction, hoping nobody out on the street was watching her too closely. The tower continued to crumble. She stopped.

"It doesn't seem to be working like I thought it would," she admitted.

"Try a different direction," suggested Melissa.

Tyler began to cross the road. It worked. The little dark tower began to build immediately, but that meant she needed to walk through a row of houses. "It's this way. We'll have to go to the end of the road and take a left."

She tucked the contrap into her coat and they set off. In this way they were able to cross the town. At a point on each street Tyler took a bearing from the contrap and they set off again, knowing they were on target. It felt like a very long way of getting from A to B but it was working. After twenty minutes they were in a part of Watford they did not recognize.

"We should've brought a map," said Lucy. "We have to find our way back somehow."

"We can use the contrap for that, too, if need be," said Tyler.

"Or we could just take a cab," said Lucy.

"Good idea," the others said in unison.

They passed a fish and chip shop with a buzzing neon sign across its front and then more houses and a few small shops, all closed on Sundays. The street was quiet with hardly anyone about as they approached a coffee shop that was open and they could see a smattering of customers being served inside through the plate glass windows. Tyler had taken a bearing a hundred metres back and to her reckoning they needed to take a right at the end of this road. When they came to the end of the road, however, Tyler took another reading which left her confused.

"It says this way is wrong." She tried going left at the end of the road instead of right. The tower appeared to be crumbling just as fast. "I don't know what's going on."

They stood in the street for a moment looking at each other.

"So what now?" said Lucy.

"Give me a minute," said Tyler. She switched the contrap to the front facing eye symbol and scoured the area, delving in and out of streets and houses. When she found no sign of anything that looked like a Nazi ghost she set the contrap to the wings symbol and checked about to be sure no one was around to witness what she was about to do. She pushed off from the ground and flew up over the houses to take a look around. A minute later she returned to her friends.

"I don't get it. I can't see any sign of a ghost anywhere. She set the switch back to the *Tower of Doom* and put the contrap to her eye again. This time she began walking a strange circle, facing outwards and sidestepping every few paces. "Got it!" she said after a moment. "This way."

"That's back the way we came," Lucy pointed out.

"Do you think it's broken?" asked Melissa.

"No. The tower is building. It's building quite quickly! I think we must be really close."

"That doesn't make sense. We'd have seen the ghost by now, surely."

"Just follow me."

The contrap led Tyler back to the coffee shop and when she passed its door she noticed again the tower began to crumble. She caught a glance of some figures in the coffee shop. She took the contrap away from her eye, hid it quickly away in her coat, and looked sideways at Melissa and Lucy.

"They're in there," she whispered. "There are three of them. They're having coffee. Don't look at them."

"What do you mean *they're having coffee*? How can a ghost have coffee?" asked Melissa.

"I don't know. I'm not making this stuff up, you know. I just saw them."

"So how could you tell it was them?"

"They're in the corner, far left. Three figures huddled round a small table. They all have big coats, hats and scarves. That's not so unusual. But wearing sunglasses at night *is*. *They* have sunglasses."

"It's a cold night. Everyone is wearing coats and scarves and hats…"

"Yes, but the shades?"

"But what we saw in the woods… The figures were kind of glowing."

"I know," said Tyler. "But I think they've found a way to cover that up. I don't know. I suppose in a lit room they wouldn't glow so much anyway. Maybe they have makeup on or something…"

They looked at Tyler as though she'd lost her mind.

"What?" she said defensively. "Look, the contrap led us here. It's too much of a coincidence. Hitler is in there having a coffee. If you don't believe me, go and ask them what their names are. Then in a day or so *you'll* probably be the ones floating about and glowing in the dark 'cause you'll be dead."

A brief moment of uncertainty passed.

Then Lucy said, "We have to go in."

"What if they recognise us?" said Melissa.

"They didn't really see us, did they" asked Lucy. "I mean, when we passed them in the forest."

"Mengele saw me," said Tyler. "He saw me quite well."

"Then we can't risk you going in. At least not until we can find out if Mengele is one of them," Lucy said. "Melissa, would you recognise Mengele from the picture you saw on the web?"

"I think so. Not sure."

"Come on. Melissa and I will go in. If we think it's all clear, we'll come and get you."

"Wait!" said Tyler suddenly.

"What?"

"One of *those* is the ghost of Adolf Hitler. Just be careful."

"We will. See you later."

"Okay."

A few moments passed. Tyler pulled at her hood to hide her face and chanced a peek into the shop. Melissa and Lucy were at the counter ordering drinks. Melissa headed back outside.

"Lucy says do you want tea or coffee, or something cold?"

Tyler looked at her aghast. "What about the ghosts, Melissa? The ghosts…"

"Oh, yes. Of course. It's okay. Mengele isn't there. I'm pretty sure."

Tyler nodded. She thought for a moment.

"Do they do hot chocolate?"

"I don't know."

The two girls joined Lucy at the counter to order. They took turns to watch the three strange figures huddled in the corner around a small table laden with coffee cups.

"One of them is eating cake!" Lucy observed.

The others looked over to be sure she was right. The one eating cake was a slim man with a stubbly face. Unlike his companions he was not wearing dark glasses and he seemed less worried about wrapping up against the cold. Tyler thought he looked feeble. There was something about him she didn't like. He had a desperate air about him, as though he would do anything to please his companions. His eyes were narrow and his pointy face tipped at the chin with a tuft of scrawny hair. On another man this might have been considered quite cool, but on this guy it just looked rat-like.

"That one's not a ghost," concluded Tyler. "But the other two are. See how they're covering almost every part of their skin – hats, gloves, glasses and scarves. There's barely any skin showing, and the skin that is showing looks kind of weird. Like it's a bit flaky..."

Their drinks arrived at the counter so they found a table close to the strange trio. Lucy took out gum and wedged it under the table. The others glared at her.

"What?"

"That's gross," said Melissa.

"It's just while I drink my coffee."

"You mean you're going to put that back in your mouth afterwards?"

"Why not? Wait a minute," said Lucy. "One of the others just ate cake too."

"Do ghosts eat cake?" Melissa wondered aloud. "Maybe ghosts *can* eat cake."

"Maybe they're not ghosts after all," said Lucy.

"They're ghosts," said Tyler. "At least, they're something *like* ghosts…"

Just then, the figure sitting with his back to the girls turned and looked around the café briefly. The girls exchanged concerned looks. It was not difficult to recognise Adolf Hitler even with his heavy disguise.

Tyler swallowed hard. Melissa turned pale. Lucy swore.

To their relief, Adolf turned back to his companions.

"It's him alright," said Melissa.

"Can you hear anything they're saying?" Tyler asked.

"No. I'm not close enough," Melissa replied. "Wait a minute." She rose and went to the washroom door beyond Adolf's table, and went in. Tyler and Lucy both noticed the door did not fully shut behind her, but was held open a crack by something on the other side. Tyler and Lucy watched the trio and sipped hot chocolate.

"You like any music?" Lucy asked Tyler, nervously making small talk.

"Not that much." Tyler was trying to get a good look at the ghost sitting next to Hitler. From what she could see, his face was a little podgy and his chin small. His hair was covered by a trilby.

Silence.

"Way to kill a conversation…" said Lucy. She sipped hot chocolate and eyed Tyler suspiciously over her Styrofoam cup.

Tyler was pensive. Something was odd about these ghosts. It was like they were ghosts and yet not ghosts at the same time.

Ten minutes later Melissa returned to her seat.

"They're talking German. Planning something, I'm pretty sure. I don't know the language well enough to tell exactly what they're saying, but the skinny man with the hairy chin was talking at one point and he slipped into English. Just for a second. He said *three, two, one*, made a sound like *puff*, then said *auf wiedersehen…*"

"What does that mean?" asked Tyler.

"It means goodbye, doesn't it?" said Lucy.

"Yes. Sounded like he was describing an explosion or something… You know, like, *hasta la vista, baby,* ka-boom!"

"They're planning to blow something up," stated Lucy.

"Or some*one*," added Melissa.

"But what, or who, exactly?" said Tyler.

No one spoke for what seemed a long time.

"Come on," said Tyler. She drained her cup. "I have an idea."

Gloves

It was late. Sunday night. The woods showed no sign of the previous eerie apparitions. Trees were hushed hoarders of secret knowledge. Melissa and Tyler were dressed in black once more. They'd left Lucy on dinner duty back at Aunt Abigail's. Beyond the NVF's glassy frontage, scientists and technicians busied themselves in labs.

"So why are we here again?" asked Melissa, hungry and weary from walking.

"We need to find out what happened. We need to know what these things are," explained Tyler.

"Let me guess… The contrap…"

"Just keep an eye on the door. I don't want to be disturbed while I'm searching with it. If we get caught it's game over."

"Right."

A blind spot in the CCTV system had been hard to find, but they'd narrowed it down to the area in the shadows of the woods near a back corner of the NVF laboratory building. They weren't as close to the door as Tyler would have liked and it was a long-shot, but she thought it might pay off anyway.

Tyler switched the contrap to the left facing eye and put her eye to the viewing glass. She aimed the contrap at the back door and pulled gently downwards on the lever. Days began to roll backwards in time. Last night came and went as twilight shifted into a grey winter's afternoon. She watched for signs of movement around the doorway. Sound was a skittering noise in her ears. Nothing discernible. Tyler looked for an opportunity to learn something about the GAUNT machine ghosts, whatever they were, but she knew she might well be wasting her time. Somehow the strange beings had left the building and entered the woods. She hoped to catch the moment. She stopped when several figures huddled into view in a speeded up replay of the past. She eased off of the lever and adjusted pressure until the past was playing at a realistic speed. She heard voices. By her reckoning she had now gone back three, maybe four days.

"They better not put the blame on us," someone outside of her view was saying.

Another voice answered as two more men joined the gathering out the back of the facility. They took out cigarettes and lighters and began smoking.

"Well, they can't pin it on us. Not our fault if the machine malfunctions…"

"You think they'll get far by themselves? I mean, they don't even know where they are, do they?"

A short, rotund man with a boyish face laughed.

"I guess not," he said. "I'm not sure they even know *what* they are. They'll probably come running home when the night sets in. Otherwise they'll freeze to death. Get it? Freeze to *death*?"

"Yeah, yeah, very funny, Streicher," said a man with an army-style haircut. "Tell it to Bagshot when he takes you in for an 'interview'. He's not a happy camper."

"Yeah, I saw. Have you heard from Roger?" Streicher asked.

"I don't think anyone will be hearing from Roger for a while. They had to wire his jaw up when they got him to hospital. It's broken in two places."

"Well, we're all in deep doo-doo now…"

"For sure."

Streicher flicked a cigarette butt into the woods. It passed right through Tyler.

"What about the rest of the list? Anyone know what the plan is?" asked another of the smokers.

"I don't suppose they'll want the rest just yet, considering this mess," said military man.

Streicher lit another cigarette, sucked on it and coughed uncontrollably.

"Yep, these things'll kill you," said a thinner man with tattoos on his arms.

"Sooner the better, if you ask me," said Streicher. "The things I've seen in this place – not sure I want to see another damned day."

"Do you think it's safe?" asked the tattooed man peering into the woods. "I mean, what if they separate?"

"The gloves won't separate," said Streicher emphatically. "Why would they separate?"

The others looked at him uncertainly. Streicher tried to shrug off their insinuating stares. A few moments later they tossed their cigarette butts into the snow and went back inside.

Tyler applied more pressure and the image began to whirl backwards in time once more. She stopped when several figures appeared fleetingly in the viewer and then she backed up to watch again at a slower pace. She watched as the back door opened and Adolf Hitler came out. He blinked in the sunlight as though he'd been kept in a dark place for a long time. He looked back inside the building. He was dressed in a German uniform much the same as in the old black and white photos she'd previously seen. More figures followed. Five more. Tyler recognised Josef Mengele amongst them, also in Nazi uniform. None of them spoke, but under Hitler's guidance they left the building and entered the woods.

Their substance did appear different in the daylight. They looked almost human. They did not glow so much and now Tyler could see they were definitely more solid than, say, Albert, or Zebedee, in the contrap. She was convinced they were something more than ghosts. As Tyler watched, Hitler led the other five figures into the woods and they glowed a little more once under the shade of the trees. Soon they were all gone and a huddle of bewildered scientists arrived at the door peering into the woods, looking very unsure of themselves.

Tyler searched through days and nights but could find little else of interest. It seemed Bagshot rarely used this back door. The smokers came and went like clockwork. She set the contrap to the skull symbol and put it away.

"They definitely lost control," she explained to Melissa. "Something went wrong and they lost control of the ghosts in the GAUNT machine. Bagshot was mad about it. Now they're just on the loose and neither

Bagshot nor the NVF can do anything about it. One of the men I overheard talking said something very odd. First they were talking about a list. I think they meant the list of Nazis we now have. Only, then this one man asked something like *what if they separate,* and another said, *the gloves won't separate, why would they separate?*"

"Very odd," Melissa agreed. "Tyler, can we go now? Only, I'm freezing, starving hungry and more tired than I've ever been before in my life."

*

Lucy made a mean spaghetti bolognese. When it was eaten and plates cleared away, Melissa went back to the file. The three girls were drained and, although much was at stake, they knew they had to get some sleep. Lucy took her Aunt's bed. Tyler plumped for the smaller of the two couches and left Melissa still reading and trying to make sense of the GAUNT file by the light of a solitary standard lamp.

When Tyler awoke the next morning, it appeared Melissa had not even put the file down to rest, despite her earlier complaints.

"You been at it all night?"

"Pretty much."

"You're a machine. Found anything interesting?"

"Just this," she passed Tyler a sheet of paper. Tyler rubbed her eyes and tried to focus. "It's not much, but look down there at the bottom…"

Tyler scanned the printed sheet of German text. At the base of the page someone had scrawled a note in the margin with a pencil. It was that awful handwriting again. She took a stab at reading it.

"*Lores…* That's not a word is it? A name maybe? Could be German I suppose. Or maybe it's *loves*? But there's this squiggle before it."

"That's what *I* thought at first," said Melissa. "Then I was thinking about what you said last night. About the strange thing you heard the man talking about, round the back of the lab. You said something about gloves… Then I saw it; it says gloves. The squiggle is a G."

"Gloves, right. I see it now. That's weird. And then, below that, it says something else – *the dominant force…* What's that supposed to mean?"

"I really don't know."

"So can you read anything else on this page?"

"Unfortunately, no. It looked like German at first, but it's actually written in a code. There's not a single German word I can recognise on the entire page. Of course, it could be in code *and* in German."

Tyler yawned and went to take a shower.

When she returned to the lounge she took out the contrap and set the switch to the spiral, curious to see who was around and hoping she might find Albert. Immediately she heard her name being called from within the contrap. She was surprised to see Albert was already there, looking for her.

"Missy, there you are. I been callin' ya' for an age."

"Really? What's up, Albert?"

"Oh nuffing really. Just old Zebedee's been here waiting for ya'. 'E wants ta' tell ya' some-fing else 'e's found out."

"Oh, right. Is he there, then?"

"Mr Lieberman, sir, Miss Tyler's 'ere now," Albert said, turning to his side.

Zebedee sprang into view tapping his cane enthusiastically. He drew at length on his pipe and puffed out a great cloud of smoke.

"My dear girl, where on Earth have you been? I don't know… Why is everyone so very *late* these days? Oh well, now that you *are* here, I have something to tell you. Some news you may find interesting. I bumped into the most fascinating old girl who seemed to know some things about that device of mine, I mean, of *yours*. At first she didn't want to talk about it at all, but Albert told me she knew about the thing and so I thought I'd try a little of the *old Lieberman charm*. Well, I'm pleased to say it worked! I was trying to find out about those other two symbols, you see…"

"Right. And you can tell me what they do now?"

"Oh no, sorry to disappoint. It's nothing as exciting as that. But, I don't know. Well, it might help you somehow I suppose. It *is* about the device, though. Apparently it can be used as a kind of a magnet, you know, to draw things towards it with an unseen force. You do have magnets in your day and age I presume?"

"We do."

"Very good. Well, it works in a similar way, only, instead of attracting iron objects towards it, it has the capability to summon ghosts."

"Right." Tyler suddenly realised this made perfect sense. If the con trap was to trap a ghost through its open portal, there had to be a way of getting the ghost there in the first place. "So how does it do that?"

"The device alone does not have this power, but when it comes into contact with an artefact that has a special association with the ghost you are seeking, that ghost will be drawn to it, even against his, or her, will.

From what I can glean, the stronger the association with the artefact, the more powerful the pull."

"So the artefact would be…"

"Oh, you know, something the person owned before he or she died. A hat or a cup - it could be anything really. The important thing is the strength of the association. Just a cup someone once used, for example, might work well enough, but that person's *favorite* cup… That would be a different matter. Do you see? The more personal the item, the better it will work."

"It would create a more powerful pull. Like a stronger magnet."

"You've got it. It's a ghastly thought, but I suppose the most powerful artefact would be a piece of the deceased: a bone, some hair or something like that. Or even the whole corpse. Anyway, thought it might come in useful."

"Yes. Thank you, Zebedee," said Tyler. "That is very useful to know."

"Farewell for now then, dear girl." Zebedee waved his hat and strode off into mist.

Tyler was struck silent for several minutes, her head spinning with possibilities. The largest of these thoughts loomed above all others: Was it therefore possible for her to use the con trap on Hitler and the others? She would need an artefact, of course, and that wouldn't be easy to acquire. Bit by bit a plan began to form in her mind.

"Melissa, does Lucy's aunt have a computer in the house. We need the internet."

Melissa looked up from the GAUNT file with sore eyes. "Sorry… What?"

"Never mind. Where's Lucy?"

"Still in bed, I think."

Tyler ran up the stairs calling for Lucy. Lucy met her at the door to her aunt's bedroom.

"What? What is it? Did someone find us?" she asked. "My head hurts like a…"

"We need to get online. Now."

Aunt Abigail's laptop was locked in a cupboard under the stairs. Lucy knew where the key was kept and so it was only a matter of minutes before they had the computer on a desk and booting up. Lucy sat down. Tyler and Melissa stood behind, looking over her shoulder.

"She'll kill me if she ever finds out I used this without her permission."

"I won't tell her," said Tyler. "We need to search for artefacts that used to belong to Adolf Hitler. We'll need to do the same for Mengele and the others who are ticked off that list. But first things first."

Lucy opened up a browser window, typed *Hitler artefacts* into the search engine, hit *search*. A second later a multitude of hits filled the screen.

"The first one. Click on the first one," said Tyler.

Lucy clicked through to the first website on the list. A new page opened up titled *Museum of World War II*. It listed information and images of a host of artefacts once owned by, or associated with, Hitler.

"Why are we doing this?" Lucy wanted to know. Tyler told them both about Zebedee's latest findings.

"Where is that museum?" she then asked.

Lucy clicked on the *contact us* navigation button. "Natick, Massachusetts."

"That's no good," said Melissa. "We don't have time to travel to America. Even if we did, we'd still have to break into the Museum of World War II. I don't think we'd stand a chance."

"Go back," said Tyler, ignoring the glassy look Lucy threw her.

Tyler checked down the list of search hits. Near the bottom of the first page she found something that interested her.

"There. Second one from the bottom. It's a news website, a report on a break in at the museum. Click on it. I want to know what was stolen."

Lucy clicked and read the news report aloud.

"On the 14th July, police were called to the Museum of World War II at approximately two a.m. in response to alarms raised by a break in. The still unknown perpetrators made off with items of great value to antiquity. Amongst the list of stolen artefacts are numerous medals awarded to German military leaders during the Second World War and, curiously, Adolf Hitler's very own reading glasses, complete with case…"

"They've broken in already," Melissa concluded. "The NVF have already been there."

"Of course they have," said Tyler dropping to her knees. "They needed the artefacts to help summon up the Nazi ghosts in the first place. They used them like Zebedee said, only it was with the GAUNT machine, not the contrap." She put her head in her hands despairingly. "We're stuffed."

"Wait a minute!" said Melissa. "No, no, no. This isn't bad. This is a good thing. Listen, if the NVF have already stolen the artefacts from the museum in America, then they've saved us a job. Don't you see?"

"But we don't even know where they're keeping the artefacts," stated Lucy.

"No, we don't," said Melissa. "But I know how we can find out." She raised a finger to point at the contrap hanging about Tyler's neck.

"There's something else I'd like to know," said Tyler. "Who was the other ghost with Hitler. We know he is likely one of five others whose names are ticked off that list from the GAUNT file."

Lucy fetched the list and they entered names into the search engine. The third name they entered rang bells as pictures and information appeared on the screen.

"That's him," said Lucy. "That's the one who was with Hitler in the café."

"You sure?" asked Tyler. "It was pretty difficult to see his face."

"I think she's right," said Melissa. "I got a good look at him when I pretended to go to the washroom." She speed-read the text and summarized. "*Heinrich Himmler was Hitler's right hand man. He was a leading member of the Nazi party. During the war he was overseer of the concentration camps.* I don't want to read any more. It's too horrible. Let's just say, he's responsible for the killing of an awful lot of innocent people."

"We must stop them," said Tyler.

The Case

Several hours later, the three girls found the coffee shop again having bought a German and English pocket dictionary on the way. They went in to order drinks and breakfast rolls, glad to be out of the cold as the temperature had dropped by several degrees. As Tyler had hoped, there was no sign of the Nazi ghosts. They took the table where Hitler and his friends had sat. It was the first of two visits Tyler had in mind. This one she'd planned before leaving the café the day before. She switched the contrap to the left facing eye and passed it to Melissa.

"You just pull the lever down until you find the time period you want to see," Tyler explained. Melissa took the contrap and nervously peered into it. She pulled the lever, watched and listened. Tyler and Lucy sipped hot drinks and ate. After a few moments, Melissa dipped into the pocket dictionary and then looked back into the contrap for a while. She repeated this process several times, muttering to herself every now and then.

Ten minutes later Melissa gave the contrap back to Tyler.

"Well?" said Lucy through a mouthful of bacon roll.

"It's like we thought. They're going to blow something up."

"What?" said Tyler.

Melissa had that washed-out look again, as though she'd just seen a ghost. "What's the date?" she said. When no one responded she said, "Today's date? What is the date today?"

Tyler checked her watch. "It's the twenty-second of December. Why?"

"In two days, on Christmas Eve, they're going to blow up Westminster Abbey during the carol service. For some reason they seem to think the Prime Minister will be there. I expect they're right, along with half of Parliament and a couple of thousand other people. That scrawny guy with the hairy chin – he's a bomb maker."

The others were silent for several seconds, contemplating this news.

"So we've got two days to find out where the NVF are keeping the Hitler artefact, steal it, and get to Westminster Abbey so we can stop him…" said Tyler.

"Or we could forget everything we know, just walk away, deny all knowledge…" said Lucy. She received condemning looks. "What I mean is *piece of cake*… Of course we can do it…" She flashed a smile and took another bite of bacon roll.

"Not necessarily. We don't yet know what time the service at Westminster starts. And it's already…" Melissa checked her watch. "Ten-thirty. We might actually have less than two days. It's gonna be tough."

"Do you have any more details from their talk with the bomb maker?" asked Tyler, feeling overwhelmed and fearing a panic attack.

"No, sorry. That's about all I could work out from what they said, even with the dictionary. I'm wishing I'd paid more attention in German lessons right now… Fortunately for us, 'Westminster Abbey' in German is *Westminster Abbey*. I went over the conversation twice. I can't work out any more of it."

Tyler took out today's list and studied it for a moment before shoving it in her back pocket.

"Then we'd best get going. We have a lot to do," she said.

*

Tyler shivered and wished she'd not been so adamant about going alone. The day had been frustrating. It would have wasted less of their precious time if she'd gone in broad daylight instead of waiting for the sun to go down, but that would have been far too dangerous. Bagshot worked here as well as at the laboratory site, and at least the NVF office building was closed-up at the end of the day.

It was much as she'd last seen it. There was no light anywhere beyond the dark glass frontage and no indication of any life outside either. She took time to walk its perimeter and noticed a fire escape staircase at one side which ended at a door on the second floor. In the end she chose the front door as the best place to begin spying.

Tyler set the contrap to the left facing eye and stood before the front entrance. She brought the lever gently down until hours were ticking by in seconds before her eyes. She was not really sure what she was looking for, only some kind of clue as to the whereabouts of the Hitler artefact. She knew the glasses might well still be at the other NVF building. They had certainly been used with the GAUNT machine. However, spying on that building was difficult because of the CCTV cameras and the fact that it was never left unoccupied. This office block was different. She was free to go anywhere outside the building unchallenged and she figured this was the building which dealt with all the business. The other one was purely a lab. She thought there was a good chance the artefacts might have passed through the offices at some point.

Her first thought was to track Bagshot's comings and goings. She zipped through the last two days seeing nothing of interest, before slowing the contrap when she saw him walking backwards into the building. That was Bagshot leaving for home. Tyler calculated this must have been Saturday night and she wondered what had been so important that Bagshot felt he had to go into work at the weekend. She continued shifting back in time. Reflected in the dark glass of the building, cars went and came, but there were few visitors to the NVF offices that day. An hour or so earlier the receptionist left, walking backwards into the building. Once more in the reflection, Tyler watched a red van reverse up and stop. A man got out and walked backwards into reception, carrying something in his hands. A moment later the man came out of the same door walking backwards and climbed into his van. The van turned and reversed away out of Tyler's view.

She continued to watch time in quick rewind, now wishing whoever made the contrap had thought to fit two eye pieces. Peering intently into the strange crystal with only her right eye was hard work when done for any length of time. More men came and went. Changing shadows betrayed the passing hours. She stopped when she saw Bagshot walking backwards out of the door, briefcase in hand. That must have been him turning up for work earlier in the day. Not much to go on there.

Tyler clicked her way through days but could see nothing of any interest. Workers left and came, cars reversing in reflecting glass. She had an unnerving feeling as she watched herself and Melissa escape from a security guard and then trick their way into the building. She realised she was watching several days prior to the night when they'd rescued Lucy from the NVF laboratory. This was, as far as she could work out, before the Nazi ghosts broke out of the GAUNT machine, and so she stopped and began working her way forward in time. It was much less confusing this way. People walked forwards. She slowed several times when Bagshot was entering and leaving the building, hoping for a snippet of conversation or a sign of some sort, yet finding very little. She saw him wave to a colleague, and once he went back inside, muttered something to someone and came back out to leave. Eventually she revisited Saturday, only this time she watched more carefully and at a realistic time speed, whenever anyone was in sight.

Bagshot arrived for work, checking his watch and looking on edge about something. He didn't seem to be pleased about going in. The receptionist arrived in a hurry several minutes later, looking stressed and fumbling with the keypad in black gloved hands. She entered and then returned in a fluster a moment later to retrieve her briefcase from the pavement.

Tyler clicked through to the next discernible movement.

Two men arrived and Tyler thought she recognised one of them as the man who'd cut his arm on broken glass when she'd been cornered in the warehouse. He was carrying a silver case. It was of interest to her because this case was cuffed to the man's hand. It seemed strange to her, and the only reason she could see that someone would handcuff themselves to a case was for security. The case obviously contained something of great value to the NVF. She scrutinized the next few hours, hoping to find something of use.

The dark glass of the building was not a total blackout glass, but a dense, translucent, smoky tint. Tyler found that by placing the contrap against the glass she could see into the reception area. It wasn't a great image, being so dark, but it did allow her to see vaguely what was going on inside.

She tracked the movement of the silver case, watched the cuffs being unlocked and removed and the case being handed over to Bagshot. Bagshot disappeared with the case for a while and the two other men left the building. Bagshot returned to reception bringing the case with him. He handed it to the receptionist and gave instructions beyond Tyler's hearing. The receptionist packaged up the case and made a phone call. An hour later the red van arrived and a man with a cap and an official looking uniform entered the building. Tyler turned and saw the van right in front of her. The logo on the side read 'Safeguard Special Deliveries'. Back in reception, Tyler watched the package being handed over to the delivery man with the cap. He took the package and left the building.

This was it, Tyler realised: the moment she'd been searching for. The addressed package was about to leave the building and pass right by her. She positioned herself so she'd be able to see the package when the delivery man came out, but he was past her in a second and she didn't get time to read the address. She rewound and tried again. Again she failed to catch the address. The man was carrying the parcel with the label facing upwards. She realised that if she was in his exact position she would be able to look down and read the address label easily, so she rewound once more, but this time she walked right into the space occupied by the delivery man. It felt odd to be inside someone else. She could see her own body in her left eye and, in the right eye only the delivery man's body and what he was holding. She memorized the address as best she could and repeated the process to double check she had it right.

A sudden voice beyond the contrap made her jump.

"Find anything interesting?" It was the woman in the green coat, standing where the red van had been.

Tyler let the contrap fall to her chest, all focus on the barrel of the handgun now levelled at her. She clutched the contrap in her hand but was too late to hide it.

"I'll take that," said the woman gesturing with the gun.

"Are you the Green Goddess?" asked Tyler.

"Becky Jones, I presume…" The woman smiled sickeningly.

Tyler slipped her finger onto the switch at the centre of the contrap and, glancing down for a second, flicked it to the skull symbol.

"Uh, uh, uh… Don't even think about it. Take it off and hand it over. No funny business." The Green Goddess took a step closer and held out a hand. They were now almost close enough to touch.

Tyler looked around. They were alone. 'Where's a security guard when you need one?' she wondered.

"Okay, okay!" she said in submission. "Here you go…" Tyler feigned reaching for the chain about her neck. "Just point that thing somewhere else, will you?"

The Green Goddess let the gun aim at the sky. Tyler knew she had a long reach and could be swift. She kicked high. The gun arched through the air and went skittering to the icy ground. She ran, heading for the fire escape, launching herself up the stairs. Her pursuer was close behind.

It was clear that the steps finished in a dead end. Tyler hoped the Green Goddess would see this too. Tyler thumped into the railing at the end, bruising ribs. She turned and faced the approaching woman. As her pursuer drew level, the recovered gun in hand, Tyler let herself tip backwards over the railings. The Green Goddess shot off two rounds and ran to the edge.

Tyler fell. She already had her hand on the switch when she went over the edge and she knew she'd never hit the ground. She moved the switch to the flight symbol and tugged at the lever, dashed upwards into the dark sky and looked below to see the Green Goddess peering down in bewilderment at the ground where Tyler's shattered body should have been.

Tyler flew most of the way back to Aunt Abigail's. She descended to the streets near a pub, meaning to walk from there, but flew higher again when a police car pulled up below her. It was then she encountered a problem.

She began to drop but she hadn't released pressure on the little lever. It seemed odd at the time, but instinctively Tyler pulled the lever down further around the contrap's edge to try to climb. She levelled off and then dropped again. The contrap was not responding. Suddenly the ground was rushing up at a frightening speed. She hit the pavement with force, rolled head over heels, narrowly missing a lamppost, and went sprawling into a road. An oncoming car blared its horn and screamed to a halt several inches from her face. The driver's side door opened and a man got out, silhouetted by the car headlamps. He looked at her and took off his hat.

"What the…"

Tyler picked herself up, brushing gravel from her coat.

"Sorry, Mister," she said, before running.

"Hey! Wait!" the man shouted after her.

Tyler turned on the speed, pumping legs. She rounded a corner and skidded to a stop. Before her, the police car door opened and an officer got out. Tyler panicked. She turned and fled back the way she'd come. The man from the first car was standing on the pavement before her. Tyler tore across the road, wishing the contrap could make her invisible, or at least work again.

"Hold up, girly!" the man shouted after her.

Tyler glanced over her shoulder. The policeman was now chasing her and shouting for her to stop. Her left leg was painful where she'd bruised her knee, but she drove herself on regardless. She grabbed the contrap and tried the flight mechanism again.

Nothing.

As she neared a T-junction at the end of the road, a second police car came into view. It shot past the junction but then reappeared, reversing slowly. She'd been spotted. She noticed a narrow alley threading its way between houses to her right and sprinted down it. The alley ran through to another road on the other side of the block; a road Tyler recognised. She knew, then, she was very close to the house.

She was soon knocking quietly, yet desperately, on Abigail's back door, battered and bruised, exhausted, but very much alive.

Lucy let her in and saw that something was not right.

"What's up?"

"Lock the door. Turn off all the lights. The police are after me. I'm hoping I lost them, but who knows. And get me some paper and a pen."

Melissa found a first aid box and cleaned the grazes on Tyler's hands and face in darkness.

Minutes ticked by and nobody came knocking on the door. When a torturous half-hour had passed, Tyler relaxed a little. She took the contrap, flicked the switch to the spiral and looked into it.

"Albert!" she hissed. "Albert, where the hell are you? Zebedee! Are you there?"

But neither Albert, nor Zebedee was there. *Nobody* was there.

Underground

Melissa took the contrap and tried every switch position one after the other, peering into the crystal.

"But it can't be broken. How can it be broken?" She shook it in frustration, tapped the lens. Tyler took it back.

"Don't do that. There's people in there!"

"So we don't have the contrap anymore," Lucy stated. "I'm not sure we can do much on our own. I mean, without the contrap."

"We have to go anyway. We have to carry on with the plan or thousands of people are going to die." Tyler was resolute. "And that will only be the start."

"I don't think we should. Not without *that* thing," said Lucy. "It's the only reason we've got as far as we have. And to be honest, we haven't got very far."

Melissa looked from one to the other.

"I don't believe this is happening! It was bad enough before. Now without the contrap – what chance do we have? It's hopeless!"

"And we don't even know what was inside that package you saw," Lucy pointed out.

"Lucy's right," said Melissa. "Maybe we should wait."

"We don't have time to wait," argued Tyler. "And, really, we have nothing else to go on. Surely we have to try. They will do it all over again. You know that don't you? They will persecute and murder thousands and millions of innocent people."

Silence.

"I'm going anyway," Tyler told them. "You can come with me, or you can stay here. It's up to you. But I'm going. I'm gonna pack. You do what you want."

*

Melissa slept on the train. Lucy stared out of the window at London's moonlit wintering outskirts as they dashed by. Tyler tried to sleep but couldn't. They were out and about in public, vulnerable and exposed. It was enough to put her completely on edge. She'd been a nervous wreck surrounded by crowds at the station and had come close to a panic attack.

She ran an eye over their baggage stowed neatly under seats. They hadn't brought much with them, but the GAUNT file was safely packed in Melissa's bag along with some other research documents they thought might be useful.

The address Tyler had read on the package was on Whitechapel Road, in Whitechapel, London. Tyler had scribbled it down as soon as she'd got back to Aunt

Abigail's house. She'd also made a note of the name the parcel was addressed to.

Miss Valda Braun
Senior Assistant Manager
NVF Headquarters
South Sea House

"I wonder what their headquarters is like," said Tyler.

Lucy shrugged and stretched gum from her teeth into a long string. "Guess we'll find out soon enough."

"Listen. Thanks for coming. I mean, I know you didn't want to."

Lucy met Tyler's eyes. "Well, we couldn't let you have *all* the fun, now, could we? Besides, someone has to stop you from getting yourself killed by these freakin' weirdoes."

"Right," said Tyler, stifling the urge to say, *look who's talking.*

They were not alone in the carriage, but they had managed to commandeer one end. Tyler took out the contrap, hid behind a newspaper just in case anyone walked by, and looked into the glass.

"Albert," she whispered. "Albert, please come to me. I need you!"

Suddenly mist parted and Albert walked into the crystal view.

"Alright, Missy? Did ya' call me?" he said.

Tyler was so excited to see him that she let fly a small shriek and nearly dropped the contrap.

"Albert, what's going on?"

"I don't rightly follow, Missy."

"I mean about the contrap... Why has it stopped working?"

"Don't fink it 'as stopped workin'. It's workin' now ain't it? Or you wouldn't be talkin' to me..."

"Well, yes. I suppose it is. But it did stop working. Hang on... Do you mean to say – it's all working again?"

"I dunno. Why don't ya' test it out?"

"Wait right there, Albert. I'll be back in a minute." Tyler set the switch to the central eye symbol and levered her visual way through several carriages ahead of theirs. It was working perfectly. She switched back to the spiral and found Albert again.

"It *is* working. Can you do something for me, Albert?"

"You knows me, Missy. I'd do anyfink for *you*."

This made Tyler smile.

"Great. Can you see if you can find Zebedee Lieberman again, or even the old witch you spoke to about the contrap? I need to know why it stopped working."

"Wait there. I'll see what I can do."

Tyler took the contrap away from her eye, lowered the newspaper and saw that Melissa was now awake. She was watching Tyler expectantly, as was Lucy.

"It's working again!" Tyler said quietly. The others grinned.

"Well okay then," said Lucy.

Tyler turned back to the contrap. Zebedee was waiting for her.

"I hear it stopped working for a spell..." he said to Tyler.

"Yes. Do you know why?"

"But of course. I must apologise. In my zeal I neglected to tell you of a small weakness inherent to the device, though when I was using it I quickly learned to compensate and so it had slipped my mind completely."

"The device has a weakness?"

"Well, not so much the device but you must remember you are dealing with ghosts. It's not like a mechanical engine. We ghosts get tired from time to time. If you use the device repeatedly for an extended period of time, the ghosts grow exhausted and need time to recuperate. If they grow too weary whilst the device is in use, it will simply cease to function for a while."

"I see," said Tyler. "So you're saying, basically, don't over-use the device."

"Precisely. Don't use it too much if you don't need to. Even talking to me now will be burning energy. Use the power wisely and it will get you through most scrapes. Use it foolishly and, just when you need it most, it may let you down."

"But what if I need it for important things, for a long time? Is there no way to keep it working?"

"None that I know of. It's down to you and what you do with it."

"Okay."

"But, Tyler, do not be deceived into thinking that without the device you are powerless. This would be foolish. There are powers you possess that are far greater than those of any ghost machine."

Tyler was left to ponder Zebedee's words as the train slowed and reached Baker Street. They got off and then boarded a train to Whitechapel on the Hammersmith and City Line, hoping all the time that no one would recognise them from their television début.

*

Lucy used her credit card to pay for a hotel room with three beds. Tyler set an alarm for six the next morning. She wanted to be up and at the NVF headquarters before anyone arrived for work. She intended to spy out the place as people came and went, and wanted to figure out a way of getting in. Time was too short for much planning. She felt if she didn't get in there soon and acquire the Hitler artefact, all their efforts would have been a waste of time. She fell into bed feeling burned out and slept deeply.

The next morning they left the hotel wearing hoods and traveling light. They searched for South Sea House on Whitechapel Road. They bought an *A to Z of London* though they would never have found the house without some help from the *Tower of Doom* and Tyler was irked that they'd had to use it for such a mundane task. But they *had* found it.

The building itself was a tall brown-stone construction with three rows of huge windows on its impressive front. Either side loomed other huge buildings in red brick and black glass. Shoppers and businessmen and women were already beginning to fill the streets. Facing the road, the building's only front door was large, white and intimidating. They stood by a glass shop front across the road from the house, partially concealed by a bus stop. Tyler could not imagine any of them actually going in.

She took out the contrap and searched through the building's walls and rooms. Someone was already inside. Tyler had to look away and blink. What she thought she was seeing made no sense at all. She checked again, sifting from room to room, passing through solid matter as if it were made of transparent jelly. She found the figure again, and again was surprised.

"There's someone in there actually wearing a Nazi uniform."

The girls exchanged glances.

"You mean one of the Nazi ghosts is in there?" asked Melissa.

Tyler continued peering through the contrap. "If it *is* one of the ghosts, I don't recognise him. No wait. It's a woman."

"It's not one of the ghosts then," said Melissa. "They were all men. There wasn't even a single woman on the list from the GAUNT file."

"So what you're saying is, there is a real live Nazi in the building across the street, dressed like a Nazi and everything," Lucy concluded.

"Er, yes. I guess that *is* what I'm saying."

"Does she have a gun?" asked Lucy.

"No, she doesn't have a gun."

"Any sign of the package or the artefacts?" asked Melissa.

"Can't see anything yet, but I'm looking for a case or a pair of glasses or a handful of medals… It's not going to be easy. It's a big building."

"Someone else is going in," warned Lucy.

They watched as a man in a long coat and a brown trilby entered using his own key. Tyler followed his progress into the building through the contrap and watched him hang up his coat and hat to reveal a Nazi uniform underneath.

"He's another one!"

As the girls watched over the next few minutes, several dozen people entered the building, one at a time. Each removed a long coat which had concealed a Nazi uniform. Tyler told the others what she was seeing.

"It's like some kind of secret club," she explained.

"It's a secret underground movement!" said Melissa. "They probably get a kick out of parading around in Nazi uniforms, running their Nazi business. But it's all in secret."

"At least," added Lucy, "until they're big enough to actually do something."

Tyler was not listening. She was busy trying to focus the contrap on a logo emblazoned on a door somewhere deep within the building.

"I think I've got something," she said. "There's a door with a sign. It's the NVF logo again. Only this time it says, Nazi Victorious Federation." Then she moved the contrap down until it was focusing into a basement level where she found racks of guns and other military equipment. Some shapes looked suspiciously like bombs and torpedoes. There was also a whole bank of laptops and some other technical-looking equipment unfamiliar to Tyler.

"I can see weapons. A whole lot of weapons and other stuff."

Melissa glanced at her watch nervously. "It's nine-thirty already. Tomorrow Hitler plans to blow up Westminster Abbey. The carol service begins at three. That gives us a total of…" She did some mental arithmetic. "…twenty-nine and a half hours to break in, get the case of artefacts and work out how to stop Hitler. Look for the silver case. That's our best hope."

"No pressure then," said Lucy.

Tyler searched. Some twenty minutes passed. She watched Nazi office workers stamping documents and working at desks. Several times she saw passports in their hands and being placed on desks. In one room she watched a Nazi officer in a peaked cap and a jacket with red lapels, stomping about angrily whilst berating a subordinate who cowered before him, but in most rooms mundane paperwork seemed to be underway.

Lucy fetched Melissa and Tyler hot chocolate and herself a coffee from a café further down the road. The cold numbed hands and feet so they huddled against the shop's glass front, cradling Styrofoam cups, but then Tyler found something of interest. Through the contrap she could see what looked like a thick square box with a dial and a handle on a small door. Inside, the contrap showed her several shelves holding various items. She could see deep wads of bank notes, an assortment of files and documents, some passports and also a metal case. She adjusted focus with the lever, sharpening the image onto the contents of the case. There she saw a pair of round-lensed spectacles in a folding glasses case and she counted twelve medals with ribbons.

"I have it," she said. "I see the case with the glasses and medals. But there's a problem."

"There's a surprise," said Lucy. "Only the one?"

"What is the problem?" asked Melissa.

"Well, I can see the artefacts, but they appear to be in a safe."

The news was met with groans.

Two hours later they ate fish and chips before returning to their hotel room, somewhat bewildered. Tyler was restless.

"We'll wait 'til they lock up and then go in at night. We'll probably set off alarms and stuff, but I don't know what else to suggest. I'll fly up onto the roof, see if there's a way in."

The others seemed tired.

"We won't be of much use if we're all put in police cells, or worse, captured by Nazis. They won't just lock us up, at least, not for long."

"I'm open to ideas," said Tyler glaring at Lucy.

"At least we're out of the cold for a while," said Melissa.

"In the meantime we can stay here and keep out of trouble."

Tyler studied the *A to Z* and worked out the rough position of the Nazi underground headquarters in relation to their hotel room. She pointed the contrap that way. A few minutes later, she'd focused inside South Sea House and was Nazi watching again. It was useful to see things from a different angle. She noticed motion sensors in the top corners of corridors and rooms. She saw CCTV cameras and watched as the officer with the red lapels approached a doorway in the middle of the building.

It's Red Lapels again…

Tyler began to get a good feel for the layout of the house. She knew that beyond this doorway was the room where she'd seen Red Lapels ranting and beyond that was the room with the safe. Red Lapels paused at this doorway and pressed the palm of his right hand against a panel on the wall. The door opened automatically and he walked through.

The Angel

Tyler watched people come and go from the building, very aware that each passing minute she was draining the ghost machine of power she might need later on. Because of this, she spied on the Nazi HQ sporadically, viewing its various chambers for five minutes at a time, trying to learn something of use, and then resting the contrap (and her eyes) for ten minutes. It made for a very frustrating afternoon and as far as she was concerned, evening could not come fast enough.

It was beginning to feel like an impossible task. From what she could tell, they were all feeling it.

Melissa fell asleep, the GAUNT file open in her hands. When Lucy dozed off around mid-afternoon, Tyler switched to the ghost portal and told Albert all about the artefacts, South Sea House and the Nazi Victorious Federation.

"You'll find a way, Missy," he told her. "You always do."

Tyler considered this, but felt less confident this time.

"Albert, if I don't make it, I mean, if something goes wrong, if something happens, is there a way I could come into the machine? What I mean is, if I get killed before I get a chance to operate the contrap?"

"I dunno about nuffing like that. I can ask Mr Lieberman if ya' likes…" Albert shrugged and rubbed at a grimy cheek.

"If I could, I'd like to be with you, Albert."

Albert grinned and Tyler felt sad.

"I'd like that too, Missy," he said.

When it was approaching five o'clock and the others were still sleeping, Tyler changed into black clothes, wrapping up against the cold, and headed out to Whitechapel Road. She knew Lucy and Melissa would be angry that she'd gone without them, but Tyler knew this mission would be dangerous: more dangerous than anything they'd tried before, and she didn't want anyone else getting hurt.

It was a long walk to South Sea House but Tyler had good reason not to use the contrap to fly there. For one thing, she would have been seen in the sky by Londoners below because of all the city lights, and she couldn't risk that kind of attention. She needed to check the HQ was closed and that everybody had gone home, before attempting to get onto the roof. This could easily be done from the street without raising suspicion and then she planned to find someplace where she could take to the air unobserved and risk a short flight to the roof of South Sea House.

The bus shelter across the road from the HQ was a good shelter from the wind. At this time of day it was packed with people. Tyler squeezed into a tiny space and surveyed the house while pretending to wait for a bus. At six o'clock sharp the long-coated workers began pouring out of the white door. They mingled with crowds and were soon gone, leaving the building in darkness. Again she waited, wanting to be sure no one returned for any reason. An hour passed. Buses came and went and no one seemed to notice that hers never arrived. By that time, the cold was biting her viciously because she'd been standing around. At seven o'clock she could wait no more. She left the bus stop and began a long search for somewhere that was not overlooked. She found a multi-storey car park a block away which had a parking level on the roof. It was high, which gave her the advantage of being able to overlook most of the area, including South Sea House. At this time of night the car park was less than half full and those still using it were parking in the lowest areas leaving the top completely unoccupied.

Perfect.

She looked across at South Sea House. The contrap showed her a flat roof with several raised vent houses and a raised entrance block with a grey door. From her vantage point on top of the multi-storey, the grey door seemed a possible way in. It would be locked, of course, but that might not be an insurmountable problem. She was peering through the contrap and wondering if she'd be strong enough to kick down the door when, from behind her, came a voice with a heavy German accent which made her jump.

"Such a pretty vista..."

Tyler turned.

"What?" Before her stood a man in a long grey coat and a black trilby. Josef Mengele smiled and looked out over the beautifully lit city landscape.

"I said such a pretty vista. Do you not agree?"

Tyler did not respond. She was frozen to the spot, a cold, paralysing fear creeping up the back of her neck.

Mengele pursed his lips and tucked his hands behind his back. He strolled to the car park wall where Tyler was leaning with legs turning to jelly.

"I've been watching you. Did you know?"

Tyler shook her head as Mengele took a bar of chocolate from his pocket and broke off a piece. He placed the chocolate in his mouth and ate it, watching traffic far below.

"My, my," he shook his head. "That's a long way down." Mengele removed his hat and ran fingers through slicked hair. He waved the hat at Tyler. "I don't want to lose it over the edge, you understand…"

Tyler didn't know whether to run, fight or scream. In the end she did none of these, but clung onto the wall for support. Had Josef Mengele been alive, Tyler would have called him a handsome man, despite his persistent unnerving smile. But the figure before her was not alive, at least, not like any living person she'd ever seen before. His skin was strange, like the skin of Hitler and Himmler when she'd seen them at close quarters in the café. It had the same flaky quality, as though covered with too much makeup and, in the gloom of the night, it was now blue and glowing softly, the makeup not thick enough to hide the luminescence beneath.

Tyler swallowed and found her voice.

"What do you want?"

"Oh, you know... I just wanted to come and say hello. And I felt it only fair I should warn you; you do know your interfering will only get you into trouble, don't you?"

"My *interfering*?"

Mengele's smile broadened.

"Come, come. You know to what I refer. You have a power the others do not possess. We ghosts feel it, you know. We feel its presence. How else do you think I have been able to find you?"

"You *are* a ghost, then?" asked Tyler, recalling Hitler's glance in her direction when they were at the cafe. So Hitler had sensed the contrap...

Mengele laughed candidly.

"I am a ghost, of course. And then again, I am something else also." He appeared to be enjoying this strange turn in the conversation. "Oh, forgive me. How dreadfully rude of me. Would you care for some?" He leant closer to offer some chocolate.

When Tyler shook her head, he placed the rest of the chocolate on the top of the wall. "I'll leave it here for you. I think you could use it. You look like you've seen a ghost." For a moment he was straight-faced, seemingly unaware of his pun and he appeared honestly annoyed by her refusal. Mengele took out a silver cigarette case and tapped out a cigarette. He found a lighter from his pocket and smoked.

"You are wondering how a ghost eats chocolate, are you not? How a ghost is able to smoke a cigarette?"

Tyler nodded.

"Have you not yet guessed?" he chuckled to himself. "Oh, this is too perfect. Too perfect." He took a long drag on his cigarette and exhaled a stream of smoke.

Tyler tilted her head at him and moved her hand closer to the contrap about her neck.

"I do apologize. I always did like to play with the little ones. But then," he added turning away, "perhaps that is just *the child in me*." Mengele laughed again.

Tyler flicked the switch on the contrap to the flight symbol.

"Oh, do not worry, my girl. You will have no need to use your little toy. I shall leave you in peace and unmolested." Then he was walking away. "Auf wiedersehen. And don't forget your chocolate." He began to sing a song she did not know.

"You're the cream in my coffee,

You're the salt in my stew,"

Tyler clutched at her heart wondering if he was really leaving, or if it was a trick. She listened to his eerie song grow fainter.

"You will always be my necessity,

I'd be lost without you…"

She only crumpled to the concrete floor gasping for breath once Mengele had gone. Her breathing raced uncontrollably, a panic attack quickly overwhelming her. She checked about hoping to find someone, some normal human being who might come to her aid but, as before, the car park was empty. Her fingers began to tingle and a hideous ringing grew louder in her ears. On the edge of consciousness, she grasped the contrap and moved the switch to the ghost portal.

"Albert," she gasped. "Albert…"

An empty mist greeted her.

Not now. Not now of all times…

She tried again, but she was gasping so quickly that she could barely get the name past her lips. In the glass viewer mist circled. Her vision blurred and then left her.

Tyler drifted for a time.

"Missy…" a small voice was saying far away. "Missy? That you? You alright?"

Tyler twitched. She wasn't even sure if she'd heard the voice at all. It was all but drowned out by the ringing in her head. It came again.

"Missy? It will be alright. It will be alright, Missy."

Breath slowed. A few moments later her heart rate dropped also. The ringing began to recede. Vision returned and she flexed her fingers, trying to rid herself of the painful pins and needles.

"Albert? Are you there?" she said, still unable to focus.

"I'm right 'ere, Miss Tyler. I'm right here. You alright now?"

"I will be, Albert. I will be."

The truth about what the NVF scientists had put into the GAUNT machine hit her like a sledgehammer in the gut. She sat shivering on the car park floor for a long time. When she could gather her strength again she was more determined than ever. She took off and flew to the roof of the Nazi HQ. She searched for a way in, rattling air vents and pounding the grey door, but everything was very solidly built. There were no visible screws anywhere at the edges of the sturdy vents and the door gave no indication of buckling even when she threw her entire body at it, bruising her shoulder. In the end she flew back to the car park's top level and slowly made her way back to the hotel.

"And where have *you* been?" asked Melissa accusingly when she answered the knock at the door.

"Jeez. You sound like my mother," said Tyler, walking past and dropping onto the bed.

"We were worried about you," said Lucy. "Seriously…"

"Alright, alright… I'm sorry. I went down to South Sea House to fly up onto the roof. I wanted to check it out. To see if there was any way of getting in."

"And was there?"

"No, but I saw Josef Mengele. He found me. Has been following me. They can feel the power of the contrap – the ghosts can. They can sense it."

"Really? What did he want?" said Lucy.

"Did he hurt you?" asked Melissa.

"No. I'm fine. Just a bit shaken up, I suppose. He's a pretty creepy guy. He wanted to warn me off, I guess. But he told me something. It's about the GAUNT machine and what *they* are – the German ghosts. And it's also about the six missing kids…"

"What are you saying?" asked Melissa.

"The NVF scientists took six kids – the missing kids – and put them into the GAUNT machine. They brought back the ghosts they were looking for and somehow used the kids to give them real form, solid bodies. What I'm saying is, inside each of the ghosts we've seen is one of the missing kids."

"Six missing kids – six names ticked off of the list… The *gloves…*" said Melissa. "*That's* what they are. The kids are wearing the ghosts like *gloves.* What was it you heard that guy say? *Why would they separate?* He was talking about the ghosts separating from the children they'd been joined with."

"Yes," said Tyler. "And they're not separating at all. Not one little bit. They're walking around in a kind of human-like form with the Nazi ghosts fully in control."

"*The dominant force*… The ghosts are *the dominant force*," muttered Melissa. "I see it now. They had to use children to be sure the ghosts would be the dominant of each pair."

Lucy looked at Tyler in disbelief.

"Mengele told you all this?"

"Well not all of it. It was just something he said about *the child in me*. He was talking about himself. But I'm pretty sure he meant me to understand it. He thought it was funny that we hadn't worked it out for ourselves already."

Delivery

Tyler woke around two in the morning in a cold sweat, dreams of blue, glowing beings haunting her rest. When she focused she found reality was not much better than the conjured images of her sleeping mind.

Why is this all happening? And why is it all happening to me?

It felt very unfair. If only someone else had happened to buy the same type of bag as Lucy. It would be someone else here right now; someone else lying awake in a strange hotel room in Whitechapel on some impossible mission.

It was Christmas Eve.

She climbed out of bed and opened the bedroom curtains to look out onto nocturnal London. It wasn't so much slumbering as it was bustling. She remembered

Lucy calling London the *city that never sleeps*. Now she could see for herself why. She dressed.

Albert wasn't in the ghost machine right now, but Violet Corpe was.

"Let me out!" Violet screamed insanely when Tyler put her eye to the glass.

"As if," whispered Tyler, switching the contrap back to the protective skull symbol.

She looked out of the window again, knowing that somewhere out there Adolf Hitler and friends were preparing for the first of many planned attacks on England. She knew she had to stop them somehow. The only question was *how*?

Traffic on the streets below buzzed like insects.

She waited a while, hoping that Violet would go away. She tried the contrap again, only to be confronted with Travis the Norman knight.

"Aha! It is my little friend! Have you considered my offer? It is a fair exchange, I think." Travis wrung his gauntleted hands hopefully.

Tyler was about to switch the contrap back to the skull when something made her stop. That small voice in her head was whispering. She looked at Travis for a moment.

"Wait a minute. What are you talking about?" she asked.

"But, do you not remember?"

"I don't."

"Very well, very well. I shall remind you. My offer was to help you with something if you help me in return. You English have an expression for it I think. You pat my back and I'll pat yours."

"Scratch. The expression is *you scratch my back…*"

"Ah, mais oui! That is the one!"

"And *what*, if I agreed, would I need to do to help you?"

Travis licked his lips in anticipation.

"It is but a trifle. You would simply make an adjustment to the device you now hold and then say some words for me. It is nothing really…"

"And what *adjustment*, exactly? What words?"

Travis wiped a gloved hand down his bristly face and looked about nervously.

"You are alone, my friend?"

"Yes." Tyler glanced at her friends, sleeping peacefully.

"Then I shall tell you. You would have to set the device to a certain symbol and pull the little lever. Then you would have to say *Phasmatis licentia;* but two petite words. This is all. It will help me. What I mean is, it will help to give the device more power so that it can help you more. You do not need to worry about the technicalities. You can leave those to me."

So that was Travis' proposal. Tyler had no intention of obliging.

She switched to the skull and then, a moment later, to the *Tower of Doom*. The moody tower was tall but crumbling slowly. She started to feel that Lucy had been right; they should have walked away from the whole thing and abandoned Westminster Abbey to its fate. Then again, she considered the height of the tower and knew they must be doing something right.

Tyler kicked her bag across the room in frustration. It landed upside down and a packet of smoke bombs fell from it. She stared at it for a long moment.

Melissa muttered something about hot chocolate and turned over.

For the next few hours Tyler waited impatiently. Every now and then she would set the contrap to the front facing eye symbol and zoom through streets and buildings to check on the NFV HQ. There was no movement in the big house and she discovered nothing new. She set the contrap to the ghost portal and gazed into swirling mist in the hope that Albert, or perhaps Zebedee, would show themselves but, even after calling their names and waiting, they did not appear. The *Tower of Doom* continued to crumble slowly and she noticed it was considerably lower than it had been earlier. Several times Tyler considered using the forward facing eye, which could give her a version of the future, yet in the end she always shied away from using it. She felt it might alter the way she made her decisions and, if what it showed her was not a true prediction, she decided it could be dangerous. She suddenly knew what she needed to do.

Melissa had been tossing and turning for the past hour. She eventually sat up looking pensive.

"Couldn't sleep," she said.

"Me neither. I have an idea though, and it would be better if we could try it before the streets get any busier. We'd best wake Lucy."

Tyler told them her plan and they readied themselves to go. She intended to visit the NVF HQ before the Nazis arrived for work and then she could use the *Past Eye* with the hope of learning something that might help them get inside. It still felt like a long shot, but the girls agreed they had little else to try. Lucy was still dressing when Melissa gasped loudly.

"What is it?" asked Tyler.

Melissa was looking out of the window at the street below.

"Police! The police are here! They've just come into the hotel."

"We've got to get out. Now!" said Tyler.

"They've probably tracked Dad's credit card," said Lucy, throwing on the last of her clothes and looking miserable. "Get all your stuff and use the stairs. Keep away from the lifts."

A minute later they hit the stairs and hurried down flight after flight to the ground level. They heard voices from the reception area close by and someone mentioned their names.

"Is there a back way out?" whispered Melissa.

"We're about to find out," said Tyler. "Follow me."

They found a narrow passage behind a door marked *Staff Only* and followed it past a kitchen and utility rooms until it brought them out into a back street.

They ran.

*

South Sea House was much as they'd left it, only now lamp lit. Tyler received some curious glances from passers-by, but most people did that very London thing of minding their own business and avoiding eye contact out on the streets. The silver device was, it seemed, presumed to be some type of camera or mobile phone, and it was not unusual for someone to be taking pictures. If any of them had taken the time to watch properly, they would have observed Tyler standing in the same spot for an unusually long time and never actually taking a single photograph.

Every now and again she'd point the contrap at a different spot, but always around the imposing entrance of the large house.

She clicked through several days, slowing only when someone came into view. Melissa stood with her keeping watch on the present world while Tyler delved into the past. Lucy was off searching for a café that was open at five in the morning. Half an hour passed before she returned laden with hot drinks and Tyler stopped to rest her eyes. She received a hot chocolate gratefully and sipped.

"I think I might have something," she said. "It's not much, but there has been a delivery here each Wednesday for the last three weeks. A black van with a gold streak. I don't know what exact time it happens but it's sometime in the morning. The deliveryman doesn't bother to lock the back of his van. Last week someone came out from the building and talked with him. From what I can tell they were talking about a delivery of uniforms scheduled for next Wednesday."

"What, Nazi uniforms?" said Lucy.

"I don't know. Could be… I think we should presume they are," suggested Tyler.

"Next Wednesday… That's today then," said Melissa.

"Yes."

"So how do we use that?" asked Lucy.

"I'm not sure," admitted Tyler. "Is there somewhere we can go to get out of the cold? We need to work something out."

The café, a basic but reasonably clean *greasy Joe's*, was a short walk away. Three other customers were eating an early breakfast. The girls ordered more food than they could stomach, ate what they could and ditched the rest. Ten minutes later they had a rough plan, which Tyler knew could go bottom up in any number of ways at any point. The delivery may be late or not turn up at all. It may consist of a small package simply posted through the white door's letter box. The deliveryman could be fit and unusually careful today. Tyler may have misheard or misinterpreted what was said on the doorstep a week ago. Any of these eventualities could easily ruin their plan. It made Tyler more unnerved than ever and a stony silence assumed its place once the girls had talked through their roles to be sure everyone knew their part.

"Why me?" Lucy had complained.

"Because I need to go in. I'm the one who knows the contrap the best, and you're faster than Melissa. Anyway, you got the easy bit!"

"But your skin's gonna give you away."

"The gloves disguise themselves with makeup. If they can do it, so can I."

They headed back to South Sea House knowing they could be in for a long and potentially disastrous wait in the bus shelter. Tyler was uncomfortable under a layer of makeup.

Hours dragged. Around seven, the woman Tyler had first seen in the HQ arrived and let herself in. A few minutes later Lucy dashed across the road and tested the white door. It was locked fast.

At eight a.m. more Nazis arrived in their long coats and hats. The girls were shivering and again drinking from Styrofoam cups when the black van with a gold stripe arrived at ten-seventeen.

"This is it!" said Tyler. "Go!"

The girls dropped their cups and crossed the road while watching the deliveryman. The van was parked out on the curb directly outside the white door, hazard lights flashing. He left the cab and went up to the door. They saw, rather than heard, his conversation with the intercom and then the white door was opened and the deliveryman entered.

Tyler dashed to the back of the van and tried the double doors. To her relief they opened. She gave Melissa a nod before climbing in. Melissa joined her a moment later and they began searching through boxes. They heard a double tap from somewhere near the front of the van telling them Lucy was in position by the driver's door. Hopefully she would be poking around inside the cab, keys in hand, by the time the deliveryman came back outside. Tyler hoped that would annoy him suitably.

There were several boxes of uniforms; trousers in one, shirts in another, skirts in yet another and jackets were hanging on a long clothes rail. They heard the driver's door open and the van rocked as Lucy climbed into the cab.

The delivery man shouted.

Then Lucy yelled, "Catch me if you can, loser!"

There was more shouting as Lucy ran.

Tyler and Melissa frenziedly tried on military uniforms, not knowing how much time Lucy's distraction would buy them. Trousers? Too big. Skirt? God, no. Melissa swapped for a smaller skirt. Tyler found smaller trousers.

"Come on!" Tyler urged.

They made the best of a bad selection and, grabbing boxes, burst from the back doors to head into the building.

South Sea House was lavishly furnished and decorated. Rich, Victorian oak panelling underlined pristine white walls, punctuated here and there by imposing portraits of the Third Reich's most infamous.

"Where do you want these?" Tyler asked a receptionist who didn't even look up from her computer, but pointed to a door further into the building.

"Through there, please. Second door on the right."

Tyler and Melissa didn't hang about. They passed a palm in a huge pot and went through the next doorway.

The uniforms appeared convincing but were mostly baggy and the girls knew they looked too young to work there and that they would surely not pass for workers if closely scrutinized.

They found the store room, second door on the right, and dumped the boxes. They took a moment to compose themselves. Tyler checked her watch, figured they had little more than three minutes before the deliveryman returned and the alarm was raised. She turned to Melissa, who was now looking terrified.

"Right. Follow me. Don't speak to anyone. Don't look at anyone. Keep your head down. Try and relax."

"Oh, yeah. Relax, man. I'm just chillin' with my Nazi homies… Easy for you to say… You're an experienced criminal! Do you realize this is the third NVF building you've broken into this week?"

"Ready?" asked Tyler, picturing the layout of the house in her mind.

Melissa shook her head.

"You haven't heard a single word I've said, have you?"

"Good. Come on. Let's go," said Tyler. The building was familiar because of all the spying she'd done with the contrap. It was strange how she felt she'd been there before when she really hadn't.

They dashed out into the corridor and took a right. At the end of this hallway they found a carpeted staircase and a table bearing a pot of pens, another tropical plant and pads of paper. Tyler also found a clipboard, which she swiped as she passed and then handed to Melissa.

"Take this. It'll make you look more official."

The stairs opened out onto a landing. They turned left and went down a corridor.

"I think it's this way," said Tyler, opening a door and finding another corridor. As they went in, three Nazis rounded the doorway at the opposite end. Tyler shoved Melissa back through the door and they dashed away to hide in another doorway. The three Nazis passed them, absorbed in conversation and oblivious to their presence.

"You know," Melissa whispered, "it's scary how good at this you are."

"Did you see the one with the red lapels on his jacket?"

"Yes."

"He's the one who can open the door that leads to the room with the safe."

"I see. How are we going to get him to open the door for us?"

"I don't know yet. Let's just try and find it first…"

Tyler checked about before heading off again. They slipped down the corridor and stopped when it brought them out into a lobby area with a leather couch, two armchairs and a glass coffee table.

"Where now?" asked Melissa eyeing the six doors that surrounded them.

"This is it. It's through this door. Look. It's the NVF logo I told you about." Tyler pointed to the logo on the door with the words *Nazi Victorious Federation.*

She pulled open the door gently to peer through the crack. The room was empty except for an expensive Persian rug and a fine oak desk, behind which was a brown leather Gladstone chair. They went in and found the door they needed, along with the scanning panel set into the wall to one side. Melissa read the words engraved in the bottom edge.

"*Biometric Hand Recognition.*"

"It's set up to open when that guy with the red lapels puts his right hand on it," said Tyler.

"So what now? You gonna lop his hand off?"

Tyler switched to the *Present Eye* and began searching through the building. "He can't be far away. We passed him just a minute ago." She found him a moment later. "Uh-oh! He's heading this way…"

Intervention

Tyler checked the *Tower of Doom* quickly. It was building fast. Her heart was hammering like a machine gun.

Melissa looked like she was about to pass out.

"What are we going to do?" she asked.

Tyler switched back to the *Present Eye.* Red Lapels was already in the corridor where he'd almost bumped into them a minute before.

"I don't know. He's alone but he'll be here in a few seconds!"

Red Lapels strode purposefully into the couched lobby and turned towards the door. On the other side, Tyler and Melissa were panicking.

"Charge the door," Melissa hissed.

"What?"

"Charge the door! Tell me when he's on the other side of it and we'll do it together. It'll send him flying!"

"Okay, he's nearly there... Three, two, one, now!"

They ran at the door and drove it open. They felt it hit him without slowing, driven by their joint momentum. The door bashed the wall on the other side of the hinge and rebounded shut. Melissa tentatively pushed it open again. Before them, Red Lapels was sprawled out on his back, unconscious. They watched his peaked cap roll to a stop several metres away.

"Quick! Grab an arm. Drag him in before someone else comes!" said Tyler. Together they battled to drag his body into the room and shut the door.

"I think it's his right hand..."

Then they hauled him over to the biometric hand recognition unit and Tyler grabbed his right hand. Heaving it high enough to reach the scanner, however, was not easy. He was big and heavy, but after three failed attempts they finally reached the unit. The scanner purred into life. The door opened and they let the unconscious weight fall back to the floor.

"How long do you think he'll be out?" asked Melissa.

"Who knows?"

Tyler led the way through to the room with the safe. The safe itself was bigger than she remembered it; a grey metal box sitting on the floor in the corner, as high as her waist. She checked her watch. They'd been in the building for a little over three minutes.

"Any ideas?" asked Melissa, watching the door at their backs.

Tyler took the contrap and focused into the safe.

"I can see the case. When I was looking before, I noticed the safe locking system. I can see it all if I focus the contrap just right. I need you to operate the dial. I'll tell you what to do."

"Okay." Melissa took hold of the dial. "Ready."

"Try turning it to the right. I mean clockwise."

Melissa turned the dial.

"A little more. I'll say when to stop…"

Melissa continued turning. The dial clicked with each tiny increment.

"Slowly… Right, stop. Two more clicks." Through the contrap Tyler could see the first of five steel pins had lined up with a hole in the internal mechanism. "Great. Now back the other way."

Melissa turned the dial anticlockwise.

"More, more. Now slow down. About three clicks more. And stop." The second pin was lined up. Three more to go.

"Clockwise again…"

"Get away from the safe."

The girls spun round to see Red Lapels rubbing his head with his left hand. In his right was a pistol, aimed at them.

"Back away from the safe if you value your lives."

Tyler and Melissa backed away. Red Lapels blocked the only door.

No way out.

"Tell me who you are, if you will?" he said.

The girls said nothing.

"Alright. Suit yourselves. You *will* talk to us sooner or later. It is only a matter of time. Time, and probably an horrific amount of pain and screaming. But it's your choice. Tell me, what is that about your neck?"

Tyler's eyes flicked to the contrap.

"Yes, that thing you were looking into over by the safe. Tell me, what is it?"

"It's nothing," said Tyler. She tucked it into her shirt. "Just my new camera. I was, er…"

"…taking a picture. She was taking a picture," said Melissa.

"I'll take it, if you please," said Red Lapels.

"No you won't," said Tyler. "It's mine."

"I could shoot you and then take it, if you prefer."

Reluctantly, Tyler lifted the silver chain from her neck and handed over the contrap. Red Lapels gestured with his pistol.

"Now over there. Up against the wall." He looked down at the strange device in his hand. "What a curious thing…"

There came a dull thud. He crumpled forwards onto the floor where he remained, unmoving. Behind him, Lucy stood, dressed in Nazi uniform, chewing gum and tapping a length of lead pipe into a hand.

"Daddy always says *if a job's worth doing, it's worth doing well.* Was he annoying you?" she said. "He was bugging me."

"Lucy! Thank God!" said Melissa.

"You didn't think I'd abandon you, did you?" said Lucy. "I'll watch the door. You guys get back to the safe."

"What about the van driver?" asked Melissa.

"Oh, he won't be bothering anyone for a while. He's, shall we say, *resting* in a dumpster."

Tyler and Melissa turned their attention back to the safe. Thirty seconds later, the final bolt shifted perfectly into position with an audible snap and the safe door popped open.

"We've done it!" said Melissa.

Tyler grabbed the silver case and turned to go.

"We're not out of danger just yet."

"What are you doing?" said Lucy from the doorway.

Tyler didn't understand. "We've got the case. Let's go," she said.

"And what about all that?" Lucy pointed to the wads of paper money, the passports and the other documents in the safe. "We're not leaving all that are we?"

"But we've got what we came for," said Melissa.

Tyler took the bag from her shoulder and opened it. "She's right," she said. "We should take it all! It will slow them down. Whatever they're planning - it will mess it all up!"

"Right." Melissa opened her own bag and emptied the contents of the safe into it. When the safe was empty, Tyler closed it and turned the dial. She looked at Lucy.

"That kind of suits you," she said, nodding to her disguise.

"Thanks," said Lucy. "I quite like it. Does it come in black?"

Then they headed out, back the way they'd come. They passed several Nazis along the way and received quizzical looks, but nobody stopped them.

"We're all done," Tyler said to the receptionist as they crossed reception.

"Okay. Thanks."

Tyler raised her hand to push open the front door.

"Wait! Wait a minute," the receptionist called. She looked up from her keyboard. The girls stopped, not daring to move. "Come back. I didn't sign."

They exchanged glances.

"For the delivery," explained the receptionist.

Melissa went to the desk and handed her the clipboard.

"Just here please."

"What happened to George?" The receptionist signed her name.

"Flu. Really bad man-flu. Thanks," said Melissa. She collected the board and they left the building.

*

Tyler's watch read ten thirty-two a.m.

"We have four and a half hours before the carol service begins."

Melissa asked, "Can we use the glasses now? If it has the power to lure Hitler, maybe we can lure him here before he gets anywhere near the Abbey."

Tyler had a horrible thought.

"No. We have to get to Westminster Abbey as soon as possible. The glasses may help us lure Hitler, but what if he's already planted the bombs? We need to get there fast. At least warn somebody."

"If nothing else, we can wait until everyone is going into the Abbey, then shout *bomb*!" said Lucy. "That's always a good room clearer."

Tyler was feeling very anxious. "I'd like to get away from here as soon as possible. The Nazis will be combing the area for us soon."

They examined the silver case as they huddled on a bus, heading for Parliament Square. Tyler sat it on her lap only to find it would not open.

"It's locked." She dug around in her bag for her Swiss army knife. She jammed the screwdriver blade into the little keyhole and wrenched the haft downwards, breaking the lock with a snap. She opened the case.

"Where are the medals?" asked Melissa. Apart from the glasses case, the silver case was empty.

Tyler frowned. "I don't understand. They were in the case yesterday. I saw them through the contrap."

"They must have moved them for some reason."

"We still have the glasses," said Melissa. Tyler opened the glasses case and took out Adolf Hitler's personal reading glasses: golden wire and perfectly circular lenses. She put them back into the spectacle case and tucked it into her inside coat pocket.

"Weird to think Adolf Hitler actually wore these," said Tyler with a shiver.

"Yeah, freaky," Melissa agreed.

"But what about Himmler and the others?" Tyler asked. "We'll need to stop them all. Maybe not today. But what if they *are* all taking bombs to Westminster Abbey?"

"Don't worry about it," said Lucy. "We'll find a way. We always do."

*

Parliament Square was heaving with Christmas sightseers and shoppers carrying high street branded bags. Tyler noticed a police van and instinctively turned away from it.

Dotted around Parliament Square were bronze statues of old prime ministers and famous statesmen on huge stone pedestals. They crossed the grassy square and the road to get to the Abbey, a massive and intricate gothic building of golden stone. It was fronted by two high towers, between which stood a mammoth archway. The doors stood open for tourists and others to come and go at will.

"We'll meet back here in half an hour," said Tyler. "I'll take the outside. You two search the inside."

"What do we do if we find something?" asked Melissa. "I mean a bomb or something."

Tyler hadn't thought that far ahead.

"I don't know. We'll have to tell the police I guess. Then they can deal with it."

The girls split up. Melissa and Lucy disappeared into the ornate Abbey while Tyler followed its outer walls checking every embellishment and carving. There were many stone buttresses and it took her the full half hour to check everywhere that a bomb might be placed. Even then, she could not check up high where further levels of columns and windows rose, but those heights would also have been impossible for a bomber to reach.

Unless the saboteurs were posing as window cleaners, she thought.

By the time she returned to the archway, she was convinced they didn't stand a chance of doing a thorough check around the building. She was the first of the three to return to the rendezvous. She waited and in frustration scanned through magnificent walls and towers with the contrap, but found nothing suspicious, only countless potential hiding places.

"You're gonna have to help us," Melissa said, shaking Tyler from her search.

Lucy agreed. "This place goes on forever and there are a million and one great places for concealing a bomb."

Tyler checked her watch.

"Less than three and a half hours until the carol service begins," Melissa informed her.

"Right. I'll come and help."

Tyler paid her entrance fee and they went into the Abbey.

Izabella

Inside the Abbey, Tyler could see exactly what the others were talking about. The place was already heaving with people and offered numerous nooks and corners. The main precinct, or nave, was an incredibly tall, aisled hall with a vaulted roof, edged by a multitude of high arches and pillars. Down the centre and ending at the main altar, was a wide walkway between row upon row of chairs. The rest of the interior was a labyrinthine arrangement of chapels, altars, tombs, galleries, stalls and corners. To the side of the main altar stool the largest Christmas tree Tyler had ever seen.

She dropped onto the nearest seat and buried her head in her hands. An impossible task, even if they used their last few hours only to search the Abbey. She looked up despairingly to see Melissa and Lucy watching. Tyler wanted to go home.

"Any ideas?" she asked.

"Hey, you're the boss of this little outfit," said Lucy. "You tell *us*."

Tyler knew Lucy was right, in a way. She'd never asked for the job but, somehow, it had become hers. Now she needed to make a decision, was expected to make a decision, and she wished someone else would step in.

No one spoke for a moment. Finally she decided.

"You two stay here and continue the search. Do what you can. Switch your mobiles on. The police will be able to trace your positions, but so what. Just as well if they turn up."

"What are you going to do?" asked Melissa, taking her phone out.

"I'm taking the contrap away from here. We still have a little time. If I can draw Hitler away from the Abbey I might be able to stop him from planting explosives. That's if he hasn't already done it, of course. I'll call if I need to. You do the same."

"What if their plan is for one of the others to plant the explosives?" asked Lucy.

"What if they all turn up and they're *all* carrying bombs?" Melissa added.

Tyler nodded. "All good questions. I'll see you later."

"Right."

"Okay."

Tyler set off at a jog. She left the Abbey to follow the road to her right and crossed at some traffic lights onto the grassy square with the statues. To her side, the huge clock face of Big Ben's tower loomed over her at the end of the Houses of Parliament. Behind her Westminster Abbey sat in all its glory. But for how long?

She passed Winston Churchill and several other stately gentlemen remembered in bronze and then crossed another road into Parliament Street. When she'd walked for several minutes she turned to look back. The clock tower was as clear as ever, so was the top of the Abbey. She paused when a green coat flashed at her through the bustling crowd across the road. The coat vanished amongst bodies. Tyler sighed with relief when she found it again and saw that it was just an old lady. She didn't need the kind of interference that the Green Goddess would bring right now.

She dodged a policeman with a German shepherd on a leash and took refuge in a doorway while she dug out Hitler's glasses from her coat pocket and drew the contrap from her shirt. She set the contrap to the ghost portal and clamped it to the glasses case with one hand, waiting and watching the crowd. Hitler's disguise had been good when they'd seen him at close quarters in the coffee shop, but in this crowd she wondered how she would ever spot him. Ten minutes later she was losing her mind. Adolf was nowhere to be seen and she suspected she was doing something wrong. The ghost machine was really her last hope. If it didn't work she knew a lot of people were going to die.

Mengele's face was suddenly watching her. She caught only a glimpse, but it was enough. She ran. Her only thought was to put distance between him and herself and, if at all possible, lose him altogether. The knowledge that *they* were not merely ghosts was terrifying. A ghost can pass through walls, at least, this was Tyler's understanding. It can give you a fright, maybe even speak to you, but the *gloves* were physical; as physical as normal people and this made all the difference. She'd met

Mengele once before and he'd not harmed her. But then she'd not been any real threat. This time it was different. He was surely in on the Nazi plan and he knew that, with the contrap, she could really get in the way. Tyler did not think he would show her the same nonchalance this day.

Again she caught sight of Josef Mengele's unnatural face, now behind her in the bustling mass on her side of the street. He was smiling as though entertained by the knowledge that she'd seen him. His black sun glasses hid nothing of the pleasure the chase provided.

Tyler crossed the road and dashed between bodies. She crossed again to double-back, not knowing if he was still on her trail. It seemed to work. Ten minutes later she was back in Parliament Square standing by a towering likeness of Abraham Lincoln, risen from his bronze chair. She tucked her body in behind Lincoln's vast pedestal and switched the contrap to the *Tower of Doom*. To her utter amazement the tower was tall and building. She felt encouraged despite the palpable horror of her situation.

She tried the ghost portal again with Hitler's glasses held against the contrap. Again nothing happened. She watched for Hitler, searched crowds for that tell-tale flaky blue skin, hat and glasses. In desperation she looked into the crystal lens and called for Zebedee. She nearly dashed the thing against the stone at her back when all that greeted her was the mist. She promised herself she would find a way of summoning individual ghosts when this was all over.

If I live that long…

She searched for Hitler for several hours as a terrible feeling grew. Time was running out and the little voice was speaking.

He's here somewhere. He's not too far away. Even if he's already planted the bomb, he will hang around to watch his handiwork play out.

She tried the portal once more, called for Zebedee and then Albert. No one responded. Her heart lurched when her mobile rang. It was Melissa.

"Tyler?"

"I'm here. Did you find something?"

"No. At least, not yet. But Lucy thinks she just saw Bagshot in the Abbey."

"Bloody hell. That's all we need."

"I know. We'll keep looking though. Lucy's gonna try keep her head low."

"Good idea. I should've given you the Mace."

"She doesn't think Bagshot saw us."

"Good. Josef Mengele is here as well. I saw him in the street. He was following me. I think I lost him, but it's probably only a matter of time before he finds me again."

"Any sign of Hitler? Are the glasses working?"

"I don't know. I feel like I must be doing something wrong. I haven't seen Hitler yet."

"Right. Well. Keep trying, I guess."

"I will. See you soon."

"Okay, bye."

Tyler pocketed the phone and stared at the contrap. She set the little switch to the *Tree of Knowledge* and spoke.

"What should I do?"

She looked into the crystal, watched the words form out of mist and then vanish as if sucked down an invisible plughole. She waited. Nothing happened for a minute or so until words flowed slowly back into view.

When all you can do is what you can do, do what you can do.

"Some help you are," Tyler said aloud. She switched to the ghost portal and peered into mist.

"Is somebody there? Is anybody there? Anyone at all?" She waited, hoping to see a distant shape emerging from the murk. She called again and was about to give up when she thought she saw something tangible. The form quickly darted away and she wondered if she'd really seen anything at all.

"Hello?" she called softly. "You can come out. It's okay…"

She waited. Watched. Slowly a shape gathered itself in the far distant haze. It stood still for a moment as though looking back at Tyler, uncertain if it was safe to show itself.

"Hello? My name's Tyler."

The shape rose up and became a human figure. It edged forward and Tyler saw it was an old woman who was nervously peering at her.

"Are… Are you *the one*?" rasped the woman in a Russian accent. Her hair was bushy, grey and grizzled, her face plump and deeply lined. A shawl covered rounded shoulders and a long, patterned dress obscured the rest of her rotund body.

"I don't know," said Tyler. "I'm not sure what you mean."

"Are you *the one*? The owner? The one who is asking the questions?"

"Yes. At least, I think so. I did ask a question…"

"I mean, are you the one asking about the con-trap?"

"Yes!" said Tyler at once. "Yes, I am. Are you the one who Albert and Zebedee spoke to? Are you the one who knows all about it?"

"I was, once. A long, long time ago… It was mine, but that was long ago now." The old woman spoke at a frustratingly slow pace.

"What's your name?"

"They used to call me… Izabella. My name was Izabella."

"Can you help me, Izabella? I could really use your help."

"I don't know," said Izabella uncertainly. She took a few tentative steps closer and Tyler saw that there was something strange about the old woman's eyes. They looked grey and cloudy. It reminded her of her Nan, who had cataracts. Izabella continued, "I don't know much anymore. I used to know lots of things. These days, the more I learn, the more I see that the less I know. It's quite peculiar really. What is it you wish to know, child?"

"I need to use the contrap with an artefact. I need to draw in a ghost. It's a very bad ghost: the ghost of Adolf Hitler."

Izabella's cloudy eyes widened.

"Oh, I know all about him. He *is* an evil ghost, indeed. Do you have an artefact of his? You will need a good artefact."

"I have one right here: his glasses. But they don't seem to be working."

"I see." Izabella thought for a moment. "Well it should work. It might take some time. It depends on several factors, you see. Have you been using the con-trap very much?"

"Yes, I guess I have. But I've tried not to use it too much. I know it gets tired."

"That's right, it does. It sounds like you have a good artefact, so that is probably not the problem." Izabella rubbed her chin in thought. "Do you know how close the ghost is? I mean is he likely to be somewhere close to you?"

"I don't know. I have a feeling he is, but he could be anywhere really. I haven't seen him around here yet."

"That might be your problem, my dear. The summoning only works if the ghost is close enough to be affected by the con-trap. He needs to be within a certain radius of the portal. It really is very similar to a magnet. To attract a bit of metal, a magnet must be close enough. Do you see?"

"I see," said Tyler. "Is there anything else you can tell me about the device?"

Izabella waved her away then and turned to go.

"Wait! Izabella, please wait!"

"I must rest now. I'm tired. I don't like talking about the con-trap really. I probably shouldn't have come. Goodbye."

"Please wait!"

The old woman drifted into the distant fog and was gone.

The Summoning

An expectant queue had formed. People were already entering the Abbey to find seats although there was a further thirty minutes to go before the carol service was scheduled to begin. About the entrance steps and the courtyard beyond, hundreds began to gather. Above the resplendent Abbey towers and pinnacles the sky was ever-darkening. Christmas decorations and stately buildings were admired by all. There was an air of cheerful anticipation and people on the streets were unusually polite to one another as England's capital city began to celebrate Christmas in earnest.

The *Tower of Doom* was crumbling. Tyler turned away from Westminster Abbey and faced the Houses of Parliament to check the contrap again. Miniscule stones continued to fall. When she turned a little more to her left so the ghost machine was pointing to one side of the famous clock tower, blocks began to assemble. The *Tower of Doom* rose by tiny increments. Tyler set off down Bridge Street and could soon see Westminster Bridge and the muddy waters of the Thames beneath it. Somewhere in this direction was all that remained of Adolf Hitler.

She continued onto the bridge, checking the contrap every few moments and finding the *Tower of Doom* still growing. She searched for the odd characteristics of the gloves and for Hitler's unforgettable face, but saw neither. Halfway across the bridge, the *Tower of Doom* began to fall suddenly. She scanned the crowd.

He has to be here somewhere.

Had she just passed him without noticing? Turning back, she found that the tower rose once more and she noticed the red double-decker bus.

Of course, the small voice in her head said. *He's not walking. He's just passed by in a vehicle.*

Tyler sprinted back down Bridge Street not bothering to check the contrap again. He was here. He would soon get out of a taxi or a bus and go to the Abbey. She guessed he was on the bus. All she had to do was find him and draw him away.

When she was nearing the end of the road, gasping for breath, she saw the bus pull over onto the Square and passengers disembark. She found him: a pasty, flaky-skinned man with a blue baseball cap pulled down low over dark glasses and wearing a black leather jacket. He had a red and blue striped scarf around his neck and wore a caramel backpack, which sagged under the weight of its contents. A camera jostled about his neck also. Adolf Hitler had shaved off his famous moustache and now looked like a slightly sick tourist leaving the bus with dozens of other visitors.

"I've found Hitler," Tyler said when Melissa eventually answered her phone.

"Right. We've found nothing. I don't think they've planted any explosives yet."

"He's just got off a bus and is crossing the Square. He has the bomb in a backpack. Got to go." Tyler hung up and tore after Hitler. When she was some thirty metres behind him, Hitler hesitated. He stopped and turned to glance precisely in Tyler's direction.

Tyler knew he was sensing the contrap. She continued and, taking the glasses out of the case, held them against the contrap. Hitler frowned. He seemed to know what she'd done. He set off again, marching towards Westminster Abbey with renewed purpose. Tyler closed on him. She felt a drag from the contrap and she knew it had found its mark. Adolf slowed but did not stop. Tyler moved closer to intensify the summoning affect, wishing she'd not drained the contrap so much. If this didn't work, she had no plan B. Hitler slowed again and then stopped. It was working.

Tyler took one more step and felt the contrap tighten its grasp on the gloved ghost. Hitler took a step backwards. It was an unnatural movement and it turned a few heads. Hitler almost toppled over as the drag from the ghost portal unbalanced him. He stumbled backwards, but regained his footing and leant against the pull, his face showing exertion as though he was a contestant in an invisible tug of war contest. People were pausing to gawp now. With his strange movements and unnatural makeup he resembled a peculiar mime artist at work. Tyler had a surreal sensation as a small crowd formed, some even clapped as Hitler bent forwards to grasp at the hard grassy ground of the Square. There was no longer any point in trying to hide what she was doing. She held out the contrap in Hitler's direction and purposefully stepped backwards to draw him away from the Abbey. Hitler clawed at grass, snarling with effort and outrage.

Tyler continued regardless of the spectacle she was creating. All she knew was that it had to be done and she was the one who had to do it.

It was then that the words from the *Tree of Knowledge* came back to her, making perfect sense.

When all you can do is what you can do, do what you can do.

Well, that pretty much summed it up.

She cast a glance over her shoulder. She was edging backwards, feeling the draw from the contrap like a dog pulling on a lead, but it was working. Behind her she glimpsed Churchill's statue and beyond, traffic on the road.

Before her, Hitler snarled and fought, tearing chunks of frozen turf from the green with his bare blue skinned fingers. Where the thick makeup had worn off, his flesh shimmered in the twilight.

Tyler reached the road and cautiously backed into a stream of oncoming cars. Some members of the crowd, thinking this was all part of the street theatre, went ahead of her and stopped the traffic. Horns blared angrily. A family wearing red and white Santa hats walked by, oblivious to all.

"Thanks," Tyler shouted above the noise, not caring why they were helping her or who was inconvenienced. Her aim was to draw him well away from the crowded abbey and square, and then open the ghost portal. If she understood it correctly, the right words should send the ghost into the contrap and then she could close it with Hitler trapped inside. It seemed like a simple enough plan in theory but now she was seriously wondering if it would work at all. She realised the crowd was in danger because of the explosives in Hitler's backpack and wanted them out of the way.

"Back away!" No one moved back. She checked her position. She was nearly across the road. "He's got a bomb!"

A few of the people watching laughed. Some stared, open-mouthed.

"He's got a bomb!" she shouted at the top of her voice. "Get back! I'm serious!"

This time the crowd seemed unsure. It was the strangest piece of street theatre, if indeed, that *was* what it was. Some of them moved back and others ran. Someone else shouted, "Bomb!" Chaos ensued as the call was echoed.

Tyler backed into the curb and almost tripped. For a second the contrap wavered off target and Hitler pulled away. When she righted it a moment later he was back within its power. Tyler made it onto the pavement but people were running all around her, many screaming. Several tourists focused cameras and smartphones on the odd phenomenon.

In the distance, the last few attendees of the carol service filed into Westminster Abbey. She noticed a big black car and important looking people being ushered in, guessed that was the Prime Minister or some other VIP.

Tyler wanted to get further away from the Square before triggering the con-trap. She backed down the road and saw Hitler stumble and then latch onto the curb she'd hit moments before, but his fingers slipped and he was dragged along onto the pavement, howling like an animal. He clawed at the railings of an underpass but it only slowed his backwards progress. Soon he was skidding along on the flagstones screaming German protests. His next anchor point was an old-style red phone box. As he clung here for a few seconds, Tyler felt a presence at her shoulder. She looked up to see a second glove standing over her.

"Stupid girl." The ghost of Heinrich Himmler dashed the glasses from her hands and they skittered across the pavement. The contrap remained safely on the chain around her neck. Tyler screamed and ran to retrieve the glasses, but Himmler was closer. He crushed them under a large black cowboy boot and kicked the countless pieces into the road, laughing. Himmler was also dressed as a tourist, though a rather strange one. His clothes were an odd mismatch of styles as though he really didn't understand what went with what: high street style combat trousers with a garish pink and yellow Hawaiian shirt, a long scarf. For some unfathomable reason he'd stuck with the black trilby. Tyler noted the bulging rucksack slung over his shoulder.

"Tyler!" Melissa was there with Lucy at her side. They stood, panting.

"It's Himmler," said Tyler pointing. "Follow him! He's got a bomb too! I'll stick with Hitler."

Melissa and Lucy went after Himmler's gloved ghost, now heading into the crowded square. Melissa hesitated and turned back.

"But what are you going to do? The glasses…" she shouted to Tyler.

"They've gone. I don't know. Go! Before you lose him!" Tyler watched them go and searched for Hitler. He was easy to find now because all his struggling had worn away much of his camouflage. He'd lost his baseball cap and most of his skin glowed eerily. He'd set off with renewed vigour, now released from the draw of the contrap, and was making good progress. She saw him glance at his watch.

Tyler dropped to her knees at the edge of the road and searched for the largest of the glass shards. She would have preferred the wire glasses frame, or at least a piece of it, but she could not find any. Placing the broken glass against the contrap, she aimed it once more at Hitler. It had no apparent affect at all. Hitler had reached the other side of the road and was approaching the statue of Churchill.

Tyler dropped the shard and dashed after him, unsure of what to do next. She considered enlisting the help of some bewildered bystanders, but there was no time to explain why she needed help doing what she was doing, so she quickly abandoned the idea. Next she wondered if she would be strong enough to wrestle the bag from Hitler's back and run away with it. She felt sure she could outrun him and decided her best plan would be to get close enough to him to use the con trap to capture his ghost, regardless of the lost artefact. The rest would be easy if she could get that far, although *that* did not account for Himmler and the contents of his bag.

Tyler glanced up at the clock tower when she heard the three o'clock chimes ring out over the square. She wondered how the other girls were getting on.

Turning back to Hitler she watched him draw level with Churchill's bronze. He clearly recognized his old adversary and stared at the name inscribed in the massive pedestal. It must have been an opportunity too good to pass up, because Tyler saw him pause on his way long enough to gather spit and launch a huge gob at the statue with contempt. He reached the green of Parliament Square and strode away towards the crowded abbey.

Tyler gave chase, hurling herself across the road and meeting painfully with a cab, bringing traffic to a screaming halt. She picked herself up, surprised to be relatively unscathed. Just a few more bruises for the growing collection. Ignoring the angry shouts from cabbies and other fist-waving drivers, she passed Churchill, trying to speed up. But despite desperate pleas for them to move, people blocked her way. She came to a dense mass of Christmas revellers and realised she'd lost Hitler altogether. It seemed hopeless. She turned about, searching, but it was as if he'd vanished. She caught sight of the Churchill statue where a great dollop of Hitler spit was dribbling down the bronze figure's coat. She took out her phone and called Melissa.

"I've lost him. It's like he's vanished. He must be coming your way."

It sounded like chaos at the other end of the line. People were shouting and screaming. She could hardly make out Melissa's voice at all. She tried to see the Abbey through the bodies and caught a glimpse of masses fleeing the area. She hung up and looked back at Churchill's stoical face. She was suddenly drawn to the statue, to the man who'd run the county at the time when Hitler was doing his worst. She wanted to clean the spit from the monument but *now* did not seem like the right time. His brazen face was somehow willing her not to give up.

She had an idea. Abandoning the search for Hitler, Tyler turned back and headed for Winston Churchill.

Churchill

The statue, including its gargantuan pedestal, was more than three times Tyler's height. It was all she could do to leap up and catch a hold of the pedestal's top with her fingertips. This was difficult because she was still carrying her bag on her back but she managed to catch hold well enough to pull herself up, her face level with Churchill's feet. From here she swung a leg up onto the marble surface and hauled the rest of her body up. She stood, clinging onto Churchill's bronze cane, and wiped a hand over the surface of his patinated coat to collect as much of Hitler's spit as was possible. She smeared the slime all over the contrap and pointed it towards the Abbey. From this height, the panicking crowds were easy to see. It was only a few moments before she'd located Hitler with his blue glowing head. He was already succumbing to the draw of the contrap, slipping backwards like a paperclip within range of a powerful magnet. The drag was so strong this time that his gloved body knocked hapless pedestrians aside as it came.

Again Tyler yelled at pedestrians.

"Get back! There's a bomb!"

This time they seemed to listen and soon there was a clear area about the figure with the glowing head and hands.

Tyler dropped from the pedestal and once more backed across the road and down Parliament Street, dragging Hitler. He followed gracelessly and mostly on his back, grappling for handholds on any passing structure within reach. As he clung to an iron bench against the wall of a huge building with classical columns, the bomb in his rucksack detonated hurling Tyler into the air with immense force. A further explosion echoed from somewhere on the other side of Westminster Square as she landed in a heap. She felt blood trickle down her face and winced when she moved, wondering if her arm was broken. It hurt when she tested it and she felt dizzy and sick. The air was full of dust and so, for a while, she could see very little.

When it cleared, she saw that where the iron bench had been, there was now a crater the size of a bus, and a chunk of the building was missing. Masonry was still falling from the upper levels of windows and columns, half filling the crater.

Tyler stood up tentatively. She thought her legs felt alright, but when she took a step, her left knee buckled and she was forced to sit down. Her ears rang incessantly from the blast and her ribs hurt. A piece of paper fluttered close by in the slight wind. She squinted at it, thinking she recognised it, and grabbed it when it flew close. Unfurling it she saw that it was one of her lists, fallen from her pocket.

> ***Find the missing kids***
> ***Stop the Nazis***
> ***Track down Adolf Hitler's ghost***
> ***Spy on Hitler***
> ***Stop the Nazi ghosts from doing whatever it is they are planning to do***
> ***Have Bagshot and his Nazis arrested and put in prison***
> ***Clear your name***

What was she thinking? She balled it up and tossed it away.

Others were recovering from the blast. A haze hung in the air and a strange silence replaced the previous mayhem and traffic hum. Tyler observed the devastation knowing she'd failed. She could see people picking themselves up. The able-bodied were going to the aid of others, but everyone seemed to be alive. When Hitler's bomb had detonated at exactly five minutes past three, nobody had been close enough to be killed in the blast. Nobody, that is, except for the child who had been gloved with Hitler's ghost.

Tyler wept.

People about her began to speak again. Shell-shocked pedestrians made calls, Tyler presumed, to the police and others talked about what had just happened. She realised she needed to get out of there and tried to wipe off her hands so that she could dry her eyes. As it was, she could barely see through her tears and the haze. Voices alerted her to a new wonder.

"Look!"

"What is it?"

"Can you see that?"

Tyler rubbed at her eyes and looked about. Ahead of her, above the pavement, something was happening in the air. Shards of morphing, blue light met and joined. Moments later Hitler's ghost reformed and stood sneering at Tyler. He took a step closer.

"Idiot child," Hitler said. "You do not understand the things you are meddling with." He lurched towards her.

Tyler panicked and pulled the lever on the contrap.

"Phasmatis licentia!" she said.

Hitler continued to come at her as a sound issued from the contrap like the rush of a hurricane. It began quietly, but soon was tearing from the contrap. Tyler waited, hoping to see Hitler sucked into the ghost portal. Something was obviously happening but it had no effect on him. He had stopped his approach and listened instead.

The noise rose to a torrential roar. The contrap in Tyler's grip vibrated and jarred her arm, and it was all she could do to hold on to it. Tendrils of blue mist began to issue from the crystal lens in the centre of the contrap and suddenly Tyler knew her mistake. She hadn't opened the portal into the contrap, but instead she'd opened the portal *out* of the contrap.

Ghosts emerged from the portal. Hitler backed away. There was a quizzical expression in his eyes which soon turned to fear. Five ghosts drew themselves out to stand between Tyler and the Führer's spectre, and soon some thirty glowing figures were assembling. They rushed out of the ghost machine in a torrent, dashing through air, through brick and stone to take their place amongst the many.

Tyler was reminded of something Albert had once said to her.

Stars, I calls 'em…

Moments passed and the rushing did not end. Parliament Square filled with the ghoulish entities; a shimmering sea of sunken-eyed, skin and bone, Jewish ghosts, all surrounding Hitler, and all looking at him. They overflowed in their thousands and millions onto the adjacent streets, across Westminster Bridge and beyond.

The contrap shook so violently that Tyler could barely hold onto it. She hurt all over and was exhausted, damaged from the blast and close to passing out. She tasted blood in her mouth.

Then, at length, the rushing stopped and it seemed that every ghost that was going to leave the machine had left.

Silence.

The contrap, however, did not cease to shake. On the contrary, it shook all the more vigorously until Tyler feared that it might also explode.

About her, haunted faces regarded Hitler. The Führer turned around nervously in his small space, taking in the sea of gazes. His former confidence crumbled, falling away like pieces of shattered plaster. The entire place fell eerily silent. The longsuffering nation watched their abuser and murderer as fear overtook him. Tyler wondered at the sight, wondered why they did not say something, or why they did not attack him. Yet they were simply there and it appeared that this was enough. It was as though the Jewish ghosts knew what was in store for the spirit of Adolf Hitler.

Tyler shifted the lever in the opposite direction.

"Phasmatis licentia!" She whispered the words.

The rushing began again as ghosts re-entered the contrap. She heard Hitler's screams as he realised he was being taken into the portal along with the many others. Tyler blacked out.

Dead End

As Tyler came round she saw a hazy image of someone standing and studying something shiny and silver in their hands. She subconsciously put a hand to her chest seeking the contrap, but found it was gone. Her vision recovered enough for her to recognise the contrap in the other's possession and with much effort, she clambered from the rubble to snatch the contrap back.

"That's mine," she hissed before stalking away. She didn't know how long she'd been out for. It couldn't have been long because the scene before her had barely changed. People assessed the devastation and brushed themselves down, though the air had cleared considerably. Sirens screamed in the distance, but grew louder.

She took out her mobile to call Melissa and was surprised when it worked.

"Tyler? You okay?" said Melissa. The line died. Tyler tried again. No credit.

The wonders of Pay as You Go…

Tyler stuffed her phone in her pocket and walked, knowing the place would soon be crawling with police and other emergency services. She saw a man who was talking to a police officer point her way. She turned, walked in the opposite direction. When opportunity presented, she ducked down a side road and used the contrap to look through walls and buildings to see if the officer was following. The contrap did nothing and she found herself staring into a lifeless crystal lens. She tested the flight symbol just to be sure, but remained firmly on terra firma when she moved the lever.

Her only thoughts now were of getting out of the area. If she could get away, she could buy some time and top up her phone, meet up somewhere safe with Melissa and Lucy. She desperately wanted to know what had happened to them and what damage the second bomb blast had caused. She hoped no one had been injured or killed and each time she thought about it the pit of her stomach did a summersault.

A familiar figure caught her attention. Bagshot was approaching her from further down the street. He'd spied her, though Tyler had no idea how long he'd known she was there. She fled, turning down another street, not really knowing where she was heading. When she saw a police car pull up she quickly backtracked. The next road was no better; police dog handlers and trained dogs combed the area. Ambulances screamed by.

Tyler took the next left and found the street bustling with people. No police in sight. She figured she'd left the cordoned area of the bomb blasts. Here she was able to lose herself amongst the crowd. She weaved her way through the masses checking for Bagshot's position. At first she couldn't see him at all, but she soon found the green coat of an equally worrying individual; the Green Goddess was also in her wake. When she located Bagshot again, she saw that the Green Goddess was tailing him. Tyler doubled her efforts.

Several streets later she'd strayed into a quieter area and wondered where all the crowds had gone. Her pursuers were close now. Her many double-backs had given them the advantage and she'd been exhausted before the chase had ever begun. She ducked down the back alley of a hotel only to be confronted by a dead end. She knew she was in trouble now. She scanned waste bins and walls in shadow.

She turned to see Bagshot pausing to catch breath at the entrance of the narrow, empty service road. He seemed to sense the chase was up and she had nowhere to go. She frantically tested back doors, fire exits and service entrances but nothing offered an escape. She hammered on a door with a sign that read 'Services', but had no response.

Bagshot casually looked around. He appeared unsurprised when the woman in green joined him in the alley, flustered and exerted, but drew a hand gun from his coat.

Tyler jumped at the end wall. She tried again, took a run up, but the top of the wall was way too high for her to reach. She desperately shouldered a huge dumpster into position as the two figures approached and, scrambling up onto the dumpster lid, she reached for the wall again. She caught the top with the fingertips of her left hand but released it when an earthshattering pain coursed through her elbow. She landed badly on the dumpster and abandoned all thoughts of running as pain overwhelmed her.

"Come down from there," Bagshot said, waving his gun sideways.

Tyler slipped down from the dumpster, wincing at the pain wracking her body. She rose to her feet tentatively, nursing her arm, glaring at Bagshot.

The woman in green had also taken out a gun and now stood aiming it at Tyler.

Tyler looked from one figure to the other.

"Who *are* you people?"

"Oh, please ignore my little green shadow," said Bagshot. "She is nothing. But I suppose I should introduce you all the same. Tyler May, this is Miss Silvia Bates."

Silvia Bates glared at him.

"How dare you?" she said. She turned to Tyler. "Give the device to me. It is mine by divine right."

"No it isn't," Bagshot chuckled at the idea. He addressed Tyler. "You'll do no such thing." Then he glared at Silvia. "The device is mine. I own it. It was stolen from me. What serious claim do you have, or have you *ever* had to it?"

"I have as much right to the device as you, you old wind-bag."

Bagshot ignored these words and turned back to Tyler.

"Now, young lady…" He took out a handkerchief and mopped beads of sweat from his brow. "You *will* hand over the device to me. If you refuse, I will shoot you. Believe me, I would rather shoot you first in any case, so I suggest you do not test me further."

Tyler peered down the alley beyond them, thinking this would be a good time for Melissa and Lucy to show up. No such luck. She was alone and cornered. Outnumbered and exhausted. She conceded and begrudgingly removed the silver contrap from around her neck.

"Good girl. Now bring it here," said Bagshot. "Slowly…"

"Wait a minute!" began Silvia. "Why should *he* have it? Give it to me!" She turned her gun on Bagshot.

Tyler paused as an idea came to mind. If she could get these two idiots to kill each other, she might walk free taking the contrap with her.

"I tell you what," she said. "I'll just set it down here. You two can settle the rest between yourselves." Keeping her eyes fixed on the guns before her, Tyler set the contrap gently down onto the oily ground between the three of them. She rose and backed away. "I'll be off then." She slowly headed for a gap to one side of her captors.

Bagshot waved his gun again.

"Where do you think you're going? Get back there."

Silvia turned her gun back onto Tyler.

Tyler shrugged, returned to her place by the dumpster, hands raised.

Bates made a dash for the contrap. Bagshot moved in, but arrived late. Silvia reached out, grinning maniacally as her fingers closed around the silver casing. Bagshot's boot came down with crushing force. Silvia screamed and released. She turned and shot at Bagshot but the bullet missed, ricocheting off the hotel wall. Bagshot dashed the gun from her hand and it clattered to a halt in the gutter.

"Now, now. That wasn't nice," he muttered.

Tyler edged her way round again, aiming for the gap between Bagshot and the hotel's wall.

"*Get back*, I said." Bagshot now had control.

Silvia crawled towards her gun, sobbing and clenching her injured hand.

Tyler reluctantly stopped as Bagshot, not taking his eye or his gun from Tyler, stooped to claim the contrap.

"Alright," he said to Tyler, not caring that Silvia was even now recovering her gun. "You will tell me all you know about the device."

"I don't know anything about it," objected Tyler.

Bagshot laughed. He turned briefly to check the quiet road at his back. "Come, come, we have all night and, I fear, nobody is coming to your rescue this time. You'll tell me what you know, one way or another."

"I swear I don't know anything about it! I'd tell you if I did."

Bagshot looked down at the contrap and moved the switch. With one eye on Tyler, he peered into the contrap's lens.

"It's not working. What have you done to it?" He raised his gun higher, aiming directly at Tyler's head and lowered the hand holding the contrap.

"I don't know what you mean."

"I know you know more than you pretend, Tyler May. You *will* tell me how to make it work again."

"Give it here. I don't know what you're talking about. I don't believe it's stopped working. It never stops working."

Tentatively, Bagshot passed the contrap back to Tyler. She peered into it feigning surprise.

"Make it work. Don't try anything stupid," Bagshot warned. "It would be my pleasure to kill you."

Tyler saw that Bagshot had set the switch to the *Tower of Doom* but there was no image within the crystal. The ghosts within the contrap were still recuperating from the mass of activity she'd forced upon them earlier.

Bates, now recovered, levelled her gun at Bagshot's right temple.

"Drop your gun or I'll shoot," she threatened.

Bagshot smiled and shook his head dismissively. When he spoke, it was to Tyler.

"Miss Bates thinks I believe she has the guts to kill me. I don't. She has also forgotten I know more about the device than she does. Which, confusing as it may be, means that I am an asset and not one she is likely to eliminate. Now, please – you will fix the device before we continue."

Bates lowered her gun in a gesture of deflated resignation. Apparently Bagshot was correct.

Bagshot waved his gun.

"I grow impatient, Miss May…"

"Okay, okay! I'm trying. It's stopped working for some reason." As Tyler spoke, a light blossomed within the contrap's lens. Her heart pounded. The ghosts were recovering their power. She switched to the ghost portal and was greeted by the malevolent face of Violet Corpe. Tyler pulled the lever anticlockwise.

"What are you doing?" asked Bagshot.

"Phasmatis licentia," whispered Tyler, pointing the portal at her captors.

The sucking, rending sound began as the ghost began to exit the contrap. Blue glowing matter streamed and gathered as Bagshot and Silvia backed away.

"Stop it!" cried Bagshot above the rushing noise. "Make it stop! Make it stop or I will shoot you!" Yet he seemed too mesmerized to follow the threat through.

Silvia looked terrified as a spectral woman formed from unearthly miasma.

The ghost of Violet Corpe hesitated briefly in the air as if weighing the choice before her before plunging, with a shriek, headlong into the body of Silvia Bates. Silvia screamed and fell backwards. She began writhing on the ground. She rose grasping at her head, turned and, still screaming, ran away.

When Silvia and Violet were gone, Bagshot tilted his head at Tyler.

"Well, it seems you have done us both a favour, although, I am irritated that you disobeyed my instructions. I did tell you not to try anything. You'll give the device to me now. Do not touch it or try anything else. You may hold it by the chain only."

Tyler weighed her chances, tempted to try and fly out of the alley to escape Bagshot, but he looked as if he was about to snap. She decided he really might shoot her as she took off and so chose to hand the contrap back. She offered it to him, dangling it before him on its chain. Bagshot snatched it.

"Now, as you clearly know so much about what this trinket can do, you will tell me how you have learned so very much about it."

"Alright," said Tyler. "I'll tell you how it happened." She thought for a moment. "There is a setting with a spiral symbol. The symbol for the ghosts."

"Yes, I know this symbol."

"Well, when you select the spiral and turn the device over, you can see ghosts in the glass. You can see them and talk to them."

"Go on."

"I've learned all that I know about the device, and how to work it, from one ghost and one ghost alone. All the others are liars."

"Who? Give me a name." Bagshot waved the gun in her face, pressed the barrel into the skin of her forehead.

"Travis. Ask for Travis. He's an old knight from the time of William the Conqueror. He's *really* helpful. He'll tell you everything you want to know about the device. He knows more about it than I do. Far more."

Bagshot grinned.

"You see, it wasn't that hard, was it?"

Tyler could barely stand any longer. She crumpled to the ground, drew up her legs and hugged her knees. When she eventually looked up, Bagshot was a distant figure leaving the alley.

The Con

Tyler dragged herself to her feet and staggered after the retreating figure. It was all she could do to keep up with him and she nearly lost sight of him several times. She binned her bedraggled, dust-covered coat when she noticed people on the streets staring at her and realised she must have looked like a war refugee. She did what she could to tidy herself up whilst trying not to lose Bagshot.

He was purposefully heading somewhere and Tyler wondered how long it would be before his curiosity of the contrap got the better of him.

She trailed him back towards the blast scene at Parliament Square and was met by blue and red flashing lights and uniformed men. Still she managed to get through the area without going too close to the lines of blue and white police tape where bomb disposal units were deployed. Bagshot also appeared to want a low profile.

He skirted the cordoned zone and joined Bridge Street. No traffic moved there. Police cars, lights flashing, blocked the road to all but pedestrians. Bagshot passed the blockade and headed for Westminster Bridge. Tyler glimpsed a damaged part of the Abbey up ahead. She pulled up her hood to shadow her face and followed, relieved once she passed the police. She saw Bagshot pause to wipe his spectacles clean as he neared the bridge.

Westminster Bridge was almost deserted. Word of the explosions in Parliament Square had spread and people were keeping clear of the place in dread of further terrorism.

Halfway across the bridge Bagshot stopped. The London Eye was a vast blue-lit wheel across the water. Stately buildings were warm russet tones in the blaze of numerous spotlights. All this reflected in the shimmering Thames. On the other side of the bridge, to Tyler's right, the mighty Houses of Parliament ran along the water's edge. But something told Tyler that Bagshot was not interested in the stunning views. He leaned on the decorative barrier at the edge of the bridge and studied the contrap.

A shock of panic shivered through Tyler.

"No. Not there!"

She ran. When she'd covered only half the distance, a flicker of blue light passed in the air between Bagshot and the device in his hands. He collapsed forwards suddenly.

Tyler sprinted, pressing aching, painful legs to drive as hard as they would go. She reached him moments later to find no signs of life. The contrap rolled from his failing grasp and left the bridge even as she lunged for it.

Tyler threw herself half over the side and watched in dismay as the contrap tumbled. It seemed to fall for an age before vanishing into the dark waters far below.

Bagshot had met Travis and now the contrap was lost forever.

She pulled herself back onto the bridge and slumped against the barrier to rub sore eyes. She was ready to give up and go home. She wondered what she would say to her parents, to the police, when they came to arrest her.

When she opened her eyes and looked up a few moments later, she squinted at a figure walking away further down the bridge, a familiar figure in a black trilby and a long coat. She could not see any skin or the bluish sheen that makeup could barely conceal, but she was almost certain she was looking at the back of Josef Mengele. She hauled herself to her feet and followed. What was he doing? Had he also witnessed Bagshot's untimely demise?

Mengele was in no hurry. He strolled across the rest of the bridge as though he was enjoying a gentle walk in the county. When he reached the end of the bridge he turned left to descend some steps and sat on a bench overlooking the Thames, watching the world go by.

'WHAT ARE YOU DOING?' the little voice in Tyler's head screamed.

*

He'd been sitting there for hours. Tyler fought to stay awake. She was tired, cold, in pain, hungry and despairing. She delved into her bag and threw on a lightweight jacket.

What the hell are you doing?

Mengele was like a statue. As far as she could tell, he hadn't moved a muscle since he'd taken his place on the bench. She even wondered if he had died and was now literally frozen to the spot.

Tyler considered leaving her place on the bridge corner beneath a giant stone lion to buy food. But she'd kick herself if she returned to find Mengele gone. She couldn't risk it. She hunkered down against the plinth and tried to get warm. She had to find out what he was up to.

*

Tyler awoke, startled as a jogger dashed by. It was fully dark. She was stiff with the cold and deepening bruises. She shook herself and swore, looked over at the bench. Mengele was gone.

She checked her watch and saw that it was smashed and had stopped working. She looked up to the vast clock tower. It was one o'clock in the morning on Christmas Day. The streets and the bridge were almost empty, but for the last of the partygoers.

"Merry Christmas," she muttered to herself.

Tyler got up and rubbed at her neck. She made her way down the steps to the bench where Josef Mengele had been sitting for so long. She sat in his place and looked out over the water where he'd looked. Then she realised he'd been gazing out at the exact spot where the contrap had gone into the Thames. She rose and walked to the wall edging the river to look over. There was a drop of several metres to the water below, but there was also a small area of bank protruding from the water. Something caught Tyler's eye: a black trilby sitting, rather bizarrely, atop a folded grey coat, on the gravelly bank. It had been placed there quite purposefully, as though, thought Tyler, some sad man had committed suicide in the river and left these belongings neatly behind.

Tyler came to her senses. Mengele was not the sort to commit suicide. He had another agenda. She searched her bag and then upended it, struggling to find the small pink and black canister of defence spray.

An eerie bluish glow approached her beneath the black water of the Thames. It grew until she could make out the features of a head and then two glowing hands. The gloved ghost of Josef Mengele neared the water's surface.

Tyler searched for a way down to the bank and found a series of large stone steps set into the wall to her right where it turned to cut into the river. She rushed to the steps and leapt down them two at a time as Mengele emerged from the water. The water didn't seem to affect him very much. It was almost like watching a mechanical being. He held the contrap in his hand and looked down at it, not interested in where he was headed. Tyler met him at the water's edge. Mengele first focused on her feet, water draining across his impassive face. He blinked, leant closer before following the legs slowly up to Tyler's body and finally her face. She emptied the canister of Mace into Mengele's face at point blank range. He screamed and staggered backwards, clawing at his eyes as sticky red gel enveloped his face. The contrap fell from his hands and splashed into the shallows as Tyler charged him, shoving him in the chest with all the force she could muster. Mengele lost his footing and toppled backwards into the Thames.

Tyler dropped to her knees at the water's edge and frantically searched. She was panicked by the thought that she'd lost the contrap again. The water was a slick of suspended mud and she could see nothing beyond its shimmering surface, but a moment later her hand brushed against something solid. Snatching it up, she slipped the contrap's chain around her neck while Mengele still flailed in the water. She climbed the steps and grabbed her stuff, shoved everything back into her bag and ran.

The Pledge

"Where the hell have you been?" Lucy and Melissa hugged her tightly on the almost deserted Victoria platform.

"Oh, you know." Tyler grinned. "Here and there… Chasing bad men and playing with ghosts… What happened to you?"

"No. You first!" said Melissa.

Tyler told them about Bagshot and the Green Goddess, about the contrap being lost to the Thames and Mengele emerging from the water. She reminded them that Mengele, along with all the ghosts, was able to sense the presence of the contrap and he'd been able to home in on it, even under the murky waters of the Thames. He'd simply had to wait until the streets were quiet enough for him to retrieve the contrap without being noticed. They huddled together sipping hot drinks on a bench, knowing that few trains would run today. They did not care. They were in no hurry to go anywhere.

"What happened to you in Parliament Square?" she asked when she'd finished answering all their questions. "Were there many casualties? I heard a second explosion."

"When we left you with Hitler, we followed Himmler. He led us straight to Westminster Abbey where he began planting explosives, quietly sneaking into corners and leaving these packages he took from his bag. We followed him through the crowds and he never knew we were watching him." Melissa sipped hot chocolate.

"It was easy to trace his progress," Lucy explained. "He's an idiot really. And as for his fashion sense… The only reason he got as far as he did, was the crowds. No one could really see what he was doing, but *we* knew what he was up to. People were finding their seats for the carol service. The choir stalls were filling up. Everyone was just too busy to worry about what one little weirdo was doing. The first bomb was easy to find. He hid it in an alcove on the tomb of Edward the Confessor. We followed him there and watched him plant it."

"We got that one and saw it was on a timer. But get this. We found an off switch. So it was easy to make it safe."

"We followed him again and found the second bomb hidden behind an altar in a chapel right in the middle of the Abbey."

"That's when we lost him," stated Melissa.

"Yeah. He must have planted his last bomb over at the edge closest to the square, because a few minutes later that part of the Abbey blew up."

Tyler turned pale. This was the bit she had been dreading.

"So how many people were killed? I haven't seen the news..."

"That's the thing," explained Lucy. "No one was killed. Not a single person. Oh, yes, there were a few injuries and a few people had a hell of a shock, but nobody was killed. We did it. We stopped them!"

"I don't understand," said Tyler, frowning. "How can a bomb explode in a building packed with people and no one be killed in the blast?"

Melissa grinned.

"Have you met Lucy?" she said. Tyler looked blank. "When we lost Himmler we realised he hadn't finished planting bombs. Then we thought *what about the others?* We hadn't seen the other Nazi gloves there, but we figured they could still be there somewhere, planting other explosives, so just as the Dean is beginning the service, Lucy climbs on top of the altar in front of everyone and shouts '*BOMB!*' at the top of her voice. *That* got people moving."

"By the time the bomb we couldn't find went off, most people were outside or up the other end, trying to get out."

Tyler smiled.

"Thank you."

Lucy placed a black bag purposefully on a bench before Tyler and unzipped it. She pulled it open so Tyler could peer inside where two recovered bombs nestled.

*

They found a hotel for Christmas night and watched the BBC News on a small television while eating pizza. The explosions in Parliament Square were headlining the program with footage of the damaged Abbey, the crater in the road where Hitler's bomb had exploded and the pandemonium in the city.

"…and on our program tonight, terrorists in Parliament Square or is something far more sinister at work in our capital city? We examine conflicting reports." Other headlines ran as images flashed up on the screen. The titles closed and the newsreader addressed the viewers.

"Last night, two explosions ripped through London's Parliament Square damaging the road and surrounding buildings, including part of Westminster Abbey's north wing." A close-up of the ruined section of the Abbey appeared on the screen. "The first of the two explosions caused a section of the underpass to collapse, north of Parliament Square. So far, no terrorist organization has claimed responsibility. Accounts describing the explosions are confused. Authorities are baffled by multiple reports suggesting the unexplained appearance of numerous ghosts around the time of the detonations. Investigating officers suggest the presence of toxic or hallucinatory gases in the vicinity are to blame, although less easily explained are the multiple accounts of striking similarity, which suggest the same hallucinations were universally experienced."

The picture changed to a close-up of a businessman looking ruffled and covered in dust.

"Can you tell us exactly what happened here tonight, sir?"

"It was chaos. I couldn't see much. I think at least two bombs went off. One over by the Abbey and one on the other side of the square. The air was full of dust and it was difficult to see properly."

"Did you see an apparition?" pressed the reporter.

"I think I saw what everyone else saw but maybe we were under the influence of some kind of weird gas or something. I know I can't have seen what I think I saw."

The report cut to a grainy, shaky piece of footage taken from a bystander's smartphone. In it, Tyler was holding out the contrap and walking backwards. The camera panned to focus on Hitler being dragged along the ground by an unseen force.

"Police want to speak to witnesses of events prior to the terrorist attacks. In particular, the girl seen here in this video captured by a tourist at the scene moments before the explosions…" The clip was replayed, but it was difficult to make out Tyler's face well because of the camera's constant jostling and the poor resolution of the video.

"Great," said Tyler to herself. "That's all I need."

The studio newsreader began a new story.

"Following an anonymous tipoff, the Metropolitan Police have today issued a public warning regarding a woman wanted in connection with terrorist activities and considered highly dangerous." An image of Bates appeared on the screen. "In a press conference this morning, the commissioner made a plea for Silvia Bates to hand herself in, while asking the public to be vigilant but not to approach Bates."

Tyler showered until she could stand no longer and then plunged into a blissful sleep.

*

On Boxing Day morning the three girls caught a train back to Watford and were reunited with their families. The police were informed of the girls' return and a full investigation into their movements and various breaches of law was begun. Tyler did not care. They had enough evidence to show they'd been acting for the good of the nation and she felt this would surely quash any charges against them. Even so, she knew some things were going to be difficult to explain.

Another investigation was also launched, one which promised to uncover the truth behind the spurious and many NVF organizations, acting upon information and evidence released to the authorities by the girls. Tyler did not know much about the police force and the way it was run, but one name was familiar to her and she regarded it as a trusted establishment. She refused to talk with any authority except the head of Scotland Yard.

Tyler sat on her bed in her bedroom with her arm in a sling, relieved to be home. The greenstick fracture of the humerus had not needed to be plastered. She was warm and no longer in pain thanks to prescribed painkillers. Her parents had been lenient on her, or so she had thought, though there were a lot of issues still to be dealt with. On the whole they had just seemed pleased and relieved that she was home. It was as though absolutely anything she had done, or become entangled with, was of little consequence in the light of her return.

*

Three days later the girls met at the little café now forever known to them as *Adolf's Coffee Shop*, or *Adolf's* for short. There was something reassuring about seeing the place devoid of Nazis.

"So what's on today's list?" Melissa asked as they found a table.

"Oh, I don't have one. I… I haven't made a list for a few days now. Not since London. I'm not sure I need them anymore."

They were discussing plans and hopes for the coming new year when Tyler became pensive.

"Who do you think it was?"

"What do you mean?" asked Melissa. "Who do I think *who* was?"

"The kid who was gloved with Hitler. The one that was killed when Hitler's backpack exploded."

Tyler took out a collection of newsprint copies from her bag and spread them out on the table.

"Oh, Tyler, not this again. You need to leave it alone."

"You're obsessing again."

"That's me, obsessive compulsive. I can't help it. I feel so guilty when I think about it."

"So don't think about it," Lucy suggested.

"I can't stop myself. It's my fault the kid died."

"No it isn't," said Melissa. "It's Hitler's fault. And it's Bagshot's fault. *You* saved people. *We* saved people. Hundreds of them."

There were six newspaper reports taken from the *Watford Observer*. Each one was a news story about a missing child. The girls scanned through small print and images of disappeared children. Tyler read out each of their names in turn.

"Susan Ellis, Steven Lewis, Freddy Carter, Kylie Marsh, Emily Stanford and Harry McGrath."

"Do you notice something about them all?" said Melissa.

Lucy leant in to get a better look at the grainy black and white photographs. "Yeah. They're all white kids. They're all white kids with blond hair."

"Exactly," said Melissa. "It wouldn't do to glove the Nazi ghosts with any other than the Arian race, would it?"

"One of them died on Christmas Eve," said Tyler. "The others are roaming about still, gloved with Nazi ghosts."

"I guess we have no way of knowing which one," said Melissa.

"What about the ghost machine?" Lucy said to Tyler. "Maybe it can tell us which one died."

"I'll ask Albert. See if he can tell me anything." Tyler had not used the contrap since releasing Violet Corpe from the portal. It had two new ghosts trapped within it, both undesirable. She was nervous about the effect they might have on it and she didn't want to be confronted by Adolf Hitler when she really wanted to see Albert.

"Wait a minute!" Melissa dug in her bag and took out a brown file. She thumbed through it before extracting a single page.

"The GAUNT file? I thought we'd handed that over to the police," said Lucy.

"I copied everything first," Melissa explained. "Look here on the list, next to the names of the gloves. There's all this other information. And there are initials." She cross-referenced between the list and the photocopied news articles. "SL, that's Steven Lewis. HM, that's got to be Harry McGrath. See? They're all here! ES is Emily Stanford. SE is Susan Ellis."

Tyler peered at the list.

"And Hitler was gloved with… Kylie Marsh."

They fell silent for a while. It seemed more real now that they were able to name Hitler's latest victim.

"What about the others?" Tyler said. It was a question they had all considered but none had wanted to ask. "We can't just abandon them. We can't just let them spend their lives gloved with Nazi ghosts."

"And we can't sit back while Nazi ghosts wreak havoc throughout England," said Lucy. "Or wherever they've gone."

"Yeah, who knows what they're planning to do? Or where they plan to do it?" Melissa unfolded a sheet of paper and read from a list. "With Hitler gone there are five left: Josef Mengele, Heinrich Himmler, Reinhard Heydrich, Adolf Eichmann and Joseph Goebbels."

"So we're agreed, then," Tyler concluded. "We must do something."

"But what?" asked Melissa.

"Where do we start?" asked Lucy.

"I don't know," Tyler admitted. "But we have one advantage." She lifted the chain over her head and placed the contrap gently down on the table. "We have this."

"We should make a pact!" said Melissa.

Lucy shrugged but then nodded.

"Right," said Tyler. She picked up her hot chocolate and raised it over the centre of the table. "We pledge to rid the world of the Nazi ghosts and to not rest until the remaining five kids have been rescued."

The others exchanged glances and raised cups to clink them over the table.

"We pledge," they said.

"But how can we rescue the kids when they've been gloved?" Melissa sipped from her cup. "I mean, how do we separate them from the ghosts?"

Lucy shrugged.

"I don't know," said Tyler. "But we're gonna find out."

Mr Chapman

When Tyler went home from the café she escaped to her room and sat on the edge of her bed. The contrap shimmered in her hands as she turned it apprehensively. She decided to stop putting off the inevitable and switched it to the ghost portal.

"Albert? Are you there?"

Grey mist flowed. She tried again, waited for a few minutes. Nobody came. She didn't know if she was disappointed or relieved.

An hour later she tried again. After a moment a familiar figure emerged from the void.

"Miss Tyler May, how good to see you!" Zebedee Lieberman greeted her.

"Hi, Zebedee. Are you alright in there?"

"Never better, my dear. Never better." He puffed on his long pipe and winked. "Am I right to suppose it is young Albert you truly wish to see?"

"Yes." Tyler smiled. "But before you go I need to thank you, for all your help. I don't think I could have done it without you."

"Oh, no need to thank me, dear girl. No need at all. It was my pleasure. Now you sit tight and I'll see if I can find that boy of yours." Zebedee strode away tapping his cane. It was not long before Albert appeared, cap in hand.

"'Ello, Missy."

"Hi, Albert."

"Everyfing alright, Missy? You look sad."

"I feel sad, Albert."

"Why's that then?"

"I don't know. Everything that's happened I suppose."

"Oh yeah. Of course. Well, cheer up, my girl! Ya' can't mope around all day."

"You're right, as always, Albert. I have a lot to do." Tyler steeled herself for what she needed to say next. "Albert, there's something I need to talk to you about. It's about you and the contrap. You see, when Hitler went into the contrap it altered the balance, according to Mr Lieberman. I let out Violet Corpe to set the balance right again. Zebedee told me I should be careful not to unbalance things, you see."

"Yeah, I sees."

"Thing is, then Bagshot went into it, so I get to choose a ghost to set free from the portal. And I think I need to set you free. Would you like that? Would you like to be free, Albert?" Tyler sniffed. She didn't want to lose Albert, yet over the past few days she'd become convinced it was the right thing to do, though even now she couldn't quite put her finger on the reason why.

"You could always set anover ghost free, Missy. If ya' wanted to keep me 'ere, I mean."

"I know. But you've been so good to me. I think you deserve it."

Albert thought about this for a moment.

"What if I don't want to go?"

"That's fine. Just let me know and I'll leave you be. But it's not right, Albert. It's not how things are supposed to be; ghosts trapped in some nasty machine that makes them work for a master. You shouldn't be in there. None of you should be in there. I plan to set you all free someday. Except Hitler of course. And perhaps Bagshot."

"Suppose you're right, Missy. Suppose you're right." They were quiet for a while until Albert spoke.

"Where would I go? If you set me free, where would I go?"

"I'm not sure. I don't really know. I thought *you* might."

"Right. Will it hurt?"

"I don't think so. Though I can't be sure."

"Well, if it's what you fink is best, then we'd best do it."

"I'll miss you, Albert Goodwin," said Tyler, tears leaving her eyes suddenly and catching her by surprise.

"I'll miss you too, Tyler May."

Tyler closed her eyes and pulled the little lever anticlockwise.

"Phasmatis licentia," she whispered. When she opened her eyes again, Albert was gone.

"Albert?" She searched her room and checked the contrap but he was not there. She was left wondering where he had gone and why he had not appeared before her. Her heart sank.

"Albert, where are you?"

*

On January 1st Tyler bought a paper and read the headline story with a wry smile.

'In Watford last night, two buildings owned by the technology business NVF, were targeted by unknown activists as clocks struck midnight. One explosion occurred at the central office building and a second at the NVF's research facility on Duck's Hill, both causing extensive damage…'

She scanned further down the story.

'Representatives of the NVF have yet to give any statement or to confirm possible sources of the violence. No terrorist party has come forward to assume responsibility. Police have issued a statement saying the explosions are not necessarily associated with the recent Christmas Eve terrorist attacks in Parliament Square. Emergency services have spent the morning combing debris, now confirming both buildings were unoccupied at the time of the blasts.'

Tyler felt her journey had only just begun. Albert had been right: she did have a lot to do. It had only been a few days since she'd released Albert from the contrap, but she missed him like crazy and wondered where he was. She didn't want to forget what he looked like and so, believing she would probably never see him again, she took a sharpened pencil and her sketch pad and did her best to draw him. When she was done, she looked at the image and her tears fell to the paper.

Tyler cried herself to sleep.

When she awoke she noticed a mark she didn't remember making. In the corner of the page beneath the image of Albert and right where her tears had fallen, Tyler could see a dark smudge as though someone had dipped their finger in black dust and drawn it along the white page. Curious, she touched it, feeling the substance between finger and thumb. It was soot. She looked around but Albert was not there.

*

Tyler had that feeling again. The little voice in her head screamed.

HE'S COMING FOR YOU!

She looked over her shoulder, fearing Mengele, but saw no one. It was two o'clock, broad daylight and she was in the street returning home with newly bought school supplies. There were three days of holiday left before the new school term began and crowds out for the sales were beginning to subside.

She'd felt eyes on the back of her neck for the past few hours and wondered if she'd ever be able to go anywhere again without thinking the gloves were going to get her. Then she saw him. A hard-faced man with a grey coat and short, bleach-blond hair, watching her from a bus stop. Tyler's walk quickened, became a jog and then a run. Blondie left the bus stop and gave chase.

Tyler crossed a road, took a left and then a right, sprinting at top speed.

Nearly home!

She hurtled round the corner into her street and shivered when she saw a figure in a trilby and long coat further down the road. She turned to run but a black Mercedes with dark windows pulled up ahead of her and a man leapt out. He grabbed her as she tried to run past.

"NO! LET ME GO!"

Another man left the car and helped bundle her in as she fought to escape. She screamed until a black-gloved hand clamped over her mouth. She bit hard and was rewarded with a cry of pain, but was thrust unceremoniously onto the back seat of the limousine and pinned there.

"GET OFF ME!" she yelled.

"Tyler May?" asked a man with thinning, short, brown hair, and chiselled features. Narrow rectangular glasses perched upon his thin nose.

"Who's asking? Leave me alone you Nazi scum!" She tried to shake them off but they were too strong.

The chiselled official indicated for his men to loosen their hold. Tyler freed one hand and punched one of them in the eye, followed it with an elbow to the next man's crotch. He folded, reeled out of the car and rolled on the pavement grabbing himself, spewing a string of obscenities. She struggled again as the remaining men subdued her.

"Miss May, let me assure you, we're anything but Nazis. My name is Mr Chapman. I'm with MI5. I've been watching you and have some questions for you. You didn't really believe it would be so easy to brush aside the simultaneous appearance of millions of ghosts in central London, did you?"

Tyler glanced at the door and wondered where this was going. Was Chapman who he said he was? Or was he one of *them*? She said nothing but waited.

"I want you to tell me everything you know about the device you carry. Do you have it on you now, incidentally? I should like to see it." He hit a button on a remote and CCTV images of Tyler's exploits played on a small screen set into the headrest of the front passenger seat.

Tyler studied Chapman suspiciously, withholding any reply.

"Never mind. We have ways of acquiring such things in any case, should we choose to do so. I didn't really expect you to have the thing on you."

Tyler fought the urge to look down towards the contrap, or put a hand to her chest where it hung beneath her shirt. Chapman closed the file he had been studying and peered at her over his glasses.

"However, I do feel it would be in your interest to talk."

Tyler only stared at him.

"Fine, have it your way, but I should tell you this is of the utmost importance, Miss May." He gestured to the screen. "You have been observed, on several occasions of late, performing what can only be described as acts of an impossible nature. This places us both in a very… unusual position. In short, I believe we might be able to help one another and I'd like to offer you a deal. Now, what do you have to say for yourself, Miss May?"

The Tyler May series to date

The Haunting of Tyler May
(book one)

The Thieves of Antiquity
(book two)

The Brimstone Chasm
(book three)

Gallows Iron
(book four)

Ghosts of Redemption
(book five)

Follow the Tyler May series

www.tylermay.co.uk